This book should be returned to any branch of the
Lancashire County Library on or before the date shown

Lancaster Library
01524 580700

2 6 AUG 2008

2 8 FEB 2009

1 7 JUL 2009

- 6 FEB 2010

1 8 MAY 2010

2 6 JUL 2010

ALAN KELLY was born in Bellshill in 1961 and grew up in Coatbridge, North Lanarkshire. At sixteen, he started work as a labourer with North Lanarkshire Council Roads Department where he was to spend the next twenty years road-sweeping, litter-picking and drain-cleaning; he was eventually promoted to a tar squad, specialising in 'skills' such as tar-shovelling, tar-raking, tar-chipping and tar-rolling. Around this time he married, but he was losing his battle against alcoholism and he and Patricia divorced four years later. Then a chance meeting with an old friend, Des Dillon, changed the course of his life. Des, who was running a local writers' group, encouraged him to join and put his experiences down on paper. Tarmen's yarns formed the basis of *The Tar Factory*, his first novel. Alan now works as a school janitor. He's been sober for fourteen years and lives in Airdrie with Patricia – they re-married in 1995 – and their little dog, Mollie the Collie.

By the same author:

The Tar Factory, Luath Press, 2004

Help Me Rhonda

ALAN KELLY

Luath Press Limited

EDINBURGH

www.luath.co.uk

First published 2007

ISBN (10): 1-905222-83-1
ISBN (13): 978-1-9-0522283-4

The author's right to be identified as author of this book
under the Copyright, Designs and Patents Act 1988 has been asserted.

The paper used in this book is recyclable.
It is made from low chlorine pulps produced in a low energy,
low emission manner from renewable forests.

Printed and bound by
Bell & Bain Ltd., Glasgow

Typeset in 9.5 point Frutiger

© Alan Kelly 2007

To my auld Da, John and wee sis-in-law, Liz

Chapter One.
Killed Billy.

I've killed Billy. Aw Jesus Christ Almighty man, what the fuck've I done?

Murderer, yer a murderer, yer a dirty rotten evil bastart.
Look what ye've went an done.

Rhonda's standin over me, squeelin, howlin, wailin.
She's mad. A mad demented she-devil.
Aw man, listen to her, she's screamin, screamin like a teenybopper at a boyband gig.
Screamin so loud an painful her lips go purple an her eyeballs bleed.
Her eyeballs. Her eyeballs bulge like shiny silver ball barins.
Pain. I feel pain. I feel slashes, wet cold slashes rainin down on me.
Aw dear God, I'm bein stung to death by a billion deadly bees.
What the fuck's goin on man, what's she hittin me with?
What?
It feels like somethin hard an pointy like a screwdriver or a poker or a brickie's chisel.
But naw, it's not, it's none of them.
D'ye know what it is? It's stiletto heels. She's playin a heavy drumroll on my head with two stilettos.
Rat-a-tat a rat-a-tat a rat-a-tata. She rattles those drums like Cozy Powell. Doesn't miss a beat so she doesn't, bang-on perfect timin.
Then she stands up an sticks them on her feet an starts jumpin up an down jabbin her heels hard into my ribcage an grindin them round an round like she's stubbin out a fag. She jumps up in the air an kicks me hard as fuck on the point of my spine where it meets my neck.

Then she goes to work on me with her nails, starts tearin into my face, neck, stomach, balls, diggin those nails in deep bro, oh ya bastart ye, ya fuckin bastart, those razor sharp nails pierce my skin an sting right into the nerve ends.

Her small bony fists bounce hard on my napper as I lie there like a criminal bein stoned to death by a million chuckies.

Aw holy mother of God, yer man here's dead. Dead.

This is my death. This is it man. This is me dyin. This is me bein slowly stoned to death. Stoned to death. This is it. This is what it feels like.

The end of the road is now. Now, not nigh, fuckin now. The end of the world is now.

A long hard stonin. A slow agonisin death.

Is this really happenin, is this the end?

How'd it all come to this? Ye always wonder don't ye?

Ye always wonder when yer time comes, how it's gonni happen.

Car smash? Cancer? Suicide? Stroke? A heart attack maybe, or even a right good kickin.

Aye, ye do man, ye think of all these things. Well, I dunno about you bro, but I certainly do.

But this is different. Never this. Ye never think of this do ye? Stoned to fuckin death man. Aw Jesus. Imagine it. Standin against a wall bein slowly battered to bits with all these tiny jaggy rocks bouncin off yer forehead, burstin yer eyeballs, yer lips nose an teeth.

It's slow an sore. Aw fuck. It's far too sore. Change the record. Change the script. This is not in the script. Naw, not this.

This is a horror story. A nightmare.

Well, naw, it aint really.

Ye see, I aint dreamin man. No way. This is real. The real deal.

This aint no blackout. I wish it was. Aye, I really do. But naw. This is real. This is my life. My pathetic fucked up existence.

My whole sorry life is just one big major gang fuck.

Murderer. Ya murderer. Ya dirty lousy bastart.

What've I done? Oh dear God in Heaven, please don't let this be true.

Sonny Jim boy's frozen. Iced up. The fear is pissin out my pores. Oh Sweet Jesus please forgive me.

Please please tell me I'm dreamin. Yes, I'm dreamin. Dreamin. I tell myself I'm dreamin.

But then this wee voice in my head shouts, No yer fuckin not, I've told ye that already ya cunt, told ye a million times, yer not fuckin dreamin.

This is real. This is happenin. Welcome to the real live horror show.

I dunno what I've done so I don't. Please believe me when I tell ye, I dunno what the fuck I've done.

It was a blackout. An out an out blackout.

A real jet black shot.

I'm an awful cunt for takin them man. Terrible. Take them all the time so I do. Can't remember fuck-all.

Boozin all night long an don't remember nothin. Honest. Not a thing.

That's a fact.

It's the bevvy. The auld Don Revie.

It does it to me every time. The jungle juice is to blame. I'm tellin ye.

It's the juice that makes me do it.

I'm not a bad cunt really. Honestly I aint.

Everybody says so.

Sonny boy, they say. Ye aint a bad cunt. Ye really aint.

In fact, yer a good cunt even. Aye. When yer sober yer a real nice guy.

The drink made me do it man.

What?

What did it make me do?

What've I done?
Some cunt please please tell me.
I aint got a Scooby man. I'm puffin an pantin like an asthmatic miner.

There's a void. Yer mind goes blank. Ye can think of nothin for ten, fifteen, twenty seconds. Yer mind goes through the wringer. Who? What? Where?
Ye see faces.
Whose? Dunno.
Faces. Bloody screamin hysterical faces. Polis cars. Ambulances. Silver blue flashin lights. Sirens blarin. Coppers. Jails.

Murderer. Murderer. Crazy psycho murderer.

The blows keep bombin. Her mad bloody eyes keep starin right through mine.

All the time I'm feelin nothin. At least not on the outside. Pain no more. I'm numb from head to toe. I don't feel a thing.
But listen, see on the inside? On the inside I'm achin. The pain inside's unbearable. A dull desperate emptiness. A real scary feelin so it is. That unknown fear. That nothinness.

Murderer. Murderer.
I try an trace my steps. Think think think. Think hard ya cunt. What happened? What?
I came home last night. Well, I must've done. I'm lyin here aint I?
I came home blootered, sparkles, wired to the Moon. Aye, the Sonny Jim boy. Rat arsed. Usual.
I remember it a wee bit now so I do. The whole picture starts to unfold. The big picture, the whole fuckin horror story. The whole thing's as clear as a teetotaller's piss. I go through it bit by bit.
I'm sittin there on the couch, I'm real solid gone man, starin into nowhere.
The Billy boy's just sittin over there in his usual place, but I'm out my skull with the drink, I'm heebi jeebi'd up. The drink man, it

makes yer man hallucinate, it makes the Billy dude's head swell
up like a beachball an his eyeballs bulge like poisoned rabbits.
He starts turnin into this great big orange monster an he's
growlin an snarlin an he's gonni attack me an tear my fuckin
head off.
Oh my fuck man, a big orange monster the size of a killer whale.
It's splashin an kickin an comin to get me.
He opens his big mouth, fucksake check it out, row upon row of
shiny silver fangs as sharp as razors an they're snap snap snappin,
gonni bite me, eat me, gobble me all up.

I'm curled into a ball now, cowerin in the corner, hedgehogged
up to fuck. Boo hoo hoo. I'm bubblin like a baby. I'm gonni die,
die at the jaws of a big jaggy-toothed monster.
It's inside a big glass bubble an any second now it's about to
explode.
The monster inside is bulgin an bloatin, ready to attack.
Yer man decides he's had enough, fuck it man, if yer gonni
die yer gonni die. Yer as well goin out a hero. A huge rush of
bravado bursts through me like an orgasm. Big balls of steam
belch out my ears like pish hittin a coal fire. The auld drink man,
ye know what I'm sayin, it turns ye into a right gallus cunt.
Fuck ye, I say to it. Fuck ye ya bastart. Yer man here aint waitin,
aint waitin for no cunt.

C'mon ya big ugly fucker ye, come ahead.
I go like that an put the head down. It's time to charge, aye,
turbo charge right in there bro. I don't give a fuck now, no way,
I'm runnin on highly inflammable rocket fuel.
Pure adrenalin.
I grab him by the neck. Billy. The monster. I grab it by the scruff
of the scrawny neck. Come on ya bastart, just me an you, c'mon,
d'ye think yer a hard cunt?

Here, I say to it. Have a load of this.
Munch. In they go man, the molars. Aye, the auld molars, I sink

them right into its slimy orange neck. I dig them in deep so I do. Don't let go, don't let go, lock those fuckin jaws bro. Its eyes erupt, its tongue bursts open an blood an guts spray out its belly an arse. I hang on tight till there's no sign of life. None man, none. Just a orange slimy body hangin lifeless an limp.

The party's over big boy. Well an truly over. Time to call it a day. Yer man's the man. Victorious. The champion.

Murderer. Murderer.

That's what she was screamin. Poor Rhonda. Poor demented Rhonda.

I've killed Billy. Poor wee Billy the fish. A wee defenceless goldfish.

That's what I've done man, I've killed the wean's goldfish. The wean, the poor wee wean, she's only seven, seven years old. Seven summers. She had a little goldfish an I've went an killed it. I've killed her little fish. Killed it in a blackout. A nightmare. A horrendous night of heebi jeebis. The dreaded DTs.

A tiny little goldfish. Oh my God Almighty man. Please please forgive me.

Chapter Two.
A Pure Pisser.

Man, I should've known, I should've seen all this comin. The first time I saw her I should have sussed right there an then that she was trouble.

I was just standin. Just standin there an this big pink double-decker bus drew up an stopped right in front of me. An that was it. That was the moment time seemed to stop forever.

Off stepped the sweetest lookin angel in the whole wide Heaven. Aw man, aw man. My heart, my fuckin heart.

Honest to fuck by the way, I just could not believe it.

I had to nip myself to make sure it was happenin. Aye, I had to nip myself.

But listen, I'll tell ye what I should've done.

I should've cut my fuckin throat. An I'll tell ye why.

Because from that moment on, life was never gonni be anythin other than complete an utter madness.

I just stood there an stared. Stood there an prayed.

Please Sweet Jesus don't let this be a dream. I'm not dreamin man, this aint no dream. Naw, I won't let it be.

This is no hallucination either. The bold Sonny Jim's a dreamer. I have dreams an hallucinations. But this was none of these man. None of these at all.

Ye get these real strange vibes. Ye know what it's like. That right dodgy feelin in yer gut. A feelin ye can't explain. Beautiful but dangerous. I had a gut feelin. Ye know what they say about them. Follow them. Follow yer gut feelin.

Well, this auld gut feelin wasn't far wrong.

Normality no more man.

Hey normality, where the fuck are ye off to?
Normality's done a runner. Packed his bags an gone.
Normal? What the fuck does that mean?
I'll tell ye what normal is. Normal's a settin on yer washin
machine.

Aw man, talk about bein swept right off yer feet?
Yer man here was blitzed right off the planet by the full force of
a hurricane.
Hurricane Rhonda.
Fucksake, one minute I'm just standin starin, lookin straight
ahead. Next thing I know rockets get launched inside my arse
an explode out my eyeballs an ears. I go all dizzy an light an my
head spins off my shoulders an starts to orbit the earth. Aw holy
fuck man, there's no ground beneath me.
My head's goin round an round an I'm just standin there starin
right into the eyes of this stunnin beauty.
She's right there. Standin right in front of me.
I haven't said a word yet. Not one single word.
But listen, yer man here's in love. Love. Sonny Jim's in love.

I say hi, an she says hi back, but hers rings out forever like an
opera singer stretchin out a high note. Rhonda. Rhonda baby
makes me melt. My body is rubber. My limbs are jellied eels.
The lights go out bro. I'm weightless an the inside of my head
has a shiny white background. She fuckinwell does it to me man.
She does me over goodstyle.
She's got me. She has me. I'm trapped in her glare, her stare.
She's bowled me over big time bro. Yer man here's hooked.
Hooked, lined an sinkered.

Rhonda. My sweet Rhonda. Rhonda with the firm round tits,
Rhonda with the big brown eyes, Rhonda with the squeaky tight
arse.
Rhonda Rhonda Rhonda.
Look at her. I just stand there an look at her. She's standin right

in front of me. Poutin an posin. Aw look at her, look at those lips those dark crimson petals.

An check that walk, that cheeky wiggly walk. In fact she doesn't walk she swivels. She swivels her hips an twists her pelvis. Listen an ye'll hear the grindin.

Her smooth satin hips are grindin bro, tight jeans rubbin on soft coffee-coloured legs. An what about those jugs? Those jugs are shooglin around slowly under her shirt.

They wobble up an down an wiggle from side to side. Aye, that's what they do bro. Wobble an wiggle like two turtles bouncin on a water bed.

I've got it all in here, in my box, my brainbox, my mixed up mind, my filthy dirty lust department.

I look at her. I look an look an look. I see her an I take it all in. Her vision tattooed on my mad demented mind.

It's all in here bro. Boxed an sealed.

I'm knocked out by the first hit. Died an gone to Heaven an returned as Hugh Hefner. There's never been nothin like it. Hey God, ye better take a head count of all yer lovely angels cause ye'll find that there's one missin.

My Rhonda. My angel. My sweet gorgeous angel.

She used to have a hubby. Had. Fuckin hell. I'm thinkin he must've died. Must've. Must've fuckin pegged it.

Naw. He left, she says. Got up an left. Left me all alone. Me an my little baby girl. He left me all alone honee.

Honee. She calls me honee.

Jim. My name's Jim. Sonny Jim. People call me Sonny.

Rhonda calls me honeee. She makes it sound so sweet, like honey, real bees' honey. I can taste it as she says it. It rings out forever so it does.

A sweet-soundin elongated E.

A high E. An E sharp.

Honeee. Aw holy fuck man, doesn't it sound so mega fuckin

sexy? Honeee. Listen to it. Listen to it ching like a piece of finely cut crystal.

Aw those were the days bro. Hazy days, sexy days.
Me an my Rhonda.
Walkin in the park arm in arm, kissin an cuddlin, sittin hand in hand on park benches. We don't care who sees us, the whole wide world can watch.
Ducks quackin, birds chirpin, little silver fish makin ripples in the river. Everythin is beautiful bro, there's nothin else on this planet. There's just nothin else goin on but me an my baby. Just you an me babes, now an forever. The rest of my life man, this is where it's gonni be.

Freeze this moment. Don't let it die. Keep it an capture it, lock it up forever. Please Lord in Heaven don't let me lose this wonderful feelin.
We go drivin in the countryside. Weekends at the seaside walkin on the beach.
We go to her daddy's caravan.
Mummy an daddy's loveshack.
They like me, they do, they like yer man here. Nice guy, good guy, good for their daughter, makes her happy. Happiest they've seen her in a long time, couldn't be happier, couldn't have done better if she tried.
What a nice boy, treats her well, treats her like a queen.
Sonny boy. A real nice boy.

They gave us the keys to the caravan. On yees go. Treat it like yer own. Enjoy yerselves. Have a great time. A wee trial honeymoon. A wee dress rehearsal for the big picture.
The weddin. The weddin of the year. Our weddin.
Me an Rhonda are gonni get married bro, no doubt about it. Yer man here's in love big time. He wants to marry Rhonda. We're gonni spend the next hundred years together. Nothin's gonni stop us.

Nice wee caravan. Nice an tidy, warm an homely. A lovely place for a wee trial run.

A wee two-berth. Cozy an comfy.

We unpack an head downtown. We're dressed to kill so we are. A handsome couple walkin hand in hand, headin downtown to a wee trendy restaurant.

She calls it a rest-ronng. The onng rings out like the eee in honeee.

So chic, so sexy. Sexy little rest-ronng.

Check it out man, how the other half live. Real classy stuff. She teaches me table manners, shows me how it's done.

Ye see, yer man here just dunno. I know fuck-all bro.

Knives an forks? What the fuck? What's the fuck's the difference? Big forks, wee forks? I bet ye the big forks are for bigger mouthfuls an they just give ye two in case ye drop one. Aye, I bet ye.

Rhonda babe. Stylish an chic, sassy an classy.

She calls me honeee. You work from the outside in honeee.

Yeah babe, that's right, from the outside in, work from the outside in.

Easy peasy man, easy when ye know how. Oh for fucksake, look, I've even got a six-inch chib for steaks.

Two juicy steaks with tangy onions swarmin all over the plate. Best steaks in the business, the wee waiter says. Best in the world. Bubbly an juicy. Winner of the world's juiciest steak competition. Could cut it with yer finger so ye could. Just suck it man, no need to chew. Suck it an see. Just press it against the roof of yer mouth with yer tongue an let it slither like warm flowin lava down yer thoat. It's so juicy an soft as it gently tip-toes its way along my tastebuds an slides gently down my neck. Rich beefy nectar. Everythin is perfect.

Tasty grub, tasty lady. The light an lazy music in the background whispers sweet nothins in my ears as soft golden candles flicker in front of my eyes.

We go walkin, walkin through the streets takin in the night, the atmosphere, the busy bars buzzin with people dancin, singin, kissin, cuddlin, holdin hands an laughin.
We sip exotic cocktails, interact with locals, chat to the bar staff. Nice an easy. My luck is in bro, I've hit the jackpot. Three golden stars on the fruit machine. Fifty big ones, drinks all round folks, nights like this are few.

All the locals are lookin at Rhonda an me. People stare. Stare at two strangers.
Guys stare at her then stare at me cause I'm with her. Even girls stare at Rhonda. They do. They do that kinda thing anyway, girls. Aint that right?
It's a girly thing. Girls stare at other girls in admiration, in a jealous way, in a kinda, oh I wish I looked like that, kinda way. They do.
They look at Rhonda that way. They whisper an stare.

Oh look at that girl's hair. Gorgeous hair.
Deep brown curls that dance across her shoulders.
Aw look at her skin. Coffee-coloured skin.
You've got lovely skin, they say to her, oh you have absolutely gorgeous skin, who does yer make-up? Where do ye buy yer clothes?
Guys ogle at Rhonda an ogle at me. What does a girl like her see in a guy like him? Lucky bastart. Lucky you. Wish I was you.

We drank an danced the night away, danced an sang an bounced about under hazy orange streetlamps. Fucksake.

Watch this, she says, have ye ever tried this?
Watch the fuzzy orange balls as they bounce across the sky.
This is how ye do it. Ye screw yer face up an tighten up yer eyes.
Open them just a teensie weensie bit an no more, then look up at the glow from the streetlamps, shake yer head about an jump

up an down. It's magical. Bouncy fuzzy orange balls.

Lie on the grass, she says, I want to show ye this.
Yer man here's feelin hot an he just loves a bit of fresh air
delight so he does.
Fucksake babe, let's do it right here, right in front of every cunt
cause yer man just loves an audience.
Did I ever tell ye the Sonny boy likes an audience?
Oh fuck aye man, the thought of people watchin just blows my
bawbag to the Moon so it does.
Let's go. Let's do it, do it, do it.
Lie down honeee, she says, be patient, wait till we get home.
We lie on the grass.
Shut yer eyes, she says. Imagine really hard that we're lyin on the
sky. Now take deep breaths in out in out. Concentrate. Inhale.
Exhale. Turn it all upside down in yer head. Imagine we're lyin
on the sky lookin down. Concentrate. Focus.
Now open yer eyes an imagine yer lookin down.
We look down, we look down at blackness. A black sheet of
velvet sprayed with twinklin stars. A plane floats by. An then
another one goin that way. Thin clouds scatter an break up into
nothin. The fuzzy orange dots bounce like beach balls on a cold
dark sea. What's goin on bro?

Lyin in the park, arms wide open, we float like eagles spreadin
our wings an driftin through the night gettin further an further
away. Weightless an free. Astronauts lost in space, driftin into
oblivion, floatin through the galaxies. Time stands so still it's
scary. Rhonda an me floatin off forever an ever an never to be
found. Who cares? Not me. Not us.

Aw man. What a night. We float an bounce an stagger an laugh.
Laugh an dance the night away.
We make our way back to the caravan. The love nest. The
honeymoon suite. The passion wagon.
Passion, let's have passion baby. Yer man here's big on passion.

I'm hot, so hot, so very hot an horny. Serious stuff bro, the Sonny boy takes all this serious.

Rhonda slips into somethin sexy. A tiny pink teddy. Aw for fucksake.
Lovely an lacy. It's a see-through.
I can see through it.
I can. You can. A blind fuckin man can. Ye could see through it from Mars so ye could. I can see her tits an her nipples. Look at those nipples, brown an bold an tasty as Maltesers. I can see them man. Firm an ripe an ready for sookin.
I can see her pussy too, her neat juicy pussy. I can see it, see it clear as day, I can see it, smell it, taste it. Yer man here's just about to taste it, lick it, bite it, eat it.
Fine lacy negligée. So pink an skimpy. I'm just gonni wrap my tongue around it an peel it off with my teeth.

The Sonny boy's gonni go all night so he is. The auld hormones man, they're racin like Red Rum. Yer man here's a mule, a horse, a stallion, a finely tuned thoroughbred. A Derby winner.
I always start off in a slow canter. Aye, always. Nice an slow strokes, that's the game, get the breathin right, find yer rhythm. Soft an gentle, no rush bro, treat her like a lady. Now give that throttle a push, increase the tempo.
Give it a dig, dig the heels in, keep that rhythm, don't miss a beat. Concentrate. That's it man, steady as a rock. Push harder, more force needed, make her work faster, increase the pace.
Now giddy up into a gallup. Faster faster faster. Go go go. Go all night baby. Aint ever gonna stop. Yer man here's a stayer. Go all night.

Hey, what's that noise man?
I'll tell ye what that noise is, that's the fuckin burds chirpin.
Aye, yer man here goes all night.
Oh fuck, she screams, oh honeee oh oh fuck oooh oooh that's so so nice faster faster slow slow oh baby baby don't stop don't

ever ever ooooh honeeeee slow down honeee slowww.
Slow down, she says.

Slow down? Can't be done so it can't.
Yer man here can't slow down. Ye can't slow down a runaway train.

It's the final furlong baby, go baby go. I smack her arse for the final run in, the winnin post's in sight, I can see it bro, it's up there ahead.
Giddee up, here we come, get the auld head down son. Tunnel vision.
I take up the commentary, let my baby know what's about to come.

An it's the bold Sonny Jim comin through on the inside, he leans forward, head up, back straight he locks his legs, he's out of his saddle he can see the finishin post up ahead.
But aw man, what's this?

He starts huffin an puffin, the stamina starts wiltin, he's gonni fall at the last hurdle, he aint gonni make it, the auld coal train just aint got the juice, its fire's goin out, its engine's packin in. My balls are gonni burst, I've stopped firin on all cylinders. It's my balls man, my bladder, it's burstin, my bladder aint holdin its own, it's pushin on my scrotum, it's tweakin my sphincter muscles, it's startin to tickle like fuck.

Aye, it's the auld vinegar stroke tickle, but it aint what ye think man, it's my bladder, it's gonni spring a leak. Ahhh fuck man, yer man here's gonni have to dismount, gonni jump the saddle, I need a hit an miss, I'm gonni piss all over the place.
It's dribblin, it's squirtin an it aint gonni wait. I've just got to piss bro. Piss an piss an piss. When ye've got to go, ye've got to go. Yer man here's got to go. Auld mother nature's diggin her sharp claws into my big bulgin bawsack.
Toilets, where the fuck's the toilets?

The toilets are miles away. Wouldn't really matter anyway. The flood gates have opened. I've started a slow, leaky, dribbly piss. It's the usual. Ye can never find a piss pot when ye need one. There's one, she says. Over there on top of the sink. An empty milk bottle.

Aw yessss, ya fuckin beauty. I knew there had to be one somewhere. Every caravan should have one. I bet ye it's what her daddy uses. Ye know what the auld yins're like, they need to piss a lot. Piss piss piss.
That's got to be what it's there for. Well done auld daddy. Fine man Dan. Thank the Lord for tiny milk bottles.
Yee haaa. I'm gonni put it to the test, gonni blow it apart. I hope whoever blew this bottle done it well bro, hope they didn't go easy on the glass cause yer man here's gonni smash it into powder.

Aw yessss. Pure relief. The auld adrenalin rush ye get from pishin is nearly as good as gettin yer trumpet blown. The pleasure of it. Piss an piss an piss. Such pleasure, such delight. A nice pissy tickle. A warm golden flame caressin my inner scrotum.
Keep on goin man. One pint, two pints, three pints, four. More more more. There's always fuckin more. Fill it up an pour it out. My poor sweet baby. Sweet Rhonda lyin there waitin, waitin for the horse. Like I say, I'm a horse. Half man half horse. Pissin like a horse. A fuckin brewer's horse.
We're now big buddies me an that bottle.
Saved the day more than once so it did. Saved my bacon. Saved my bawbag. Saved me an Rhonda's fantastic fuck sessions.
It saved so much time so it did. Fuck that havin to jump off an run away to a toilet. Just piss in the bottle an jump back on. All weekend we done it. On an off. Pissin an shaggin. Eatin fine food an drinkin fine wine. What a time, what a real fine time.

But then it was time to come home bro. All good things come to an end. Me an my Rhonda. Headin back home. Back to reality.

But that wasn't the end of it. There was more fun to come.
Fuckin fun an games.
I'm tellin ye. Listen to this.

We were only back home a day or two when I walked in through
the door an got pure shocked to fuck.
Well, ye see, the thing is, ye don't really think about what yer
doin or what ye've done. Well yer man here doesn't. Ye go on
a tidal wave, ye go on a fuck spree, ye need a piss, ye piss in a
bottle. D'ye know what I'm sayin? Ye think no more about it. Ye
don't. Ye don't man, why would ye?

Rhonda was sittin on her chair. Sittin lookin up at me. Lookin at
me nice. A nice smile but she also had a stare. It was a strange
look bro, a look I aint ever seen before. It's a look so cute but
with a rugged edge.
Somethin aint right.
She smiles, shuts her eyes, shakes her head an tuts.
Oh see you, she says, what a man, yer a right rascal.
She was at her auld daddy boy's house earlier. Says she was tellin
daddy all about our holiday, was tellin him we had a great time,
only thing that spoiled it was the toilets, the toilets were miles
away.

Then daddy says yes, that's the only thing that annoys him, that,
an the fact they only sell cartoned milk an he fuckinwell hates
cartoned milk, hates it so much he keeps a bottle on top of the
fridge. The milk tastes cooler in a bottle. Daddy just loves his
milk from that bottle.
Oh fuck man. Oh gulp she says. Rhonda goes gulp.
Oh man oh man. What about those auld guys?
The auld daddy boy. Doesn't like cartoned milk. He always keeps
a fresh bottle, keeps it on the fridge. Milk is nicer an fresher an
cooler in a bottle.
Oh my fuck. Don't auld daddies just think of everythin?

Chapter Three.
Happy Daze.

Those were the days. Happy days. Big fun days. So much fun we
laughed until our hearts stopped.
We had it so good once. Rootin tootin good. Me an my honey.
I loved it when she called me honeee. She sung it like the
sweetest nightingale so she did.
Aw man, it had this sexy ring.
Honeeeeee. The eeee bit pinged like a fine ming vase.

Oh I love you, she says.
I love you too, I say.
I said it first, she says.
But I told you at two minutes past twelve last night, so I said it
first.
Oh I love you honeeee.
I love you too.
Our big love. Our love shack. Our love nest. Our beautiful blue
room.
Soft sounds, low lights. My angel in a soft silky negligée with
eyes like Maltesers meltin into a pale creamy backdrop.

I knew I couldn't keep it up man. I fuckinwell knew. I just knew.
I can't. I never can. C'mon ya cunt. Behave. I can, I can if I try.
Naw ye can't. That's the fuckin truth. The Sonny Jim boy just
can't behave. Aw man, I try but I just can't. Ye know what it's
like bro. Ye try yer fuckin best but sooner or later ye waste it big
time. How do I know, how do I know that?
Wait an I'll tell ye how. Because I always do it. I always fuck
things up. Aye, big time. Yer man here's a full time fuck-up.
I contaminate beauty. I take sweetness an drain it dry, I squeeze
out all the sugar. I've done it all my days bro. That's what yer
man here does best.

Give me a call honeee. That's what she'd say. Yeah no probs, just a phone call to let me know yer comin home.

So I'm thinkin to myself, it's a skoosh case. A novelty at first. OK baby, that's me just leavin. I'm on my way, on my way home. I take a fast cab home an there she is, my sweetheart, standin waitin for me at the window. We do all our usual lovey dovey stuff.

Hi honeee, did ye have a nice day?
Missed you.
Missed you too.
Love you honeee.
Yeah, love you too.
Oh, but I said it first.

Yer shower's runnin honeee, bathrobe's on the radiator.
Big fluffy polar bear bathrobe. Soft sweet-smellin towellin, so warm an sensuous. Like a Persian cat's tail strokin my damp naked back. Oh an that smell, that delicious tonsil tinglin smell. My mouth droolin at the edges, saliva runnin riot round my tastebuds. The aroma sendin lovely tangy shockwaves down my throat. Check it out man. Check it out.

In the kitchen there's spicy Italian sauce bubblin an poppin round tomatoes an mushrooms all laced in pasta trimmins. Aw man, I'm tellin ye, I'd crawl a mile of barbed wire for to poke my nose in there bro.
Tasty cheesy dips an fancy cut bread. The dessert sits at the side.
Waitin, waitin, teasin the skin off the roof of my mouth.
Sticky toffee sauce an sweet cherry toppin.
Jesus Christ Almighty man. I wonder how the poor folk are livin? This is the life.
This is the life yer man leads. Fuck the poor folk. Fuck yees. Yer man here likes to lord it. Too right man. Too right.

Here she comes. My sweetheart bringin me my pleasure on a

snazzy silver tray. Check it out, shiny bright silver. Delightfully decorated in all my favourite treats. A can of beer, a glass of voddy for the body, a wee jar of cashew nuts, twenty smokes an a can of diet Coke for a wee mixer.

All this brought through an served on a plate to yours truly. Fit for a king. Aye yer man here's the king. The king of kings. The boss man. The bold Sonny Jim.

Haw King Faruke. Go fuck yerself ya peasant. I'm the new man. The new kid on the block. The new king is born. King of the fuckin castle bro.

But like I said, like I told ye earlier, it was never gonni last, all that lovey dovey stuff. I could never keep it up. No way could I maintain it. The writin was on the wall bro. Big fuckin bright white letters against a dirty black background.

DESTRUCT.

Do ye ever hear cunts talkin about pressin the button?
Ye know the one I mean.
The one that bleeps an flashes an screams out, hey all you crazy cunts, roll up roll up, looney tunes unite, join the crazy bastarts club, do any of yees want to self destruct, any cunt, any cunt interested? That one. The big red fucker.
Yer man here's got his own personal button bro. Don't need no coaxin. Press here. Okey dokey. BOOMM.
Aye, that's what I do. Self-destruct. Give me an inch an I take a million miles. Give me yer hand an I'll rip yer fuckin arm off. Give me a smile an I'll steal the teeth right out yer fuckin head. Yip.
That's me mate.
That's what I do.
That's what yer man here does best. Better than any cunt I know.

Chapter Four.
Nothin Stronger.

Ye see, the real problem is the Sonny boy's a headbanger. Aye, a real headbanger.

Yer man here sticks the head on walls so he does.

Bang bang bang.

Walls an doors. Punches kicks an headers them. Temper. It's the red stuff that causes it ye see. Not the cheap wine. Naw. Well it is that too, but it's the other red stuff I'm talkin about.

The mist, the auld red mist man. That's the real problem. Down it comes like heavy sodden clouds fallin out the mountains. The deep red mist. The mad mental temper.

Just look what it does bro. Take a look around ye. Look at the state of this house man. Check it out. What's it like? The surface of the fuckin Moon. The walls, aw fuck, look at them. Lunar landscape walls. Rhonda cracks up man, screams an bawls an shouts.

What the fuck've ye got against walls ya crazy bastart eh, walls an doors, what the fuck've they ever done to you?

Dunno really. Dunno. Walls don't hit back. Smack. Fuck ye. One way traffic with all these headers an punches. They throw no blows back so they don't.

Got to get them fixed but, the walls, the holes. Oh fuck aye. Out of sight out of mind. Too many flashbacks, too much pain.

I know a guy, a big handy guy. Big Joey, I always call on Joey. The big man fills them in, smoothes them over with his nice shiny trowel.

Nice an smooth.

Don't worry, I'll see to it sweetheart, yer man here'll get it sorted.

Rhonda's goin haywire, doin her fuckin dinger.

Get it sorted ya cunt. Ye better get it fixed. Look at the place, my lovely wee house. Look at it, just look at it. Aw fuck, aw fuck. Sunday mornin first thing, phone big Joey. Aye, big Joey boy gonni sort out the problem. Smooth out the walls, smooth out my mind. Out of sight out of mind.
Take away the pain man, all those holes, holes in the walls, holes in the doors, holes in my memory. Aw Jesus Christ.

Get yer arse down here big man, help me out, help me out for fucksake.
Yer man here's head's like a machine shop. Drillin bangin boomin flashin.
All sorts of stuff goin on in here bro. There's mad screamin motorbikes flyin over my head. Don't fuckin touch me, don't rub against me.
I'm fragile. I'm delicate.
I'm chokin for a swally. Chokin man. The Sonny boy's gaggin.
Aw fuck I need a drink, need one, aye, I do man, need one, just a wee sip, a wee sook, the hair of the dog an all that. That's all I need. That'll solve the problem.
Aye.
Naw.
Naw, it aint that simple. It'll cause a greetin match. Rhonda's on her high horse, she's gettin fuckin ratty.
It's the mornin drinkin ye see. Mornin drinkin.

Fuck you an yer mornin drinkin, she says, I've had enough of it, yer not startin any o that shit in here. This aint no pishy stinky ale house. We don't want no alkies livin here.
See, see what I'm sayin? A wee hair of the auld mongrel's arse aint as straightforward as you an I might think mate.
I need a drink but. I'm chokin. But how am I gonni get one? How?

I'll think of somethin. I always do. Aye. The bold Sonny Jim thinks of somethin.

Big Joey boy. Big man, I say, I'm fuckin choking. Gaggin. Need a
swally.
He tells me to go ahead, says he'll have one too.
I tell him it aint that easy, naw it aint man, aint as easy as ye
think. Ye see, I can't just go an have a swally any more, naw, it
aint like it used to be in the good auld days.
She's goin haywire, she's a cat on sticky black asphalt. Got to
tread easy. The auld jacket man, know what I'm sayin? The auld
nail's hangin on by its baw hairs.
Aye, honest, it's that bad so it is. Can't push it no more.

So I tell him that I've got this plan, It's dead easy. Honest to fuck
man, it's pure lemon squeezy.
I tell him I'm gonni let him get started, get the tools an that
out. Then I'm gonni say to him d'ye fancy a wee cuppa tea an a
biscuit?
But when I ask him this, he's to turn round an say, have ye not
got anythin stronger?
Well, there ye are man, doddle. I'll pull a couple of tins out
the fridge. One for you, one for me. I mean I'd have to join in,
wouldn't I? Ye can't go an ask a guy down to yer house to do
some work an let him sit there suppin away on his jack.
No way man, not this dude. Fucksake, what kinda cunt would
do that now? The big guy smiles an says, See you ya cunt ye, yer
some fuckin man.

The plan's all set.
The big man gets to work plasterin away, smoothin out the mess,
the holes, the pain, the memories. The walls all nice an smooth,
no more holes, holes no more. Rhonda's chattin away, givin it
all the small talk. Oh yer doin a grand job Joey, oh yes, smashin
lovely marvellous. She's talkin all hoity toity. She does that when
cunts come to visit so she does. Snobby cunt. Fucksake man.
What's all that about eh? Dunno. You tell me.

So the big yin's smoothin away, slippin an slidin that shiny trowel over those silky smooth walls.

It's time man, time to put the master plan into action. Here we go bro. Watch this, watch yer man playin an absolute masterstroke. A true fuckin genius at work. Watch. Watch an learn.

Hey big yin, yer doin a grand job there, c'mon take a wee break, aye, have a wee blaw. D'ye fancy a wee cuppa Rosie?

Hey check it. Check the Rhonda blade. What's she like man? Check the boat race. None the fuckin wiser so she aint, in fact she's even givin it a wee, aw that was nice of you to ask, kinda smile. Hehe. Ya beauty. Ale time. Ale time here we come. Aw man I can fuckin taste it so I can, taste the auld golden honey drops brushin the edges of my lips.

I'm just waitin for my big buddy now, my big partner in crime to do his bit an add the finishin touches. C'mon big guy, c'mon to fuck, let me hear it, let me hear those words, have ye not got anythin stronger? Go on, say it, it's easy, just say it, have ye not got anythin stronger?

The big guy but, fucksake, he just keeps workin away, smoothin away at the walls, doesn't answer, doesn't even turn round.

Come on ya cunt, say it, say it, six fuckin words man, a piece of piss so it is.

But naw, nothin, nothin happens for ages an ages an ages.

An then he stops. He puts his trowel down, turns round with this big cheesy grin on his face that's so fuckin wide it pushes his ears round the back of his head.

An then he speaks. Aye he fuckin goes an speaks alright.

D'ye know what he says, d'ye know what the big cunt goes an says? He turns round an says, Aw I could just fair choke a cuppa tea mate, go on, milk an two sugars.

Aye that's what he done man. That's what the big bastart went an done. Milk an two sugar. Fuck ye. Yer man here. Dyin. Shakin rattlin rollin. Dyin for a drink. Bastart. Ya bastart ye.

Fuck it. Two cups of tea. Milk an two sugars.

Chapter Five.
Chibbed.

I was alright at one time. Honest, ask any cunt. I was an alright guy. Normal. Ordinary. Fine. Just yer average Joe.
But all that changed after I had my accident. Aye, it all changed big time.
Cunts tell me that all the time so they do. They tell me I'm not fuckin right anymore, not right in the head. Ye've never been the same since ye had that accident Sonny.
That's what they tell me.

Accident? What accident?
All I did was stagger out onto the street. I didn't feel a thing. Nothin. The only thing I felt hittin my face was cold air.
I felt dizzy. Then lightheaded.
Then bang. This almighty explosion erupts inside my head. My eyes pop, fireworks go off in front of my face an bright screamin stars snap crackle an pop through the back of my eyes.

I start screamin. Aw my God I'm gonni die, I'm gonni die right here in the street.
I've been shot.
Shot, stabbed, punched, kicked, jumped on. Aw Jesus Christ Almighty I'm bein murdered. Murdered, aye that's what I start screamin man.
I'm screamin blue murder but not a soul can hear it.
Nobody's listenin.
Well, see if they are, then they aint givin a fuck cause no cunt's stoppin it, no cunt's comin to my aid. A desperado in distress.
Help me help me help me.
I'm bein brutally beaten up man. Battered to death big time. Stabbed in the head, neck, shoulders an back. Blunt an sharp objects.

The pain runs through me like an ice cold wind.

Aw my fuck, I've been stabbed man. Somebody please please help me.

Don't let me die, please don't let me die, not here, lyin in the street in a pool of my own blood pish an shit an chokin on big fat jellied lumps.

My keks are full of shit. That's what happens to ye by the way, I'm tellin ye, the auld bowels, they just empty their load so they do. Bowels belly bladder, the lot. That's a fact. See when yer just about to pop yer clogs, that's what they go an do. The auld bowels, they just give up lock stock an barrel an hand themselves in at the station.

Did ye not know that?

Well it's a fuckin fact.

An I'll tell ye another thing. Ye don't have to die first.

Yer man here's a dead man. Well not quite. But just about.

Holy Jesus God I've been stabbed. Stabbed in the head neck an face.

Short sharp stingin stab wounds. Burstin my belly an breakin my back. The short shiny blade keeps slashin an slicin through me like bullets from a gun.

Zip zip zip.

Stingin an burnin like splashes of electric rain. The stabs, the slashes, they keep on comin man, whizzin through the moonlight, they take no break.

I stagger across the street, bangin into wide-eyed strangers an dodgin in an out of skiddin cars.

I crash down face first an my head bounces twice on the cold black tar. Hot blood spews out onto the cold mucky slush an hisses like a snake as it turns it deep dark burgundy. The pain man, aw the fuckin pain, it's a pure pain in the arse so it is. Pain in the neck, the head, the back, the arse. Pain in the fuckin arse. Ye've no idea man. I'm tellin ye, ye've no idea. Even after all this time. Eighteen months now, eighteen sore an sorry months an I still can't bear it. Honest. Ye dunno what it's like. Man, it just aint bearable.

An I'll tell ye somethin else. That's only on the outside. That's only the outer pain. The scars. The scars all heal. Well near enough, near enough that ye can't really see them. Take a look at me now man. Take a look. Not a close look. But just a wee quick glance an ye'll see that I look like any other dude. Aye I do. I look no different from yer average guy. But don't come too close mister. Don't dare come too close.

Ye might not like what ye see.

The scars paint a horrible picture. The inner scars I mean. They're the real psycho killers. The mind-eatin demons. They're the ones ye don't see. Can't see. They're the ones that torture yer sorry soul. They break ye down so they do, a wee bit at a time. The wee mental pain soldiers. That's what it feels like. Wee soldiers with big sharp bayonets on their rifles an they're twistin an turnin them an grindin them right into yer mindpiece.

Stab stab stab. Stabbin me still. Stabbin my head. Stabbin my head on the inside. Openin up my wounds, my poisoned mental stab wounds. Openin them up an lettin all the yellow pus pish out. Openin them up in the dead of night when no one else is around. They come an visit me at two, three, four, five in the mornin. Uninvited guests bro. Come without an invite. Gatecrash the party. Who the fuck invited you cunts along?

Wakey wakey ya bastart, they say to me. Remember us? We're yer inner scars my son. We're yer mind's tormentors. We've come to give ye the bastart of all nightmares.

Yoo hoo. Wakey wakey. Time for terror.

Big black red-eyed daggers come screamin out of the darkness. Laughin like loonies while they stab me through the eyeballs. They piss boilin blood that sticks to my flesh an smoulders away like a shit covered corpse.

Their pricks are three feet long electric eels that start whippin me to death.

They scream pure dog's abuse right into my face. Say yer sorry ya bastart, they scream. Say yer fuckin sorry ya dirty rotten fuckpig. Ye deserved to die so ye did. Yer the most dirty rotten cunt that ever walked the face of this earth. Scream ya bastart. Ye better beg for mercy ya pail of pish cause we're gonni set fire to yer little midge-sized prick ya dirty horrible filthy piece of pig shit. Scream, go on ya scumbag, scream in fuckin pain haaaarrgghaaargghhh.

They piss on me man. They piss pure poison. Hot sticky black acidic poison.

It burns deep into my open pus-filled wounds givin off a eye waterin stench that peels the skin off yer face an turns the air toxic makin me boak up big lumps of raw liver.

Chapter Six.
Mickey Mulrooney an the Slinky Siamese.

Compensation is no consolation.
I know, I know. But hey, it softens the blow.
It does man, it sure fuckin does, it eases the pain a bit. Nothin like the feelin of smooth silky greenbacks to sooth yer sorry mind.
Yer man here needs a curer. I go for a walk to clear the head.
I walk up to see our man Mickey. Mickey the man. Mickey Mulrooney. Criminal lawyer. Aye too fuckin right he is. Bigger fuckin criminal than the Kray twins.
The bold Mick. Lay it on thick Mick.
That's what he says man, says it all the time. D'ye know what were gonni do here son? We're gonni lay it on thick.

His eyes light up like a smackhead in a poppy field.
He takes one look at me an says, fucksake Sonny boy, what the fuck happened to ye, did ye have a square go with a gang of gorillas?
Jesus Christ man, look at the fuckin state of ye. Yer face is like a patchwork quilt. It'd be easier to put Humpty Dumpty back together.

Would ye like a wee dram? he says.
Would I like a wee dram? I say.
I'd like a big dram, I say.
What the fuck happened? he says. Tell it to yer daddy. Tell it to me straight.
I give it to him straight. Straight between the eyeballs. Fuck ye man.
Ye asked for it. Here we go.

I got bladed man. Chibbed. An unprovoked attack.
I was walkin out of Mucky's bar carin not a jot an the next
thing, bang, I'm sliced into slitherines. Gutted an filleted an left
lyin there in a heap. Some fucker done me man. Done me over
goodstyle. Perforated like a tea bag.
Look at me man. Look at me. What the fuck am I like eh?
I show him my sheet, my medical sheet. I show him pictures
taken before an after my operations. Look at my face man, what
a stitch-up, what a fuckin mess. Stab wounds an slashes. Eighty-
seven stitches. Fourteen fuckin stab wounds. Fucksake man, look
at me, I'm a freak show, I'm the man with the face like the map
of Ireland an the body like a dot-to-dot book. Every fucker looks
at me, they all stop an stare. C'mere an see the state of this cunt,
has any cunt got a camera, fucksake don't let the weans see it.

I put it to him straight. Money. How much are we talkin about
here mate?
A hundred quid a stitch. A grand a stab wound. Easy man. Easy
fuckin peasy. We're in the money. We're in here big time bro.
Cruisin on all six cylinders.
It's an absolute doddle, he says. Easy peasy, skoosh case, piece of
fuckin cake. An open an shut case.

Well, I heard that last bit. That's one thing about the Sonny boy,
there's fuck-all wrong with his ears. Absolutely fuck-all bro. I can
hear a snail draggin his balls along the grass.
Open an shut case did ye say my man, open an shut case?

Hey listen, that was his first mistake. Mistake No. 1. Mickey's
boy's a real fly guy. Second flyest guy in town. Aye, second. Guess
who's first. Guess who's number one.
Well, I'll be OK for a wee bit up front then, I say. A wee kinda
sweetener, a wee sort of daily allowance just to keep me tickin
over eh?
As ye say, the money's in the bag. An open an shut case.
Skoosh case, doddle, piece of fuckin cake.

At this point the wee cunt changes his tune quicker than the orange walk passin by Scruffy Murphy's. Aye, he fuckin does by the way, honest, his mood changes quicker than a schizophrenic.

Oh, eh, I dunno about that son, he says. I mean I've a wee business to run, ye know how it is, I don't like to count my chicks. I mean it's really just a figure of speech that, open an shut case, no such thing really. I dunno, I really dunno.

Well I'm sittin there quite chilled, quite serene an relaxed, sippin on a whisky that tastes like Miss World's love juice. I stretch out an spread my arms across the back of his leather couch, when *ziiiiiing*. Pain man. Unbelievable pain.
What the fuck was that, delayed reaction or what? This pain like a zillion volts of electricity blitzin through my brain blowin out my eyeballs. Holy fuck man. What happened, what the fuck happened?
I'll tell ye right now what happened.
Simon. Simon the slinky Siamese. That's the bold Mickey's cat. It was lyin across the couch havin a few zzzzzz's an yer man here must've invaded his territory, must've gave him a wee fright. Right?
Well bro, now the fright's on me. These two big slobbery fangs just went piiiing, like that man, like a two-pronged electric plug bein jabbed right through my arm an turned on at full power. Fuckin hell, as if I aint got enough holes in me as it is. Aye, honest, my body's like a fuckin colander an this wee bastart goes an sinks two more holes in me. Oh ya bastart. Call me lucky.
Aye, call me lucky man. Why's that? Why's that, I hear ye ask?

Wait an I'll tell ye why. It leaps across the table an right into wee Mickey's arms. He stands there smilin an strokin it slowly like the wee baldy baddy in the Bond films.
Oops a daisy, he goes. Sorry about that son, did she bite ye there, are ye alright? Did ye get a wee fright? Sorry about that young man.

Well there's the bold Simon curlin round Mickey's arm hissin away like a big hairy snake. Ya bastart ye. The fuckin thing's givin me a sleekit stare with its big luminous greeny yellow eyes. He's lovin it so much he's smilin.

Aye, honest man. I could swear the fuckin thing was smilin. Oh ya fucker. Look at ye, look at ye. Bet yer fuckin lovin it, bet ye'd take a hard-on if ye hadn't been snekked.

But ye see, all that electricity that just shot right through my body has brought on a mindblowin brainwave. Aye, a brainwave. Genius, yer man here's a genius.

I look up at Mickey. I look at Simon, then back at Mickey.

I give him my favourite dead man stare. I show him my arm. Two tiny rivers of blood dribble down like snot wigglin out a wean's nose.

Look, I say. Look at my arm Mickey. Yer wee cat did that. Yer cat just caused me grievous bodily harm. It did by the way. A real serious injury. Look, yer man here's bleedin like a burd on her bad week. Aw my fuck man, two holes in my arm, two slits, two fannies. Fuckin hell, I'm deformed. I'm a freak show. Listen, this is not what I meant when I wished for a couple of bits of fanny on my arm, d'ye know what I'm sayin?

Just be careful what ye pray for bro, ye might just get it.

Aw holy mother of fuck. I start sweatin, shakin, cryin. A panic attack is on the way bro, it's fuckin comin through. Aye, yer man here's the world champion panic attacker.

Rabies!!

Aw Holy Mother of God man, maybe I've got rabies.

Jesus.

I stare right through Mickey's head an out the other side.

I stare for ever an ever without breathin then I say, Listen Mickey my man, ye couldn't do me a favour could ye?

What's that son, he says, what can I do for ye?

I look at him an give him a wee squinty smile.
Ye couldn't give me the name of a good solicitor?

Aw for fucksake, he goes. He turns an throws Simon out the door. See you Sonny, yer a cunt so ye are. A pure fuckin cunt wee man. Honest.
OK, he says. Fifty a day's the limit. Fifty quid an not a penny more.

Chapter Seven.
Fishin for Falsers.

It was a beautiful day. A beautiful day in more ways than one. A nice wad of cash in the pocket an the sun spreadin its big cheesy grin across the sky.

It was burnin down so hard that my big baldy napper was nippin like acid under yer foreskin.

Hot hot hot. I'm tellin ye, It was so hot the dogs were shittin hard baked turds.

A lovely day, a perfect day an ideal day for a nice cold drink. Time for a swally. Aw my fuck man. Ye know what they say? Mad dogs an Coatbridge men go out in the midday sun. Well this mad dog from Coatbridge has a thirst in his throat an money in his pocket an he's headin down town bro. Down to the river me an Peezi boy go. Two bags of booze under each arm.

Party time.

Time to treat the rats, the auld river rats. That's what they call them by the way. Mad Deek, Shoogly, Boaby Breach, auld Stan an Ernie. They call them the river rats. They spend more time down here than the rats.

They're sittin at the river bank fishin. Fishin fuck-all. A piss up round a fishin rod. The rod does nothin. It's never saw a fish in its life. But the thing is, ye need it there, ye need it there in case the Polis come. We're just sittin fishin officer. Honest.

Look at all the troops man, they've left all their happy heads at home, what the fuck's up boys, why all the long faces? They look like they're havin a gloom an doom contest, they're all starin at the water an squeezin the last dregs out a couple of cans an a half bottle.

But their eyes light up like hundred watt bulbs when they see yer man. Well to put it better, their eyes light up when they see what yer man's carryin.

Their laser eyes zoom right in on my bag of tricks.

Oh ya beauty. Blue bags, blue bags are a dead giveaway. They're too big to be the rolls an papers an they're too wee to be the dirty washin. An they're clinkin. Blue clinkin bags can only mean one thing.

They're so excited to see me so they are. A long lost soulmate. Return of the prodigal son. Aw for fucksake boys, I never knew yees cared.

How's it goin Sonny boy? Long time no see bro. How's things bud? Yer lookin good. We were just talkin about ye there, aint that right troops? We were just sayin, I wonder how the auld Sonny Jim boy's doin, wonder what he's up to?

Hey, c'mon join the party dude, this aint no private affair. C'mon down.

Join in man.

I open the bags. Check their faces now. Like a classroom full of kiddies watchin Santa open his sack.

Six bottles of Buckfast, six litres of cider an two dozen tins. Party time. I'm yer man. Get stuck in boys, fill yer fuckin boots. The drinks are on me. We crack open the bottles an cans an Peezi skins up some joints.

The icy cold lager's like angels' teardrops fallin on my tongue. My grey misery clears as the soft sun keeks its cheery face through thin pink clouds. A cool breeze runs its fingers along my face an God winks down an gives me a big cheesy grin. The ripples from the river sound like cans openin as they gently smack their arses off the rocks. I look to the sky an smile as I suck gently on a joint an blow big puffs of happiness back up to Heaven.

Auld Ernie starts givin it laldy, downin the bevvy good guns. He's bangin down the cans like bullets. Bang bang bang. Take yer time ya greedy auld bastart, ye've got all day.

Fuck that all day patter, he says, Ye want blootered now. Aye, that's all ye've got lads. NOW. Tomorrow? What the fuck does that mean? There's no tomorrow, no such thing Sonny Jim. He hugs me an squeezes me an kisses my neck with his slobbery auld face. Aw for fucksake man, the auld cunt smells like a soggy fanny.

Ye need plenty lager to quench the auld thirst. Hey, listen by the way, it's hard work lyin here in this hot blazin sun. I'm tellin ye, ye've got to watch ye don't dehydrate.

What time is it? Is that the time? Fuck me man it's Buckfast time. Ernie doesn't like sookin out a bottle. No way José, that's for poofy fairies. He's got half a can of lager left. He pours the Bucky into it.
Aw ya clatty auld cunt, we call him. Take yer time ya greedy auld bastart.
Fuck yees, he goes. Give me more give me more give me more. C'mon to fuck get it down yees.

The auld yin starts chantin Bing Crosby tunes an tellin us how he knocked fuck out of Hitler durin the war.
Ya shower of cunts yees. I fought for yees durin the war so I did. Yees're only pups for fucksake, I've got string vests that're aulder than yees. Don't tell yer grandpa how to suck tits. Who the fuck d'yees think yees're talkin to? I'll fuckin knock yees out. Yoodee haw yoo deee heeee. Yahoo ya bastarts c'mon. No wonder the fuckin Germans ran away from us.

The auld yin's on a roll.
Who wants to fight? he shouts. I'll arm-wrestle any cunt in Britain.

Check him out. What's he like? Look at him. He's Status Quo.
Aye, Status Quo, rockin all over the world.
Auld Ernie gets blootered in ten minutes so he does, ten minutes man, that's all it takes.

He always blames the heat too. Aw it's the fuckin heat, see that heat it just goes for ye so it does, it must be a hundred an twenty degrees easy.

Or it's the fresh air, he'll say. Aw fuck, I was fine till I hit that fresh air. All I had was a couple of bottles of Bucky an a dozen cans. Aw see that fresh air it's a pure bastart so it is. I mean I just walked out into it an the next thing I'm in hospital gettin my stomach pumped. Dunno what the fuck happened. Aw an see this fuckin arthritis, he says. Those painkillers make me fuckin woozy.

He's bouncin about like a rubber ball.

Auld Ernie boy. Check the boat race. Check the colour. Casper the friendly ghost hasn't a look in. Honest. He makes Casper look a lovely golden brown. He starts turnin yellow like an auld pished bed sheet then he starts turnin green an then last but not least his eyes go all red an runny.

So we're sittin waitin on it. Aye, the usual, we can see it comin.

Oh fucksake lads the auld sea's a bit rough, he whines. The auld sailor's legs aint what they were. Aw man aw man aw
yeaaaauurghhhhhhhhhh
up comes the whole lot, the full monty.

Aw ya cunt, all that good drink goin to waste.

He's a greedy auld cunt auld Ernie. He's that greedy he likes to taste it twice. Once goin down an once comin back up. Fuckin glutton. Aye the auld yin barffs up the lot so he does, the works. A half bottle an three cans go right down the fishes' necks. Partytime for fishes.

His puke's full of big fatty lumps. Big bits of tatties an streaky bacon.

There's bits of chewed up sausage an beans mixed together with all this lovely green slimy elasticated snot.

The fish are onto it. Munch munch munch.

Even the frogs an the flies join in.

The auld yin's flat on his belly emptyin his guts. Gurgly boaky noises splatter on the water. He's spittin an choakin.
Serves ye right ya auld cunt, we're tellin him. Serves ye right. Ye won't listen ya dopey auld tit.

He rolls onto his back. There's gungy bits of bile smeared all over his coupon. He starts gruntin an groanin. Aww ya bastart he goes, my fuckin teeeshhh, I've lost my fuckin top teeeshhhhh.

We're rollin about pishin our pants laughin. Mad Deek starts boakin at all the boak on Ernie's face an Peezi laughs that hard he shits his trousers.
The auld yin flakes out. Fucked. Big ZZZZZZZZZZs fly through the air.

There's never a dull moment down by the river bro.
Auld Ernie man. Star turn.
The laughter dies down an we carry on skinnin up an swallyin away goodstyle. The sun plants some more hot kisses on our heads an dishes out nice warm cuddles all round. Even the fish an frogs have got their happy heads on. They smile an rub their bellies then disappear under for an afternoon nap.

We're feelin good man. Feelin happy. Happy heads all round. Fun time. Time for fun. Time for mischief. Time for a wind-up. The bold Deek. The wind-up wizard.

Deek goes like that to auld Stan, c'mon auld yin get the teeth out, c'mon, just the top set, just till we play a wee joke on the auld yin.
C'mon to fuck man we'll give ye them back.

Auld Stan's none too keen at first but hands them over.
The Deek dude sticks the teeth on the hook. Watch this lads. Wait an see this. He jams the teeth on the hook.
Cast off, *wheeeeesh*. Plop. In they go.

We sit back an wait. We sup more ale an suck the arse out a few loose joints an watch the silver river flash slithers of sharp light into our eyes as the sun does a samba dance on the ripples. We watch it man. Stare at it. Caught in a soft an sensuous trance. Aw man, look at that big orange ball doing golden wiggles on the water.

The joints do their job so well. Every single click an hiss is magnified a millionfold. Every bird chirp, every plink an plonk on the water sounds like the sweetest tinkle on the richest ivory an every breeze that brushes through the air feels like like soft warm sand bein slowly poured across my face.
Time just slowly takes its time. Time? Naw, there aint any. No such fuckin thing bro.

All of a sudden there's a bit of rough shufflin.
The auld yin starts comin round. He starts coughin an splutterin an rubbin his eyes an scratchin his baws. He starts chumpin his chops like a wean munchin soggy bread.
He's comin round, he's comin too, he's re-enterin planet bonkers. Right boys, let the show begin.
Deek grabs a hold of the fishin rod an just sits there. He starts givin it the patter, starts givin it the auld, awright auld yin? Hey, yer a greedy auld cunt so ye are. Well, I told ye didn't I? I told ye to take yer time. Yer gettin past it auld filla, yer drinkin with the big team now so ye are, drinkin with the A division. That's a right cunt what happened to yer teeth all the same. A pure fuckin shame. We did warn ye but. We all told ye.
Deek's a classical actor. I'm tellin ye. A fuckin multiple Oscar winner. Just watch the cunt, what's he like? He's playin a pure stormer.
He gives the rod a wee jag, fucksake he goes, what the fuck was that? What the fuck? Hey troops check this out, I've got a bite, I've got a bite, I'm sure I did, I definitely got a wee tug there so I did.

He starts reelin it in an watchin Ernie out of his side view.

The Auld yin's not givin a fuck at this time. He aint interested. Then all of a sudden he becomes very interested. The Deek dude just goes like that an whirls in the reel, wheekin it out the water sharp. And guess what? Guess what's on the end of it? Guess what's on the hook? We all jump up. One at a time. Me first, then Peezi then Stan then Shoogly then Boaby Breach.

Yaaaaaaaaaaahooooooooooooooo, ya fucker, Deek's screamin. Check it out troops. Check what's on yer man's hook.

Haw Ernie, Ernie my man, c'mere an see this, check out what I've just caught. I've caught yer fuckin teeth. Aw man, aw in the name of the wee man, what the fuck's the chances of that ever happenin eh? Must be a hundred million to one.

Ernie springs to his feet an shoots forward like a venomous snake zappin its prey.
Let me see, let me see, let me fuckinwell see, he goes.
He grabs the teeth, tears them from the hook an jams them right into his mouth. He wriggles them about a wee bit like he's tastin somethin to see if he likes it.
Then all of a sudden his shoulders drop an a sign of sadness hits his sorry auld face. His eyes go empty like a guy who's just nearly got the winner in the big race but just been pipped at the post.

He spits them into his hand, looks at them an shakes his head. They're not mine, he says.

Auld Stan leaps up an he's just about to tell him the score. Just about to say, It's awright man we're only kiddin, they're really mine an we were only playin a wee joke on ye.
But hey, listen. Auld Stan wasn't quick enough. Naw. Too late. Yip, too late mate. Stan's face goes whiter than Ernie's was two hours ago as he watches in horror as the bold Ernie boy drops his shoulder like a shot putter an sends the teeth spinnin through the air like a mini UFO. They make a dull soundin PLOP an ripple as they land in the river.

Naw they're not mine says Ernie.

Aw ya bastart ya bastart ya silly auld cunt.
The two of them square up. Ya auld fuckin tit ye, Stan says, they
were mine.

What the fuck d'ye mean? Ernie says, What the fuck're ye on
about?
An then the penny drops. Ernie's noticed us all lyin there pissin
our pants.
I'm tellin ye, talk about pishin yerself laughin? We were pishin
that much the river was risin to dangerous levels. I swear to fuck
bro, any more pishin an the auld river's gonni burst its banks an
flood the whole town. Easy does it boys. Go easy on that pishin.
Stan an Ernie start snarlin at each other, slabbers flyin
everywhere, not a set of teeth between them.
Square go ya auld cunt.
They square up. Fists up in the air, elbows out.
Two geriatrics fanny dancin round handbags. John L Sullivan eat
yer fuckin heart out.
They circle each other. Deek's dancin round about them refereein
the fight.

LET'S GET READY TOOOO RUUUUMMMMBBLLLE, he shouts.

They keep circlin. Ten times, twenty times, thirty times. A slow
jab gets thrown, they do an occasional bob, an odd weave. An
then right out of the blue they take a right mad lunge at each
other. They start grapplin an spinnin an spinnin. Soon every
fuckin thing in the whole wide world starts spinnin. Everythin,
Deek, Stan, Ernie, Peezi, Shoogly, Boab, the sun, the trees, the
river, the whole fuckin shebang man, all spinnin into space. It's
real fuckin top of the league cakey bakey time.

It's the dope I hope. Naw it's not, it's the drink I think. Aw holy
fuck man. Deek grabs the two of them an they start birlin an
huggin each other. Fuck the fightin, it's party time, fuckit man

we're too auld for all this.
The three of them are all huggin in a huddle. We jump up an join them, birlin like Morris dancers but without the bells. We're bouncin round an round.

Everythin's birlin man. Next thing there's this almighty splash. Fish, frogs, flies an any other fucker livin in the river do a runner an dive for cover as seven alcoholic dopeheads make an almighty plunge into the water arse first.

We climb up onto the river bank. Gurglin, boakin an spewin up all sorts of muck an shite. I lie flat out on my back an let my lungs get their breath back. I feel the big orange ball in the sky pressin its hot hands down on me. Aw yes man, nice nice nice. I'll be dry in no time. As I feel my head gettin lighter an my body gettin limp, that lovely warm air presses its thumbs lightly on my eyelids. Sweet dreams are comin bro. I put my hands inside my pockets to see if I've caught any fish. Aye, fish. I'm tellin ye, see the kind of luck yer man's been havin lately it's a wonder the auld pockets aren't jam-packed with the fuckin things.

Chapter Eight.
Hows About Some Money, Honee?

I'm a real funny guy me. I am, honest, everybody tells me so.
Ye think yer a funny cunt don't ye?
That's what people say to me, the auld Sonny boy. Ye think yer a right funny cunt.
Rhonda says it all the time.
See you, she says, ye think yer a funny cunt. But she says it with a look on her face that says, well yer fuckinwell not ya bastart.

Life was good bro. I'm tellin ye. Life was rootin tootin good.
Too fuckin good. Well we can't have that now, can we? Naw, no chance. Get the finger on that button. Mind that wee red button I was tellin ye about earlier? Aye, that one. Go for it. Press it.

Life was good. Yer man here likes the good life, likes the best of all things goin. King Faruk's a pauper compared to this dude. What about these daft cunts that say ye can't have yer cake an eat it. Fuck off. Of course ye can.

What's the point of havin yer cake if ye can't fuckinwell eat it bro? Dunno. What's the point man? You tell me. Yer man here has his cake seven days a week an eats it so he does. Oh fuck aye, eats it all up every time too.
Yum yum.

Rhonda starts gettin sick of it but. Starts gettin a bit tetchy, a bit hot under the auld collar.
Sonny boy can suss it. I'm tellin ye. Honest, yer man here's a pure dab hand at it. See if anythin's wrong, if there's anythin needin sussed, yer man here susses it. He can tell at a twitch of a midge's dick if all aint well so he can.

What's up my baby, what is it? Tell it to yer daddy. No probs. We can work it out honeychops. We can, course we can.

Rhonda's stuck for words, doesn't know what to say, doesn't know how to go about it. People say yer man here aint approachable. Who says that? Fuck off ya cunts. Go fuck yerself. I'm dead approachable. C'mon to fuck. Approach me.
What is it honeychops, what's the matter?

Well, she says, it's just like this honee.
By this time I'm just called honee. Not honeee. Not as many eee's at the end of it now. Naw, her sweet soundin honee doesn't ring out as long as it used to. Ach well.

It's just like this honee, she says. Ye've got it real good here, ye've got the best of everythin, good food, good drink, an nice clean clothes that have that nice soft baby smell the way ye like them. Yer made to feel part of the furniture honee, aint that right? Treat this place like yer own, I've always told ye, what's mine is yours. This is your home honee, she says, yer built in with the bricks. Good food, good sex, good drink. Washin, ironin, cleanin all done for ye. Lifted an laid in general honee. So what I'm tryin to say is... what I have to ask ye babe, an this aint easy, is, what about some money?

Well yer man here's completely an utterly fuckin gobsmacked. I'm pure taken aback to say the least bro. There's many things ye can call the Sonny boy. Many many things. An most of them aint too nice. That I will admit. But hey, listen, yer man here aint no cunt. No way José. Yer man here aint no Shylock, he takes no cunt for granted.
He hates cunts who squeeze other fuckers' balls.

Money? Aw for fucksake honey. Money?
I look at her, I look at her so sincere.
Look sweetheart, my sweet little honeybunch. Listen to what I'm gonni tell ye cause I mean it from the basement of my ticker.

See after all ye've done for me? An ye have done so much babes, no doubt about it, the sex, the food, the drink, the nice clean clothes, the lot. Listen. An I'm serious an don't think about tryin to talk me out of this. There's just no fuckin way I could possibly take any money.

Aye, honest to God. That's what I said. I can't take money honey. Hahaha. Naw. No way. Not after everythin ye've done for me. I can't take money.

Rhonda aint too impressed bro. Aint too amused. I mean Rhonda's quite a thick cunt. Aint the sharpest tool in the shed, but there aint no way she's buyin that one. No chance. She aint buyin all that shit. She knows fine well that I know what she meant.
Ha fuckin ha, she says. See you, ye think yer a funny cunt. Well, let me tell ye this. Then she gives yer man that look. The one I told ye about earlier. Ye think yer fuckin funny? Well yer fuckinwell not.

Chapter Nine.
Daytime Stops and Nighttime Starts.

It's make or break time, she says. We can't go on like this honee.
We're breakin each other's hearts.
Let's be good, you an me babes. Aw my wee sweetheart.
Fucksake.

I love you. You love me. I said it first. What's wrong sweetheart?
We can work it out. Our love will see us through stormy waters.
I tell her all that shit. Yer man here tells her sweet stories, sweet
nothins.
Nothin, it means nothin. The Rhonda babe aint buyin it. Buyin
no more shit stories. Rhonda babe aint daft, she's havin no more
misery. She's had it up to here. Time to get it sorted out, she says.
Listen to this. Rhonda babe comes up with a stoater.
Listen, I think it's the drinkin, she says.

My drinkin? The bold Sonny Jim boy's drinkin? What the fuck
d'ye mean babes?
There's no more drinkin durin the day, she says. Aint havin it, ye
aint ruinin our lives no more honee. No way honee. Me an little
Petals aint havin it.

Her an cute little curly-headed Petals are wantin peace an quiet,
she says. No more shit no more hassle. Any drinkin durin day an
yer man's arse is in the shitter.

She wants me to promise, wants me to cross my heart, wants
me to hope I fuckin well die a horrible death in a car smash if
I take another drink durin the day. Aye, that's what she wants
man. The Rhonda blade. Wants the Sonny boy to swear on all
his weans' lives so she does. Wants them all struck down with a

flesh-eatin disease if I'm standin here tellin porkies.

Well fuck me. Listen to it. Three words spring to mind I tell her.
Kettle pot an black. Aye.

The Sonny boy doesn't need drink. Doesn't need the stuff at all.
I mean, that's the way ye take it aint that right bro? That's the
way ye react, when some cunt suggests that ye should take it
easy on yer drinkin, ye take it like it's some kinda insult don't
ye eh, like they're insinuatin that yer some kinda fuckin alky or
somethin?

So ye convince yerself without thinkin, don't ye?

No probs, I tell her. No problemo sweetheart. No sweat. Do not
fuckinwell sweat it. The Sonny boy's as solid as a rock. Stands on
his own two feet at all times. Needs no thing or no cunt. Faces
life square on so he does. Doesn't need no crutch. Fucksake man.

Stop drinkin? Easy by the way. Easy peasy slutty an sleazy. Aint
no fuckin sweat mate. No way. Won't ever let ye down sweetie
pie. Yer man don't need drink. Never have done never will. The
Sonny boy don't need drink to enjoy himself.

It's OK. Forget about it. Bury it. Put it out yer mind. Outa sight
outa mind. But the thing is, ye can't always keep it out yer mind.
Yer man here sits an thinks about this. The Sonny boy's a thinker.
Did I ever tell ye that the Sonny boy thinks things through.
No drink durin daytime? OK. Okey dokey.
But it aint that simple. Naw it fuckin aint. Not in this life anyway.
Naw in this fuckin life nothin ever is. It's one thing sayin ye'll do
somethin an another thing doin it. Innit?
Fucksake stop drinkin durin the day?
Problem.
Naw, no problem.
No problem to the the Sonny boy.
The Sonny boy's a charmer, got the gift of the gab. The bold
Sonny Jim boy can wrap Rhonda round his pinky like a python.
No daytime drinkin? OK. But listen, let me ask ye this.

When does daytime end?

When, when? You tell me.

You tell me babe.

I'm all ears.

When does daytime end an nighttime start?

She says nighttime kinda starts when it gets dark, round about, say seven, half seven.

Mmm, dunno about that. Let me ask ye this. Let's put it another way. When does daytime finish? Daytime finishes, say, four o'clock, OK.

No no, she says, that's afternoon. Late afternoon.

Yer man here thinks about it. Gives it real deep thought. The Sonny boy's deep in thought. Late afternoon is four o'clock, four thirty is late afternoon. So later than that, say five o'clock, is evenin, early evenin.

Rhonda thinks about it. Shrugs a bit. Hmms an haws. Screws her face up curls her bottom lip out. I've gave her food for thought, ye see. That's what it is. I've got her fuckin thinkin.

Mmm, well, I suppose five o'clock is early evenin, she says.

Well, I tell her, would I be right in sayin that evenin is the early stages of night, aint that right, I mean it's sometimes black as the crack of a coalman's arse just after four. An ye did say that just after four o'clock is goin into early evenin. I mean, think about it. Think about the word. Evenin. Eve. The eve of night. Aint that right? Evenin is the early part of night.

Rhonda's goosed man. I've got her fucked. She just nods an shrugs an looks as confused as a dyslexic doin a crossword.

OK, she says, OK honee, fair enough.

See what I mean bro? Talk about a silver tongue.

Yer man here could charm the pubic hairs out a shaved fanny. I'm charmed, I'm blessed. Yer man here's got it made, got it sussed, got the whole wide world at his fuckin feet so he has. Listen by the way. Call me Mister Lucky.

Chapter Ten.
Call Me Lucky Lucky.

I'm Mister Lucky Lucky. Two luckies. I'll tell ye why.
We were gettin it on good this night. Saturday night. Saturday
evenin. It was after four, that's late afternoon, early evenin.
It was party time, time for me an my baby to have some fun.
Saturday nights aint right for fightin. Saturday nights were fun
nights, love-in nights. Every night was a love-in night down there
so it was.
Well, at least it was at that time anyway. What a difference a day
makes. A week makes. A month makes.
What a difference two bottles of vodka, six super lagers, some
marijuana joints an a porn film make to a relationship eh?
Fucksake man.Take it easy. The good life burns ye out big time so
it does. Trust me.

I'm sittin skinnin up on the couch. Feelin fuckin good bro. Feelin
lighter than an anorexic astronaut. Rhonda baby. Sexy lady.
Check her out man. Kitted up to the nines. Lady in black. Black
an red. Black sussies n stockins. Tiny red panties an black lacy
bra. A silky black see-through nightie clings on her shiny brown
shoulders. Lazy brown eyes float on a pearly white backdrop.
Hey, is my name Mister Lucky or what?

The porn star on the screen's givin it big licks. Big bronzed
up hunky cunt with a dick like a middleweight bodybuilder is
slurpin on a smooth pink pussy. She's lettin rip with high-pitched
whines an urgin him to suck harder on her tight little clit.
As the big guy with the top hat an tails would say,

SHOWTIME.

Rhonda baby's watchin. Watchin the big picture. Lickin her
lips. Her ruby red pouters. Her eyes are sinkin heavier onto the

horizon. Her tiny little irises are like pinheads. The smaller the better bro. That's a fact. Little irises equal big hornyness. She can't wait, my baby just cannot wait.

Wanna be an actress honee bunch? Wanna play the part? Wanna be a tart? C'mon baby, live the dream.

Rhonda baby's heart's meltin. She wants to be an actress. She always did ye know. She loves to play the part.

Let's make movies baby. Yeah yeah.

Three two one an
        ROLL IT.

I'm lookin down on her. I'm up here in Heaven so I am. The Sonny boy's in Heaven. Room number seven. Oh look down there bro. A satin-clad angel. Soft warm lips devourin my muscular manhood.

Brown fluffy curls bouncin up an down on short jaggy pubes. Oh what a night. What a sight. A sight for hot an horny eyes. Check those eyes man. Soft sexy sad little puppy dog eyes watchin me, lookin up checkin me out, seekin my approval.

How am I doin honee, am I doin OK?

Yer doin better than OK baby, yer man here's just died, died an gone to Heaven. One way ticket bro. There aint no way back for this dude now so there aint. No way. That big bright sign that says point of no return is way back there so it is, it's one hundred miles back that way. Aye, it is. Keep on goin man, keep on drivin. The Sonny boy passed it three fuckin hours ago.

I aint comin back to Planet Earth so I aint. No way José.

Bye bye to Planet Fuckup.

A warm set of moist burgundy lips like big juicy bloodworms wrap themselves round my knob slidin up an down makin soft lappin slurpy sounds like somebody walkin through porridge in a pair of brand new wellies.

She starts off with long, slow, sensual moans. Fucksake listen to

it. What a show, what a part she's playin. Who's that moanin?
The porn star on the telly or my sweet Rhonda?
So hard to tell man, it sure aint easy.
She ups the tempo to a howl. Yeah baby let it rip darlin, give it
big ear-piercin high-pitched howls.

I know who it is now so I do, an it aint the burd on the telly. Yer
man here would know those howls anywhere.
Listen to it. Listen to her howls. Can ye hear them?
Fucksake, try not hearin them. Mr an Mrs Suckmanobski in the
eastern plains of Siberia can hear them. They're pluggin up their
ears cause they can't get a wink of kip so they can't.

Rhonda babe's a screamer.
She howls like a banshee in a howlin contest. My eyeballs are
flickin back an forth, back an forth, back an forth.
Telly. Rhonda. Telly. Rhonda. Who's playin the best part here?
Hard to tell mate. Who's gonni win the Oscar?
Back an forth man. Porn film. Rhonda. Porn film. Rhonda.

A big mop of soft fluffy curls devourin a ten-incher.
Who's who?
Is that yer man here or the big tanned dude in the porn flick?
Tell ye what bro, there aint no difference. Naw. None. Ye can
turn that fuckin telly off now so ye can, cause there's a bigger
show goin on right here. Right here.
Me an my wee honeybunch are doin the little people proud.

Raunchy Rhonda's Romp volume two hundred. Hey man
welcome to Hollywood.

The dope kicks in bro. It starts takin charge. The Sonny boy's
head is on freefall. I'm floatin off the surface of nothinness, I'm
feelin more numb than an amputated knob.
Beneath me there's nothin. Just my crystal clear magic carpet.
The sound of soft warm waves slush slowly round the rocks
beneath.

I just keep feelin lighter an lighter, so strong an hard. Fuckinhell man, hard, harder than Chinese arithmetic.
I'm stayin like this forever. Forever an ever an ever.
The softness of lips squeezes easy on my hardness. A warm orange glow surrounds me. Me an my baby float off on a mindbendin neverendin love romp.

Just you an me honee, me an you babee.
I love you.
I love you too.
I said it first.

Sex baby sex sex sex. The softness, the warmth, the slippiness, the oiliness of two hot bodies, the smell, that fruity slightly stale smell of orgasm after orgasm.
I'm comin I'm comin, this big bad daddy's comin so he is, it's on its fuckin way bro, like a big runaway train, yer man here's comin an he aint turnin back, no way man, no sirree.

Don't tell me, she screams. Don't. Don't tell me, just do me, just blow my fuckin brains out.

But there's a smell, a smell that's doin my box in, what the fuck's that smell? It's like, like, dunno man, like a smell I've never smelt before.
I mean, yer man here's been around so he has. Around the world an back again ten times over. But that smell is a strange one, so strange, so strong. Strong, must be strong man, I mean it's so strong it's interruptin a hot violent fuck.
A mixture of marijuana an love juice. A burnin smell like a hash leaf on hot coals only stronger, like hot sweat only staler. It's like a pissy smell, aye pissy. That's it, piss. A smell of burnin piss an burnin hair.

What the fuck is that, we ask each other, what the fuck?
Let's go check it out man, see what's the score. The fuckin stuff's stingin my eyes now, nippin my nostrils. It's comin from up there

too. Up those stairs. Waftin through the night an strengthenin by the minute. I'm still floatin bro. Sonny Jim still walks on water. Well wouldn't you after a shag like that?

The light brown pishy stench floats like a vagrant's ghost through the air. It's clearly visible. It is, honest. Quite a pretty colour too. A mixture of coffee cream an light lemon. I can see it clearly. Look. Fucksake man look. Look at the curly wafts of smoke smoothly shakin their hips in the night. Raunchy dancin.

We dance along with them.
Hey babee, are ye dancin?
Are ye askin?
I'm askin.
Well, if yer askin, I'm dancin.

We shake our arses slow. Me an the Rhonda, what're we like? Higher than Kilimanjaro. We follow the dancin lines of brown an yellow up the stairs like two little kiddies trailin the Pied Piper. Out the door up the staircase into the love nest. It's suckin us in like a snake charmer enticin us into his basket.
My mind's gone man, it's offski pop. It aint here no more. Dunno what to do, what to say, what to think.

Me an Rhonda babe stand there starin down at blackness, at our bed, our love chariot.
Our love nest is lookin back up at us, starin back out its big fuckin ugly black eye. Yeah man that's what it is, an eye. A big black eye starin up at us.
Jesus man, the eye of the panda. Look at it. It's starin, starin an starin, gettin bigger an bigger by the minute.

This is where it's comin from man. It's comin from out of there so it is, that hole, aye, out of that big black starin eye comes that smell, that brownie yellow dancin stuff stingin holes in our eyeballs bringin us back to reality makin our senses slowly slip their way back to our minds puttin things back together.

What the fuck man? The dope, the drink, the horny mind-numbin fuck has gone bro, gone, gone forever an it aint comin back.

It's back to life, back to reality. Reality man. Yip, that's where we are, me an her. Me an my Rhonda lookin into this big brown hole hissin an smokin an sizzlin an puffin. Spewin out these horrible smells of pish an sex.

Reality is here to haunt us once more.

It's no dream. No nightmare.

Well it could've been, could've been a nightmare. Maybe worse. Death.

Me an Rhonda normally lie there, on our big lazy fuckbed, stoned, drunk, shagged out, you name it. We normally lie there, right bang on top of that big black hole. Would've been burned alive mate. Both of us fried like death row darkies smoulderin like the furnaces of Hell on a hole the size of a hippo's arse.

It's that fuckin blanket. I've told her, I'm sick to fuckin death tellin her. It's the wires, the fuckin things have corroded down the years with beer, pish, spunk, you name it. The poor thing finally gave way under the strain. Yip, the wires finally snapped. They've had enough abuse an fuckin popped. Pop. Just like that. Aye, popped then started smoulderin. Well electricity an piss aint the best of fuckin mates bro, d'ye know what I'm sayin? The cunts hate the fuckin sight of each other. It's ten rounds of boxin whenever those two fuckers meet.

Me an Rhonda. A pair of lucky bastarts. What a lucky fuck. Yeah that one we had down there. That porn flick. Saved our lives so it did. We would've been burned alive man. Slow sizzlin death. We fuckin would've.

Aye, two Kentucky Fried alkies. Fuckin hell man.

The bold Sonny Jim boy.

Call me lucky. Aye, call me lucky lucky. Tell ye why I'm lucky lucky. I'm lucky twice now man. Not just once but twice.

54

Ye see, we fucked it out the back so we did. The auld mattress.
Fucked the auld hippo's arsehole out the back, then we phoned
the claims man. Insurance claims. Aye, we claimed Rhonda's
insurance.
The man with the briefcase came to see us. Suave guy. Smooth
an sensible. The gold rimmed specs an nice neat hair. Family
man. Of course he is. Ye can tell. Of course ye can. Ye can tell no
bother.

He's in for some serious abuse of the auld lugholes.
Me an Rhonda attack him.
What's the fuckin score mister?
Look at this. Look at this fuckin mattress. Lucky lucky eh?
Me an the missus could've been a pair of goners. Fried. Ye know
what I'm sayin? Fuckin horrible. Horrible. Ye should've seen the
smoke man, aw I'm tellin ye, me an the good lady are lucky to be
here. We're still havin nightmares to this day so we are. Aw fuck,
see all that black smoke burnin into our lungs. Can still taste it
yet. We wake up screamin every night so we do. An what about
the wean? Aw the poor wee wean. Fucksake, might never be the
same again. Scarred for life. Honest. Lucky to be alive. Just got
out in the nick of time. Ten minutes later we would've been in
bed. What would've happened to the wean then eh? Orphaned.
Orphaned at eight so she would've been, aye.
Fucksake what a nightmare.

The guy writes out the cheque right there an then so he does.
The poor cunt's only too glad man. He can't get away quick
enough. Can't. Hard luck stories he's had enough of. Fucksake
where's his hanky? He's gonni start cryin his eyes out any minute.

Me an Rhonda lay it on thicker than shit stuck to a hobo's arse.
Three hundred bucks, he says. There you are sir. Mr an Mrs
McConaughy. This will compensate for your terrible ordeal.
Oh yes, thank you very much, we say. Of course it will, of course
it will.

So why am I Mr Lucky Lucky? I hear ye ask. Why two times, not once? Wait an I'll tell ye why.

Yer man here just happens to know a cunt who delivers mattresses that fall off lorries, an he just happens to drop one off at Sonny Jim's house for a mere hundred bucks.

OK, that's why I'm Mr Lucky.

Here's why I'm Mr Lucky Lucky.

I gave the auld burnt one to the Peezi boy. Aye, I gave the auld one to the wee man. The wee Peezi filla then went an phoned the insurance man.

The boy comes out a couple of days later. A different man from ours but much the same kinda dude. Know what I'm sayin?

The man hands Peezi three hundred bucks an tells him he's sorry for his very near catastrophe.

So sorry Mr Peezi, he says.

No worries Mr Smartsuit, says Peezi boy.

I hope this will compensate, says Smartsuit.

Oh I'm sure it will, says Peezi, I'm sure it will.

The Peezi dude then sticks it in his hipper an takes a wee run round to see yer man here.

One hundred an fifty to Peezi boy.

One hundred an fifty to the bold Sonny Jim.

Fair? Of course it's fuckin fair.

That's what happened bro. The mattress, the auld hippo's arsehole ended up goin right round the town so it did. Peezi passed it on to some cunt who passed it on to some cunt else. Right round the town ten times an back again. That's why I'm lucky man. Aye, call me lucky. Call me Mr Lucky Lucky.

In fact call me Mr Lucky Lucky ten times over.

Chapter Eleven.
Mucky's Bar.

Mucky's bar. Mucky's shithole.
It's a jungle, a rat race, a zoo. Go an have a wander round.
There's all sorts of everythin, loads of different species, a complicated assortment of oddities.
Wee Mucky man. What a dirty little fucker. Take a look at his jumper. What's it like?

Wait an I'll tell ye what it's like, it's like an auld crumpled pizza.
It's all covered in bits of greasy bacon, fried eggs, tomatoes, beans, wee bits of sausage, mushroom, black puddin an some fried bread. He'll never starve will the bold Mucky.
Haw Mucky I'm fuckin starvin, gonni give me a wee bite of yer jumper. Aye, c'mon troops, big feast time, let's all tuck into Mucky's cardigan.

An I'll tell ye another thing. Wee Mucky's tight. Tighter than two coats of paint. Check his pockets, the wee miserable bastart's still got his first shillin.
Well to be honest with ye, if yer lookin for money, don't bother yer arse checkin his pockets because there's fuck-all in there.
Yer best bet's to pull his dick out an peel the skin back. That's where ye'll find a fortune. Aye, under there, under his foreskin, the wee cunt keeps his money under his foreskin.

Hey Mucky take yer dick out an pull the skin back an give me a loan of a tenner. Fucksake man, look what's just fell out. An auld photo of Winston Churchill.

He won't pay no cunt so he won't. The wee cunt won't even pay attention. Mucky doesn't even have to worry about payin his bar staff. He aint got none. Naw, no cunt'll work for Mucky.
Just his two daughters.

Aw my fuck man, what the fuck are they like? Two stoaters.
Their names are on the backs of their T-shirts. Up The Arse Agnes
an Clitoris Kate. Twenty two stone each. Their tits are water
balloons an their big cellulite bellys waddle about under their
joggers. Big baggy grey joggers all pish stains an skid marks.
Honest to fuck by the way, they make the two fat ladies look like
the Cheeky Girls.
They work for Mucky.
They get no pay. Just a roof over their head an eight meals a day.

Mucky tells them straight. Ye don't need money. What the fuck
do ye need money for? Money's the root of all evil. Ye've got
to work hard. Work work work. Ye get fuck-all for nothin in
this life. Work work work. I had to work hard for my faither. All
this will be yours some day girls, all yours. C'mon, get yer heads
down an yer big fat arses up.

Mucky's bar is boggin. Honest to fuck by the way.
Listen to this.
I walked in one day an shouted up a pint. Give me a pint of
heavy auld bean, aye, a pint of yer best Don Revie.
The wee man starts tryin to pull a pint but nothin's happenin,
nothin, it's a pure non-starter.
Gurgle gurgle it goes. The beer font splutters an coughs an takes
a right serious asthma attack. There's no beer comin out of there
bro. Beer don't live here no more.
So guess what he starts doin next man?
He starts blowin up it. Aye, he starts blowin up the pipe where
yer ale comes out. The bold Mucky man's standin there blowin
up it like a whore on a bell-end. Blow blow blow. Nothin man,
nothin.
Must be somethin stuck in it, he says. Blow blow blow. Huffin an
puffin.

Aw fuck that. Hey listen ya auld cunt, just give me a bottle of
beer.

He gives me an ice-cold bottle of beer out the freezer. Aw yes
man. Nice an chilled it is, straight out of God's own personal ice
box. The dribbles of condensation wiggle like mini belly dancers
slippin an slidin down the frosty green glass. I lick my lips. I kiss
the bottle neck. I hold it firm against my lips, tilt it over an let it
run softly through my tastebuds.

Ahhhh, nectar.

Coool tinglin honey kissin an lickin my tongue sprayin soft liquid
gold against my tastebuds. There's a rush through my veins an
a hush in my brain. A bright golden glow zooms right round
the room. Everythin is beautiful. Even wee Mucky's brown,
black, mustard an green teeth. Check them out man. A row of
condemned houses. Aw man do I feel good or do I feel good?

Mucky's bar. This is the place bro, I'm tellin ye, ye aint seen
nothin till ye've seen Mucky's bar. Ye aint drank in a pub until
ye've drank in here.

A piss-stinkin alehouse full of shit-talkin winos an wankers.

One day The Pub Spy came callin. Aye, been here, seen it, done
it, wrote a book, made a film. Done the lot man. Wrote a book
about Mucky's. He did.

It was front page headlines. Dirty wee clatty bastart of a
landlord the headline said. Rogue landlord. Scum landlord. The
dirty auld bastart drank his tea from an auld coffee jar.

Check the fuckin gantry. An auld Adidas trainer sittin hand in
hand with a withered crust of bread. Both been there forever
bro. Wee manky maggots screamin for a bath.

The world's dirtiest stooriesty gantry.

Don't dare complain in Mucky's. Don't ever complain. Don't.
Complain about the beer? Ye fuckin better not ya cunt.

One guy tried it. He went like that an said to Mucky, hey auld
yin, that beer's a bit cloudy.

Cloudy? Cloudy? Mucky says. Naw son, the beer aint cloudy,
it's just a dirty glass. Anyway what the fuck d'ye want for these
prices, thunder an lightnin?

Ye need no cash in Mucky's. Naw, put it in the book bro. Big thick tick book. The tick book's thicker than a Tory back-bencher. The place got screwed one time ye know? They came in through the roof. In an out in no time. Wouldn't have known they'd been here.

An guess what? They never stole a thing. Naw, nothin. They just scrubbed their names out the fuckin tick book.

Mucky's bar. A cheese an wine bar. Aye, it says it above the door. Mucky's cheese an wine bar.

Check the menu. Wee penny-sized pizzas that ye nuke in the micro an a big glass of Buckfast tonic wine. Soup of the day. Special offer. Fifty pence a bowl. Ten pence for pensioners.

We send auld Ernie up. Aye that's what we do. Five bowls of soup, he says. Sticks down fifty pence on the bar.

Aw for fucksake come on lads, says the Mucky man, he won't eat all that. Mucky man's doin his dinger. Costin him a fortune. Come on to fuck now lads, what about my profit? What about my turnover?

Haw, c'mon ya stingy bastart, we say, the auld cunt's starvin. Give him five bowls. He fought in two world wars so he did. That's the law. You said it. Look, look at the board. Says it clear in black an white.

TEN PENCE FOR PENSIONERS

The place is full of deadheads an delinquents. Deek, Peezi, Shoogly, Heed, auld Stan an Ernie.

They're all sittin over there in the corner. Sittin in Tin Pan Alley. The banter's flyin like fat-arsed pigs.

They all know it all. They all know every fuckin thing. Nothin they don't know. What they don't know aint worth knowin.

A bar full of barroom lawyers, doctors, professional boxers, footballers, jockeys, snooker players an comedians.

The topics are widespread. They talk about anythin. They can do anythin. They've all been there an done it an played the part in the film.

D'ye think ye could beat a Rottweiller in a square go? Shoogly says.
No probs, says the Deek. I'll tell ye how it's done. I'll tell ye the easy way to kill it. I'll even show ye how to skin it and cook it once yer finished so I will.

Question an answers are flyin through the air like fuck. They're comin fast an furious.
Who's the greatest singer? Who's the greatest footballer? Who's the greatest boxer?
Boxer? Sugar Ray Robinson. Muhammad Ali. Joe Louis. Rocky Marciano.
Ask auld Ernie somebody says. Ernie's an expert. Ernies an ex-boxer. Could've been the greatest. Could've been. Should've been. He took to the drink an couldn't resist the temptation of all the gorgeous fanny that kept throwin their knickers at him.

Ernie's sittin in the corner. Ernies's startin to doze. Startin to snooze. He's got the heavy eyelids on. All that lovely soup he ate made him a bit drowsy.
An another thing, he's goin a bit deaf. All those bombs that just missed his arse durin the war an all those times he got his ears boxed have started catchin up on him.

He looks up. Screws up his face an tightens his eyes. Grumpy auld fucker.
What the fuck d'yees want?
What d'ye make of the all time greats? Deek asks him.
Ernie thinks about it, chomps his auld chops together, shakes his head an goes, Ach they're not worth a fuck, too messy. Yer better with a gas fire any day.

Shoogly's at the bar. He's tellin Mucky to decorate the mahogany. C'mon to fuck wee man, there's a lot of thirsty troops waitin here. He starts shoutin up the drinks. Three half pints of lager, four half pints of heavy, three glasses of Bucky, six vodkas, two with lemonade, three with Coke, one with orange. Two whiskies, two packets of nuts, three packets of crisps.

Wee Mucky gives him two trays. Two. Aye he needs two. Shoogly looks at him. Looks at the trays. Looks across at the troops. Smiles a big fuckin cheesy Cheshire cat grin an goes, I hope my name's good.
He walks back to the table like a dog with two dicks. He shakes his head an draws Mucky a dirty stare. That cheeky wee bastart was about to ask me for money there, he says. Cheeky little cunt.

Drink drink drink. Get it down ye man. More feelgood juice. I want more. I need more. I take more. More more more. More of the same only better. That fine red wine. The lovely ruby red. It cooks in my mouth an turns my blood electric. Look at my veins bro, pure AC/DC. Look at them movin. Wrigglin an twistin. Dancin a slow sexy samba.
A soft shock shoots through my central nervous system. Keep it comin. Yer man just can't get enough. He's wired to the Moon. In fact naw. I'm not. I'm way past that. I'm fuckinwell spinnin round Jupiter.

Here comes Paddy Pie. Paddy Pie tells some lies man. I'm tellin ye. Top man for porkies. Paddy Pie's lies. Half the lies the wee cunt tells are not true.
Guess what I'm sellin? he says. I'm sellin beautiful burds bro. Burds? Heh ya dirty wee cunt ye, auld Stan shouts. Yer nothin but a wee fuckin pimp.
Naw, not those kinda burds ya fuckin silly auld todger. Burds. Burds of a feather. Canaries. Aye, I'm sellin canaries. But these are not yer average Joe cunt, run of the mill canaries these ones. No way. No way sirree. These are Africana Reds. Rarer than a Coatbridge proddy. An just like everythin else the bold Paddy Pie sells, they're goin cheap.

Deek looks at him an goes, What the fuck ye on about ya wee cunt? They all go cheep. Chirpy chirpy cheep cheep.

Wee Pie man shakes his head an squints a sarky grin at Deek. Aint got time for small talk. Paddy Pie means business. The very man I'm lookin for, he says to me. Heard ye had a wee unfortunate incident with a goldfish Sonny Jim. Heard all about it. Ye see, yer Pie man here has a wee set of specially designed earplugs that are directly connected to the place where the auld grapes are picked before they squeeze them into Buckfast tonic wine bottles. D'ye get my drift?

Listen, he says, one of these wee beauties are all yours for thirty smackeroos. They're worth at least fifty. Maybe more. Maybe sixty, even seventy. Who the fuck knows what they'll fetch. They're absolutely pure awesome burds mate. Awesome whistlers. Listen, there's not a fuckin tune in this whole wide world that these wee stoaters can't sing. Wait till I tell ye this, he says. But keep it under yer bunnet. Last week I was deliverin a rake of them from London up to Glasgow Zoo. So I'm drivin along with two hundred an fifty of the fuckers caged up in the back of my wagon. Well, all of a sudden I hits this hill. Honest to fuck Sonny, I mean, this aint a fuckin hill. Naw, it's more of a fuckin mountain. A one in five million gradient. Honest to fuck, ye'd need Sherpa Tensing an all his wee mates to get ye up this fucker.

Well my auld chuggabug truck aint gonni make it mate. It just aint. Naw. No chance. It just aint happenin. Well, what the fuck am I gonni do, I thinks to myself. I decides I've got to delve in deep to the talented auld pile of brain matter the good Lord blessed me with. So I just goes like that an leans out the window an clatters the side of the wagon. Boom boom boom. Big hollow boomin noises vibrate across the countryside.

Next thing ye know these little fuckers all spread their tiny wings an start flappin like pure fuckin panic merchants. Aye, all two hundred an fifty of them at once.

Well was I not gobsmacked or was I not fuckinwell gobsmacked? *Whoosh*, I went. Honest to fuck Sonny, the auld G-force blew my scrotum up like a fuckin hot air balloon. Off up the hill I went like Apollo Nine.

Flyin on the wings of a dove I was. Or should I say on the wings of a canary. Well, two hundred an fifty canaries to be precise. Unbelievable, they just all flapped their wings at once man, took me to the top of the hill faster than a turbo jet so they did.

Now that's the kind of wingspan I'm talkin about here mate. Where in the world do ye get that kinda power in a lovely wee canary?

So listen, it's all yours for thirty bucks bro. Look, I'm fuckin givin them away so I am. A fuckin free gift. Go on, he says, treat the wean to one. It'll be Brownie points too bro. I've heard through those wee special ear plugs of mine that ye've been a bit of a naughty boy of late. Tut tut tut Sonny Jim, when're ye gonni grow up?

Here's yer big chance to get back in the good books. Buy the wean a lovely wee canary. Aye, a wee Africana Red. I mean, I know it aint the same as a goldfish.

But, then again, neither's a monkey.

Wee Paddy Pie. What a guy. What a legend. A bigger bum than a dozen arses. Wee Paddy Pie. He hasn't a clue what the truth means. Honest, he doesn't know the meanin of the word. See if he's ever up in court on a charge an his lawyer tells him to just go up an tell the truth, the wee man'll end up gettin a lifer. Won't be able to do it so he won't. Honest, an absolute stranger to the truth.

Hey truth, my name's Paddy Pie. Who the fuck're you?

The wee dude could pen a book so he could. Easy. No probs. A fuckin bestseller.

I'll tell ye a good title for his book. *Paddy Pie's One Million Best Lies.*

The place is in an uproar. All the troops rhymin off their favourite Paddy Pie's porkies. What's the best? I dunno. Who's gonni judge?

I know what mine is.

Wait an I'll tell ye it.

Listen, it might not sound right comin from me, comin from the Sonny boy. Don't get me wrong, yer man here tells a good yarn, can tell a tall tale with the best of them, but I prefer to tell ye my own. I don't like doin someone else's.

But hey, I've just got to tell ye this. It's my favourite. A pure classic. The best. Listen to this.

The wee man decided to take up planespottin once. Just a wee hobby like. So he gets a camera an heads into Glasgow Airport. He walks right through Customs an out onto the edge of the runway. He's standin there. He whips the camera out. He starts takin pictures of all these planes landin an takin off. Always wanted to be a pilot. A boyhood dream.

Well I'm standin there takin these pictures, he says. Click click clickin away man. Gettin good pics. Real close-ups. Whooo, check that fucker landin. Look how close it is. Look for fucksake, there's my Auntie Maisie at the window. Can zoom right up her nostrils.

All of a sudden the big plane trundles out onto the runway. Check it out bro. Check it out big time. I can't get the whole fuckin thing into the camera. Well I'm click click clickin away like fuck, got the Nikon zoomed right in.

All the passengers on the plane are lookin out the big windows, ye can see them clear as ye like so ye can. Cheese, say cheese. They all smile an wave at the Pie man.

Well, what happens next ye'll never believe so ye won't. What d'ye mean won't believe it? Of course ye fuckin will.

Swear it man, this is the truth. Cross my heart an hope to go to the big bad fire. Doesn't it just go like that an slow down. Aye, the big Concorde chappie just drops down the gears an comes to a grindin halt. The Pie man's thinkin, Hey, what's up bro? What the fuck's goin on?

Next thing ye know the window gets rolled down. Aye, the big pilot guy goes like that an shouts across at me, Hey ya wee cunt ye, how's it goin?
Well, as they do bro aint that right?
Aw fuck man, look who it is. It's big Jeff. Big Jeff an me go back donkeys, known each other since we were wee enough to stick the head on a midget's baws.
Wee man, he goes. Where the fuck're ye off to?
Well the Pie's well chuffed aint he? Aint seen the Jeff boy for yonks. So I tells him I'm just takin a few more snaps an then I'm headin back up to Glasgow.
Big Jeff goes like that an looks at his watch. Bites his bottom lip an sucks in through his teeth. Givin it real serious thought. He looks at his co-pilot then shouts out, Listen, I'm just headin back to New York buddy, but hey fuckit, what're friends for? I can go round that way. Jump in an I'll drop ye off.
What a guy. What a guy that big Jeff is.

What a fuckin guy Paddy Pie is. Aye, what a guy.

Chapter Twelve.
Sick as a Canary With a
Squinty Beak.

Poor Rhonda. She fell an broke her fuckin neck.
She did, honest.

Well how did she do that, I hear ye ask?
I'll tell ye how she done it.
She fell over her face so she did.
What d'ye mean?
She fell over it. Her face was so long it tripped her up. Aye, her face was fuckin trippin her.
What's with the big long face baby?
Big long-faced Rhonda.

Ye can always tell, can't ye? Ye can always tell when somethin's wrong.
The minute ye wake up, or come to, or whatever the fuck ye care to call it. It takes ten seconds for it to hit ye that somethin just aint right.
Like I said, yer man here susses things quick. Razor-sharp at feelin bad vibes.
It's her movements, her body language. Her auld face is down there so it is, aye, she's draggin her chin along the floor.
She's gonni trip over it.
Fucksake hen, watch what yer doin.
Ah fuckit man, crash, too late. She just stood on the edge of it an fell flat on her face.
Think man, think think think. What have ye done eh, what?
The thing is, yer man here usually doesn't have to think too hard, he usually gets a right fuckin rude awakenin, like a dunt from the Polis or Rhonda tap dancin on his balls. But this time

it's different. Yer man can't think what he's done an Rhonda aint tellin him. Naw, she's sayin nothin, doesn't need to, her auld torn face says it all.

What the fuck've I done man eh?

Think ya cunt, aye, yer man here's thinkin his fuckin head off. It's jigsaw time. Aye, let's do a wee jigsaw, let's put all the tiny bits together. Make a nice big picture.

Well I'm here for a start right? I'm in the house. Definitely a house. Carpets an curtains are a dead give away. This aint no Polis cell this time mate, no way. Not unless they've done them up good style, all wall to wall carpets an curtains eh? Nice an fancy. Naw, doubt it. Fucksake man, behave yerself.

What time did I get in? Who was I with? Think. Fucksake man, think like fuck.

Hey, hold it, I wasn't out, naw, was I fuck. We had a big love in. Me an my baby. Me an my Rhonda. Big sweet love in. Played sweet tunes.

Aye. Blue movie, remember? Yer man here played the part of Big Hot Rod. Played a double part so he did. Hot Rod/Moby Dick. Half man, half whale.

Aye, we lay an watched a skin flick. Big bulgin dicks an hot juicy fannies all round. Me an Rhonda babe made our own movie. Flashbacks. I lie an watch the flashback.

Rhonda kitted up, sussies, stockins, lacy knickers. I chased her round the room with a flagpole. Me an her were stoned, had the happy heads on. Went to bed all lovey dovey.

I love you.
I love you too.
But I said it first.
Aw but I meant it more.

I check downstairs. Nothin. Zilcho. Everythin's where it should be. There's nothin broken. Naw, nothin. Everythin's nice an warm, no force ten gales comin through the hole in the wall where the window used to be.

Naw, none of that. All the doors are still on the hinges. No freshly punched holes on the walls.

What the fuck's up hen? What? Why ye trippin over yer pretty little face? What's up honeybunch. What?

Ya bastart ye, she screeches. Ya fuckin dirty rotten bastart. Poor wee canary. Ya fuckin dirty rotten fuckpig.

Aw for fucksake. I'll tell ye this. See the Sonny boy, he aint got much luck with animals.

Animals? Listen, don't fuckin talk to me about animals. See if it wasn't for bad luck I'd have no luck at all. I'm tellin ye. First a fuckin goldfish now a canary. Aye, a canary for fucksake.

The Rhonda blade's havin a hairy canary. She's doin her tit bouncin routine so she is. Hey, check them out but. That's one thing about Rhonda, she's got a pair of tits that any man would die for. Aw they're fuckin bouncin bro.

Bounce bounce bounce boing boing boing.

They do that all the time so they do. She makes them do that. She does. Then she blames me. Says it's me that makes her go loopy an causes her to jump up an down an make her tits explode. Can't seem to stop them so she can't. Naw. Can't stop. Once they've started they just don't stop. Big fuckin bouncy castles. Come on kids, roll up, play on the bouncy castles. Bounce bounce bounce. Bouncy castle tits.

Anyway, she's pointin at the canary. Tweety, aye, that's its name. Wee Tweety. Wee Tweety's lookin a bit on the glum side. She don't look too pleased. Hey Tweety, what's up? Why so sad? Yer wee sad face is nearly as twisted as Rhonda's.

Look at it, she screams. Look at it. It's fuckin sick. The poor wee soul's really sick. Look at its beak. Poor wee thing aint eaten in a week. Sick, she says, sick sick sick. Gonni have to get put down. An Africana Red, she says, check it. Africana Red my fuckin arse ya cunt. Look closer. An Africana red an yellow fuckin dots more like.

Aye well, true, but an Africana red an yellow aint got the same ring to it, has it?

Look at its beak. Fucksake man, its beak, aw its poor wee beak. It's twisted like a pair of crossed legs. Fuck me man what the fuck's up? Well I mean I thought I'd seen it all so I did. I've heard about bein sick as a parrot with a hare lip. But not this man. A red an yellow canary with a squinty beak? Holy lumpin fuck man. Strange.

Ya bastart ye, she says. Ya bastart. Poor wee defenceless animal. She says she took it to the vet. The vet told her there's a scam goin on. The lovely red plumage is a fake. It's caused by these cunts forcin pills down their wee necks. It turns the auld plumage red. Africana red, redder than sky in the mornin shepherd's warnin. Beautiful it was, beautiful bloomin red when I bought it.

Fifty fuckin quid, she's screamin. Fifty fuckin brick.

Aye, well, I mean yer man here told her fifty. Fifty quid. A wee bit of commission like. Fucksake, that's what ye do innit?

Fifty fuckin brick it cost her, she's screamin. An its wee beak, aw look at its wee beak. It can't eat, it's gonni die. Aye, the wee Tweety filla's gonni starve to fuckin death. Aw my god man, the poor wee defenceless animal.

The auld beak's too weak. It's because of the pills. See the pills they stick down its throat to turn the feathers red? Well, they fuck up its insides.

They drain out all the calcium an weaken its beak. A weak beak is bad news when yer a canary bro. Know what I'm sayin? Poor wee Tweety can't fuckin eat, can't peck its seeds. Bye bye birdie. Hairy canary no more. Yer man here's a pure rotten cunt. Feels a real bastart so he does. Poor wee defenceless animal.

Well ye can tell the wean yerself, she says. Tell the wean it's all your fault her wee canary has to die. Tell her it's your fault it's dead. Tell her ye murdered her wee Tweety. Ya bastart. You tell her. Ye fuckin better. If you don't I will.

Aw fuck man. Me. All my fault. Dirty rotten bastart. What kinda cunt have I become? Aw my God man. Killed her wee Tweety. It's me to fuckin blame so it is. All my fuckin fault.

Hold it. Naw it's not. Not my fault man.

I got it off Paddy Pie. Wee bastart Paddy. His fault. Not mine. He killed Tweety.

I'm gonni kill wee Paddy, the wee bastart. Wee lyin cunt. Wee Paddy Pie tells lies. He sold it to me for thirty bucks. Said they fuckin cost eighty. Sold it to the Sonny Jim in good faith. Bastart. The wee bastart. Wait till I see him. The wee cunt'll have a new story to tell. Aye, he will, honest. An it'll go somethin like this.

Listen lads, did I ever tell yees about the time I had to get emergency surgery to remove a dead canary out my arsehole? Did I?

Wait till I get the wee cunt. The Pie man. Wee lyin bastart. Paddy Pie's lies. The Sonny boy's gonni kill the pie man.

Chapter Thirteen.
Falsers an Keys.

Rhonda got bad advice.
Put his dinner in the bin, some cunt told her.
Aye, see if he aint home on time, fuck it, straight in the bin.

So the bold Rhonda like a right daft cunt goes an horses my
dinner into the bin.
Well, what a silly fucker.
Listen, it was a complete an utter waste of time by the way.
She shouldn't have bothered her arse, cause yer man here just
barged straight into the bin after it an whipped it back out an
onto a plate.
Aye, no bother. Get right in there bro, in ye get, head down
arse up, cold n greasy chips, a pie like a half brick an wee baked
beans as hard as bullets. They're burnt so black they look like
wee rabbit shites.
Still, never mind. Splash on a wee drop of salt an vinegar, a big
blob of brown sauce, mmmmmm, fuck ye man, lovely jubbly, let
the flavour flood out.
Munch munch munch, right down the hatch it goes. I'm fuckin
starvin.
It's the swally innit? It makes ye Hank Marvin.
The auld tastebuds go right out the window when yer bevvied
so they do. Aye, they just get up off their arse and do a runner.
Offski pop man. They don't stand a chance. The auld swally
fuckin murders them. Kills them stone dead. They've no chance.
Pishin against a force ten gale.

I tell her it was a real bad idea puttin yer man's dinner in the bin.
Bin it all ye like babe, bin it every night of the week, go ahead, it
don't bother me none, naw, it don't bother yours truly. The bold
Sonny Jim boy cares not a jot.

In fact I'll tell ye better than that, I thoroughly enjoyed it, fuckin lapped it up. Munched it down like a rabid dog. Munched it down so fast it didn't even touch my tonsils on the way down. Whose idea was that doll, one of yer silly pals? See whoever it was, tell her to go fuck herself, haha.

Rhonda started gettin desperate. She started the auld lock-in routine.
She decides to lock yer man in this night.
Fuck ye, she says, fuck ye, yer not goin out. No way. If I'm in, you're in. Yer stayin in.
She says it dead firm an arrogant, says it like she means it, says it like she even believes it's gonni happen.

Well listen, there's no fuckin way it's gonni happen. No way, no way José. Aw for fucksake, I mean, ye can't man, ye can't stay in. Especially when ye've been fuckin told to, right?
Can't have her tellin ye what to do bro. I mean if ye do it once yer finished. She's gonni start thinkin she can do it all the time. If ye let it go once yer fucked.
Don't tell me what to do ya cow. Naw, no cunt tells yer man what to do.
No cunt. Fuck ye.

Right at that point yer auld mind goes for a walk. Ye start thinkin about the boozer. She planted the seed. Ye weren't even thinkin about it so ye weren't. But she's put the thought in there hasn't she? It's her fault. All her fault. An see because ye've been told ye can't go, well that makes ye worse, ye know what I'm sayin?

Ye start to see it so ye do, the ale, ye see it flowin like golden showers of angel juice. Aw fuck man, ye start to smell it, smell that tasty ale. An in yer mind ye start to see all the troops at the bar an ye hear all the patter, aw the fuckin craic's good so it is, an look man, look, the place is jumpin with loads of gorgeous fanny, check it out, fuck me, wall to wall nanny wearin big high heels an little pussy pelmets. Fuck me man, all that fun goin on an yer man here's missin it.

Missin it?

Naw, no chance, fuck it, there's no way the Sonny boy's missin nothin.

So the next thing ye know yer man's offski, aye, offski pop out the window n down the drainpipe like a horny tom cat with its baws full.

See, it doesn't work, ye can't keep a chokin horny man in.

So then she goes an shifts the goal posts.

OK, she says, ye can go out. Get to fuck out all ye like. But ye aint gettin back in. Naw, no way. Not unless I say so. I will decide if an when ye get back in because from now on I will have both sets of keys.

Aye, Rhonda went an confiscated my keys.

Out ye go, she says. Aye, no problem. Go wherever the fuck ye like.

So yer man here's jumpin for joy. No more problems gettin out. Problem no more bro, I can go out all the fuck I want so I can.

But now it's the gettin IN that's the problem.

Curfew. Rhonda set a curfew.

Eleven o'clock, she says, aye, that's right. Eleven bells. If ye aint in here for eleven the doors'll be dubbed up, arsehole.

That's what she said man.

Yer man'll be slummin it rough if he aint in for eleven.

What am I gonni do now fuck? What the fuck am I gonni do? Eleven? Eleven bells? Fucksake man, the night's just heatin up. Most cunts are just comin out at eleven.

Keys. Keys. She's got my fuckin keys. How did she get them? She nabbed them when I was sleepin the bastart.

Where the fuck's the keys?

I can't find them. I start searchin, searchin everywhere an anywhere.

She's planked them. She planks them all the time so she does. I always find them but. Always. But not this time man, this time I can't find the fuckers.

I search in all the usual hidin places. Inside the mattress, inside the laggin on the pipes, in the cat's litter tray under the shite an gritty stuff, in the freezer, in the hoover, inside the linin of the curtains, every fuckin where. You name it, I've searched it.

Where are they man, where the fuck can they be?

Up her own arse maybe? Aye, it's a possibility bro. I wouldn't put it past her.

I'm fucked man. Fucked. Can't find them.

The doors'll be locked at eleven, she says.

What am I gonni do man? I'm scoobied. The bold Sonny Jim boy's fucked.

Beeeeeeeng, a light goes on a firework goes off an yer man here's hit the fuckin jackpot.

Got it. I've got it, I've got it, I've got it. I need a new strategy, a new game plan.

A bargain. I need to be able to bargain, right?

Well, she's got somethin belongin to me that I really really need. Now I need somethin belongin to her that she really really needs, so that we can do a wee swap, d'ye know what I'm sayin? But if yer gonni do a bit of bargainin ye need somethin to bargain with, right?

So whatcha got? Not a lot.

What can I get, what can I get that she really really needs?

Somethin she needs big time man, somethin she can't do without, somethin she'll trade a set of keys for.

Or even better still. Somethin she'd sell her fuckin arse on the street for.

What the fuck can I get man? What?

I'm lookin right at her an thinkin. Think think think.
What's she got, what's she got that I can take?
Like myself, not a lot.
In fact to be honest, other than a set of keys, nothin.
So I strolls into the bedroom an she's lyin there zonked man.
Blitzed n blootered. Not a pretty sight. Her mouth's hangin open
an she's snorin like a twenty-stone, hairy-arsed lorry driver. A dull
snore like a long lingerin fart comes purrin through the space
where her two front teeth used to be.

BINGO. Bingo bingo Yippppeeee, fuckin bingo. Yer man
here's won the bingo. Single line, full house, link up the lot.
yessssssssssssssssssssss
Her teeth. Her treasured two front teeth. She once fell down
three flights of stairs pished so she did an knocked out her two
front teeth.

Nobody knows about it, she'd say. Nobody. She used to go on
an on about it all the time. Oh I'd never let anybody see me
with them out, oh I'd fuckin die, fuckin die of embarrassment,
pure mortified I'd be. See when I die, she'd say, promise me ye'll
make sure my teeth are in when they bury me. So no cunt knows
about it. No cunt.

No cunt, that is, except yer man here. Yer man knows. The Sonny
boy knows all too well about the teeth. He knows she's mega
conscious about them, knows she won't leave home without
them, an even better still, an this is the really juicy part, he
knows where she keeps them. Ye see, she won't sleep with them
in, naw, not since that time she choked on them an nearly died.
So she keeps them in this wee plastic half-moon shaped box next
to her bed. Aye, she keeps them in there. There it is. There. Lying
next to her. Easy meat.
I tip-toe over.
Aw fuck man, what am I doin, why am I bein quiet? She's
blootered, she's out like a burnt out bulb. See when Rhonda's

out, she's out. Ye could ram a hundred sticks of dynamite up the crack of her arse an light the fuse,

3   2   1   boooooom   nothin.

Honest to fuck man, nothin would happen, ye wouldn't waken her up. Ye could drive a Sherman tank though the bedroom so ye could.

So yer man here clicks opens the wee case. There it is. The wee pink plate. Like a little pink jellyfish floatin on a pond.
Out ye come wee fella, out ye come. Yess, got ye, got ye hook line an sinker little chap, come to Daddy.
Right into the hipper it goes.

The next mornin she's marchin up an down, up an down, up an down.
Look at Rhonda, check her out, what's she like man?
Marchin. Pacin. Pacin the floor. Up an down, up an down.

I watch her. I stare at her. I keep on starin.
She's thinkin. She's thinkin hard.
She looks like she's lost somethin. Aye, that's what she looks like.
Lost somethin. Which she has of course. She's lost her fuckin falsers, lost her pride, lost her dignity, lost her life. Aye her life.
She would die if she was seen without them. Remember?

I sit an stare an don't say a word.
Take yer time, take yer time.
The auld Sonny Jim boy sits there waitin, waitin, watchin.

She doesn't say nothin. She aint sure yet, she aint got the full script. She doesn't want to drop her guard an give fuck-all away, she doesn't want to let me see that she's lost somethin, she's still tryin to find her barins. It's the drink ye see. It's the six super lagers, half bottle of voddy for the body an two joints she had last night that's numbed her skull. Aye, it numbs the mind so it does, wipes the old mind slate clean bro.

So she just aint sure man. Her plate, her falsers, where the fuck's
her falsers?
She's determined not to say nothin. She just keeps struttin in an
out the kitchen. In, out, in, out.

She says nothin.
I say nothin.
In, out, in, out.
Nothin said.
Not a word.

Fucksake, I can't keep it up much longer man, who's gonni blink
first?
Not me, not yer man here. The Sonny Jim boy don't blink for no
cunt.
Clunk clank doink.

See that big loud tinny noise ye just heard there?
Well that was the sound of a big metal guard hittin the tiles.
Rhonda's guard. It just dropped like one of those crushed motors
fallin out a crane in a scrapyard.

Fuck ye, she says. Fuck ye. Where's my teeth? What the fuck
have ye done with my teeth? Ya bastart, ya fuckin lousy bastart,
gimmee them, gimmee them, gimmee back my fuckin teeth.

She's fucked. Trapped. Bent over a barrel with her G-string
garotin her arse.
Rhonda babe is well goosed. A prisoner in her own home.
She can't go out without them ye see. Can't. No way José, no can
do, I'm tellin ye.

So I'm standin there shruggin the auld shoulders big time.
Shruggin slow. Shruggin smug. Grinnin. Sonny boy's grinnin like
a tom cat that's just licked the sweetest cream off its baws.

Honest, listen, yer man's so chuffed to fuck he's got a big achin
hard-on.

Ya sicko, she says, ya fuckin sick cunt, yer the lowest of the low, yer lower than an ant's arsehole, yer lower than the hairs on a snake's baws.

Sick bastart. Lowest of the low.

Fucksake, I've heard it. Heard it too many times. It means nothin. All the fancy names in the book don't faze yer man.

Dog eat dog, aint that right? That's the way the biscuit breaks hen, that's the way the crumbs fall.

I look at her hard. I grit my teeth. Gimmee the keys.

My left palm's out, my right hand's pointin to the door.

Keys first baby. I get the keys, you get the teeth. Fair do's don't ye think? Fair swap?

Ya sick bastart, sick cunt, fuckin wanker, prick, arsehole, homosexual fuckpig.

She's upset man. The Rhonda blade's upset big time. Check her out. Check those nostrils, they're steamin up an firin flames like a bull facin the cape an ready to charge.

Take yer time honeybunch, I tell her. Take as long as ye like. The Sonny boy's got all day, no sweat, I'm goin nowhere. Not for now that is.

Rhonda starts beggin.

Like I say. It's a woman thing. Pride, vanity, all that shite. Life just aint worth livin without her teeth, her beloved Cowdenbeath. Can't leave home without them. Aint that right?

Gimme the teeth first, she says. Teeth first.

Yer man just shakes his napper. No deal, no deal.

She swears to God an crosses her heart an says she hopes to die if she doesn't hand over the keys once she gets the teeth.

She crosses her heart the sexiest I've ever seen. She runs her forefinger through her tits twice. She crosses her heart an hopes to die.

She can hope to die all she likes, yer man here don't trust no cunt.

No deal doll. None. All that swearin yer life away means fuck-all to Sonny boy.

Swear yer life away? So what eh? All that strike me down dead shit? Fuck off. Die all ye like. It happens to every cunt. Ashes to ashes.

Throw them over there, I tell her. Over there.

You throw the keys. I throw the teeth.

Dead easy. Easy peasy.

After three, I say,

1 2 3

Nothin.

Nothin man. She jerks her hand out to throw them then pulls it back. She doesn't let go, she's still got the keys.

Ya bastart ye, ye weren't gonni throw them, I tell her.

Naw an neither were you ya cunt, she says.

This time. OK?

Go

1 2 3

She lets go, I let go.

Airborne. Everythin is flyin man. Teeth, keys, Sonny boy an Rhonda go flyin through the air like wee Paddy Pie's magic canaries.

There's a high-pitched tinkle as a cluster of keys are majestically plucked from thin air.

Rhonda catches the teeth. Clunk click they're in her mouth.

Tinkle clatter clump, we all fall down.

I land neck first on the floor.

Rhonda lands on top of me.

There's this awful fuckin pain man, pain. High voltage pain. Forty thousand fireworks shoot right up my arm an blow the head off

my funny bone then they do a U-turn an blow the tips off all
my fingers. Next thing I know the pain starts screamin out my
knuckles. Aw fuck man my knuckles.

Listen, there's this crunchin grindin sensation, a kinda gristly
squelch an a sound of bone scrapin bone. A hot flow of Buckfast-
flavoured blood starts squirtin through these crimson-coloured
teeth. Teeth. I've seen those teeth before somewhere. Where?

Oh fuck man, look. Look who it is. Rhonda's head's hangin from the
teeth hangin from my hand an she's takin big bites. Bitin into my
hand prizin the keys from my grip. Her face is knob-end purple.
Her jaws lock like a pit bull tastin the hot salty wetness of fresh
blood an her head twists an shakes viciously like a devil dog wringin
the neck of its victim.

I'm screamin an howlin an slappin an kickin. The pain man, aw the
fuckin pain, I can't stand it, can't take no more, I'm finished. I'm
about to let go, about to pass out when these squeals, these E sharp
high-pitched howls ring through our ears.

E sharp, they were. High. Higher than the squeals of me an
Rhonda.

Mummy Mummy Mummy.
It's wee Petal. Aw my God, wee Petal. Her Mummy's little Petal.
That's what she calls her by the way. Petal, Mummy's little Petal.
Her little girl, her little baby girl. Rhonda's girl. Not mine. Not
Sonny boy's baby. Fuck-all to do with me man. Who's the daddy?
You tell me. Ask her.

But it's the tears man. Real tears, wee Petal's tears. Petal's just
a baby. She's just turned seven, she's been put through far too
much shit already so she has. So much shit in her wee short life,
an now she's just opened her eyes an sees Mummy lyin on the
floor battered an bruised. It's seven in the mornin an she's got to
get ready for school.

Mummy Mummy Mummy.

Sonny Jim boy's offski. Offski pop man. Can't stand the horror. The blood, the pain, the wean. Aw the poor poor wean. She's only a little girl. Just a nipper. A wee innocent girl gettin up to go to school an seein two sweaty bodies wrestlin on the floor bitin an squealin an covered in blood.

Yer man can't take no more bro. Aw man, the guilt, the remorse. I'm terrorisin weans now. Sonny Jim's a bastart. A real top of the range cunt. A one-off. A limited edition. A fuckin rare collector's item.

Biggest bastart in town. Too right man, too right. She's got a point so she has, Rhonda's got a rock solid point.

She's screamin an bawlin.

Listen to the racket. Sonny Jim an Rhonda.

They love to fuckin hate each other.

Cunt bastart prick.
Slut bitch cow.

Screamin up the street. Busy busy street. Well it wasn't at one time but it fuckin is now. The whole street's out in flyin colours an they're all wantin to catch a piece of the action.

What's goin on up there? What's the fuckin script they're shoutin.

It's seven in the mornin. There's a full-scale battle goin on at number 57. Jesus Christ man. This used to be a nice street. It used to be.

Aye. Used to be.

Chapter Fourteen.
Twelve Boings.

It's the company ye keep.
That's what my wee maw used to say. Aye, yer a good boy son,
it's just the company ye keep.

The Rhonda blade kept dodgy company. An I don't mean me.
Naw, I wasn't meanin that. I'm talkin about her friends. Yes, her
friends.
I have real friends, she says, not like you. No, you have fair-
weather friends. You have riff raff. I have true friends. I have
friends for life, my friends are real friends.

Oh aye, they're real alright. Real fuckin cunts so they are. See
with friends like Rhonda's, yer man here don't need enemies.
Honest to fuck. I'm tellin ye, I fuckinwell don't.

Just phone the Polis, one of her real friends told her. If he
harasses ye phone the Polis.
Now that's what ye call a real friend. A real friend indeed.

Well, doesn't the bold Rhonda go an play that one to the fuckin
limit? Aye, she fuckin boots the arse right out of it so she does.
Goes an plays all her trump cards at once. I'm tellin ye.

I just stoated in the door this night. Tenish. Nowhere near pished
so I wasn't. No way man. I just walked in, sat down, never said a
word to no cunt. Honest, was sittin there cool, calm, collected.
Carin not a jot. I sits back, puts the feet up, lights up a fag an
cracks open a can. The Sonny boy starts chillin. Who gives a fuck
eh? Not me man. Not this dude. Not the bold Sonny Jim. Peace
man. Peace on earth. No hassle.

Ya bastart, she says. You, aye you, yer a bastart. I must be fuckin
mad. Must be. I'm too fuckin soft, she says. Ye treat this place

like a doss house. Yer nothin but a whore master, aye, a fuckin dirty rotten whore master. I dunno how either, dunno how ye get all yer whores to hump cause yer a pure shite ride ya no use cunt ye.

Chill out man. The Sonny boy sits an keeps his calm. Chill. Ignore the cunt. I take another mouthful of the golden liquid candy. *Ahhhh, yessss.* Down the hatch it goes man, so juicy an sweet like chilled angel's pussy juice.

I look along the can like a marksman starin down the barrel of a gun. There's this chequered bunnet sittin at the end of my can. Underneath the bunnet there's a pair of specs an a big red sweaty face. Then there were two. Two chequered hats. Two black coats an two sets of shiny shoes. Two Polis.

One speaks. Aye, one speaks an the other one nods.
What's goin on, it says, what's the problem?
Rhonda starts roarin an greetin an goin hysterical. *Boo hoo hooo.* That dirty rotten bastart beats me up every night so he does, I'm fuckin sick of it.

Look at me, I'm fuckin black an blue. Look, she goes, look. She shows them her arms, her arms are all bruises from fallin down the stairs pished last night. Fuckin look, she goes, look. Dirty rotten bastart.

Check the two Polis now. Tutt tutt tuttin in perfect timin an shakin their heads in tandem. Aye, Coplympic standard synchronised head shakin.

D'ye think yer a fuckin big man? says the first one.
Aye, d'ye think yer a big man do ye? goes the second one.

I'm tellin them to chill out, take it easy, the burd's a fuckin loony tuner. She's pure fuckin looney tuned up to Planet Cookyboo. I aint done a fuckin thing officer, nothin man, zilcho. I swear on that wean's life.

They're havin none of it man. Rhonda's playin a stormer, she's puttin on a pure Oscar winnin performance now.

Oh officer I can't stand it, I'm terrified of this monster, terrified in my own home, terrified to go to bed at night, I'm in fear of my life, me an my poor wee wean are absolutely petrified.
That does the trick man. The two Polis do synchronised get-yer fuckin-jacket-on-yer-leavin speeches. But yer man here's a fighter. Aye, the auld Sonny boy takes snash from no cunt so he doesn't, an he's not gonni stand here an be fucked out for somethin he aint done, d'ye know what I'm sayin? I tell them I'm goin nowhere. Goin nowhere, I've done nothin man, ye can't charge a man for doin nothin.

It's her house, the first one says. If she wants ye out, yer out.
Aye, it's her house, goes the second one.
I get halfway through tellin them if they want me out they'll have to throw me out when the next thing all I can hear is

> boing
> boing
> boing

Twelve times man. Twelve boings. Each boing is yer man here's arse bone bouncin off the steps.
The two Polis have an ankle each an they're draggin me down the stairs. What're the two daft fuckers like? An award winnin partnership at pullin drunk cunts down sets of stairs. What a team, what a double act.

Oh ya bastart ye. Fuckin excruciatin. The old arse bone hittin cold concrete. It's a mixed pain. A dull bone grindin sharp piercin pain. A mixture of bein hit by a sledge hammer an stabbed in the arse with a javelin.
Hammered an jabbed up the jacksie twelve times. Aye, twelve times man. There's twelve stairs. I've fell down them hundreds

of times so I have. But I'll tell ye what man, I'd rather fall down them than be dragged down them. Honest.

We get to the bottom an it's arms up the back an bundled into the van time. The two of them start givin it, ya wee bastart ye, ye think yer a big man. Yer a fuckin hoodlum so ye are. All the fancy names start flyin.
Thug, scumbag, alky, woman-beater.

Aw hold that result, I tell them. Hold it, I fuckinwell resent that remark. Don't give me that woman-beater pish. Yer man here's no woman-beater. How can I be when I aint fuckin married eh? There ye are, haha, fuck yees, got it wrong again ya pair of cunts.

No sweat. The Sonny boy don't sweat. Ye never sweat these things so ye don't.
Domestic. It's a fuckin domestic. No probs. No charges. Ye spend the night in the jail an yer out first thing in the mornin.
Ye see, the thing with a domestic is it costs too much cash. It costs the taxpayer millions man. An ten times out of ten the feudin couple always square it up so they do.
Aye, see by the time it hits the courts, they're all lovey dovey again. D'ye know what I'm sayin? She goes up an gives the guy a squeaky clean reference, gives him a fuckin glowin report. She starts sayin the guy's totally reformed, totally. This whole sorry mess has brought him to his senses so it has. He's a wonderful father an a great provider.
An see that word, provider? That's yer trump card.
Provider. As soon as the auld dude in the wig hears the word provider, ye've cracked it. Bob's yer auntie, yer off an runnin. I mean he doesn't want to rob the children of their provider, now does he?
Who the fuck's gonni feed those wee mouths of theirs if their auld daddio's dubbed up in the nick.
Who's gonna feed them? The fuckin tax payer, that's who.

D'ye get my drift?

Aye, domestic is a doddle. As long as there's no violence that is. As long as ye don't do a wee Barney Anderson. Aye, wee Barney. Ex boxer. Ex middleweight champion. Ex could've been the world champion if he hadn't hit the bevvy.

Wee Barney an the missus were at it eight nights a week so they were.

Aye, honest, him an wee Elsie were doin ten an twelve rounds every night when they were pished.

Anyway, the Polis are phoned for the five thousandth time. Wee Elsie's lip's bust an her eye's blackened.

Fuck it, they say. That's it, enough's enough. No more ya wee cunt, no more.

One fat lip too many. They can't turn a blind eye on it this time. The wee Elsie blade's been left lookin like a panda for the last time. Fuck it ya cunt, we're chargin ye. So wee Barney's up in the dock an the wiggy dude is ready to throw the fuckin book at him, there's no way he's gettin out it this time.

Fuck it, says the judge, he decides he's gonni make an example of the wee man. Professional fighter an all that. Fuck ye, bully boy. Think yer a hard man throwin yer fuckin weight about?

He asks wee Barney what he has to say for himself.

What is it with you Mr Anderson, he says, how come you keep beating up your wife?

Wee Barney just looks at him, shrugs, an goes, Superior footwork yer honour. Superior footwork.

So like I say, there aint even the slightest sign of a tiny wee bead of sweat showin on the Sonny boy's napper. Naw, don't sweat it, cause ye'll be out first thing in the mornin.

In fact they don't even take me down the Station. Naw, it aint worth it. They have to fill in all that paperwork plus listen to yer man here bawlin a lot of shite all night an wantin to make phone calls, speak to lawyers, threaten to commit suicide, blast out forty of his favourite karaoke numbers then lie an snore an soak the

bed with pish. Think about it. Fucksake man, aint worth it. The
two screws want an easy night. Get him to fuck man, drunken
cunt, fuck ye, aye. They drop yer man off at Mucky's.
Yess ya fuckin beauty. Thank you very much kind officers. I
couldn't tempt ye in for a small refreshment could I?

They tell me to get to fuck out an don't come back.
Listen Sonny boy, whatever ye do, don't you fuckin dare go back
to that house. Go back down there an we'll take ye down the
road for the night.
Fucksake, I tell them. Go back there, are ye kiddin?
The Sonny Jim aint ever goin back. The Sonny Jim is headin to
one place, an one place only, an that's right into clatty auld
Mucky's for more juice from the big black jungle.

I stoat through the doors, I've still got a wee stagger on me, still
feelin good, a bit light in the head but not light enough.
Peezi's proppin up the bar. Wee greasy Peezi. He hits me with his
usual pish.
Hey Sonny boy, how's it goin, listen, have ye got good eyesight?
Aye? Well, could ye see yer way clear to buyin me a drink?
Ya wee cunt, get yerself to fuck.
Big Clitoris Kate comes over with two double Buckfasts an two
pints of cider.
Stick it on the slate hen.
Me an Peezi are pourin it down our necks goodstyle. Aw go'n
yerself bro, let it slide down there, let it blow all the rough edges
off the surface of my tongue an haunt all the banshees out of
my brain. Aw man, this is magic, I'm back where I belong, back
at the bar, birlin.
Stop me birlin. Stop the world. Naw don't, keep it spinnin.

I take my medicine. A big glass of ruby red tonic.
An immediate hit. Smack. Bang. Bullseye, right on the button,
right on the fuckin epicentre of my brainbox. Gimmee the same
again an again an again an again.

The red raw jungle juice sets me on fire an burns like nitroglycerine.

Jesus Christ Almighty, yer man here's a staggerin inferno. I'm too hot now, I'm burnin up, I'm fuckin overheatin.

Cool me, chill me, gimmee somethin cold. Freezin cold cider, so cold it makes me shiver, makes my tongue stick to my lips, makes my head feel like two frozen knittin needles are bein stuck in my temples. So cold it hisses like a hot coal hittin ice.

Slowly the boozer starts whirlin like a waltzer. Every cunt's talkin an laughin an singin. Music's blarin out the walls, a mixture of sounds, a mixture of faces. All eyes on me, all starin, all glarin, smilin, singin, laughin.

Happy people havin fun.

Spinnin spinnin spinnin out of control, makin me dizzy, makin my insides churn.

All that cheap wine, all that sickly sweet cider is mixin inside me, churnin its way up like concrete inside a Jaeger.

Well, ye know what they say? What goes down must come up.

Up it all comes, my whole insides explode like water hittin a boilin chip pan. Spew sprays into the air like a ferocious firework display. Every cunt starts duckin an divin for cover.

Get out the way ya cunts, get the brollies up, get the fuckin waterproofs an wellies out.

Fucksake man, there's nothin ye can do is there? I mean ye can't hold what aint in yer hand. Anyway, it's only water. Aye look, it's watery as fuck. No muck. No heavy stuff, no chewed up mince an carrots.

Aw fuck man that was good, I needed that. That can't be good for ye all that poison in yer belly. It's good for ye to be sick, ye've got to get it all up.

Ye know what it's like man, after yer sick yer a new man. Ready to rumble once more.

I'm still flyin out of my skull, but no more dizzy turns, no more poison in the belly.

I'm in the twilight zone an I'm stayin here forever. Aye that's a fact. I'm livin in the zone, the twilight zone, where tomorrow never comes, where demons can't find me, where bad days're dead an good days last forever.

But listen, the good days don't last forever, naw they don't. Like the sweetest smellin rose they wilt an shrivel up an die. Aye, they die. They do man, they fuckin well do.

Enjoy the good stuff while it's goin cause it don't last long.

Hang on in bro, hang on o that feelgood.

Yer man feels good, yer man feels brilliant, I love it here, love love love it. Love the whole wide world an every cunt in it.

I want to shake yer hand, I want to kiss ye, hug ye, shag ye. That's what the juice does to the Sonny boy, makes him want to shag a soapy sponge.

Aw fuck, look at that arse, look at the arse on Mucky's daughter. Up The Arse Agnes's got some arse on her. Check it out, it's a fuckin sweet juicy peach. Oooohhhh, an those nice firm buns an those pert an pretty titties. An would ye feast yer eyes on Clitoris Kate? Man, she aint half pretty.

Fuck me yer man's got a dose of the auld Abba syndrome. D'ye know what that is, the Abba syndrome? Ye know those two lovely Abba lassies? Well isn't it always a pure cunt tryin to make up yer mind who ye'd shag first? D'ye know what I'm sayin? Aw fuck fuck fuck, decisions decisions, redhead or blonde, redhead or blonde? Eeeny meeny miney mo.

Ach fuckit, I'll just have to fuck the two of them at once, fuck them both with the one hard-on. Aye, that's what I'm gonni do, gonni do it right now. Right here, right now, right in front of every cunt, no worries bro, yer man just does not fuckin care.

The auld drink, it poisons the bowels of yer mind. This man's mind is a shithole. A sewer. A dungeon. The dirty filthy thoughts start reelin off like fuck. Hey, take a look inside an see, but be warned, what goes on in here will slaughter the faint hearted. It's a pure multi triple super xxx show.

Rock solid hardcore porn. Adults only.

I'm humpin Aggie an Kate. I've trapped them in my dungeon. They're draped in chains, crackin whips, they're covered from head to toe in skin-tight leather.

Shiny silver studs stuck through ruby red nipples, moist juicy pussy flaps covered in clit rings.

We're havin a baw-burstin threesome. The Sonny boy, Up The Arse Agnes an Clitoris Kate all rollin about on a waterbed. Me an the gruesome twosome, my two dirty sex slaves are suckin my doaber an sittin on my face.

Bang bang bang. There's this loud bangin. It jolts me. I escape from my mind. Back to reality. I'm sittin at the bar.

Fuck me man, the bangin's still goin. It's my hard-on, it's bangin on the bar like a heavy brass door knocker. Aw fuck, yer man here's got a big brass lion's head down his strides.

Aw check the fuckin head on it. Yer man's got a big snarlin lion on the head of his champer snarlin an roarin. A ferocious caged beast. Aggie an Kate. Up The Arse an Clitoris. They're behind the bar pullin pints. They see me. They're watchin me. They're watchin me watchin them. Readin my disturbed horny mind. They're smilin at me, teasin me, encicin me in.

Oh my God in Heaven man. A wailin siren explodes through my eyeballs zappin me back to my senses. A big fluorescent baw starts bleatin on an off an howlin like a war siren. D'ye know what that is? That's the red alert signal, the final warnin, the point of no return. The sign that tells ye that if ye don't stop here then the end of the world is now. A one way ticket from here on in bro. A one way ticket only, there will be no return. The final countdown. The grand finale. The end. It's time to leave, time to call it a day man. The party is over forever. Please vacate the premises usin the nearest exit. Do not collect yer belongings. Leave the buildin immediately. Oh for fucksake man. Listen. The bold Sonny Jim boy has just left the buildin.

Chapter Fifteen.
The Blazin Arsehole.

Me an Peezi stoat out onto the street carryin a cargo that would bulldoze a block of flats. Six bottles of Buckfast, two dozen tins of super lager, four litres of cider an sixty smokes.

The sun's jabbin two hot pokers into my eyes, pushin them in deep, grindin them round an round. I can't see man. My eyes are nippin like Victory V's. Aw fuck I'm dizzy, I aint too steady on the auld tent pegs bro. Rock steady Eddy aint my name right now.

It's true what they say about the heat. It's the heat that knocks ye off yer feet. It's the fresh air, it's the people walkin up an down the street that make ye dizzy. I'm starin at them. Where the fuck're yees all goin ya cunts? Faces. Empty lookin faces. Walkin. Every fucker walkin.

Goin somewhere. Somewhere to go. Not like me. Naw, not like yer man here.

Yer man here aint got nowhere to go bro. All the doors are closed. All the people walkin. Walkin somewhere, walkin anywhere. Lookin at me. Lookin away quick.

Who the fuck're ye lookin at arsehole? Me? You lookin at me? Fuckin bastarts. Every cunt. Shower of dirty bastarts.

I'm Status Quo, as Peezi would say. Aye, that's one of the wee man's favourite sayins. Yer Status Quo ya cunt. Look at ye, yer rockin all over the world. I'm rockin man. Rockin all over the place. Backwards an forwards, side to side, you name it, I'm rockin it. I aint too steady on the pegs an the ground beneath me aint helpin none.

It's the pavement, the fuckin pavement's to blame so it is. It's bumpy. It's movin. The fuckin pavement's movin. Oh ya bastart ye. Stop it. Stop the world an let me jump off.

Aw man. Aw my fuck. Yer man here aint well. The Sonny boy's

feelin really sick. Feelin Pat an Mick. I should've stayed where I was.

See? See what I'm sayin? No wonder ye stay in the pub. Yer absolutely fine till ye leave the boozer. It's a true sayin that.

Rhonda says it all the time funny enough. See you ya cunt, she says. Yer fine till ye leave that pub.

Aw my belly. My belly's rumblin, it's makin noises like boulders bouncin about in a tumble dryer. Aw fuck, aw fuck man. It's rumble in the jungle time. Sharp short stabbin pains. The auld belly starts feelin like it's being stabbed, only the stabs are comin from the inside. The rumblin an gurglin is gettin sharper an more severe.

Poison, that's what it is. Yer man here's got a belly full of highly toxic waste. It's workin its way down this time but. Usually it comes up. Well it's got to go somewhere innit? Oh my fuck it's on its way an it aint takin its time so it aint. The poison train's comin chuggin through the tunnel an it aint got no fuckin brakes. I'm gonni have to act quick here. Fuck me man.

Quick quick quick what am I gonni do? I need a shite, I need a starry night an it's not the kind that's gonni wait, naw, it's not the kind ye can bake in the oven till ye get home, wherever home is. Where is home goin to be tonight bro? Fuck it, I'll find that out later.

My main problem is right here right now. Where am I goin to dump this big mucky load?

See to be perfectly honest with ye, this aint no load. Naw. This is a spray job. This is eye of a needle material. Swear it. The Sonny Jim's arsehole is a steam power jet. The sheer force of this stuff could take yer two eyes right out yer fuckin head man. Honest. I could sandblast a block of flats so I could.

Think think think. Where am I goin to go?

I can't go back into the pub. Back into Mucky's? Fuck off. Have ye ever seen the state of Mucky's toilets? Well, I'll give ye a rough idea. Try an picture the backstreets of a South American slum area. Think about it. Aw holy fuck man. Big fat rats samba dancin through the sewage. That's the same stuff ye get in Mucky's lavvy. I can't go back in there. No chance. Aw for fucksake what am I gonni do. Think ya cunt. Ye better come up with somethin fast.

Peeeeeng. It happens. *Peeeeeeeeeng.*
See every now an again, yer man here get one of these wee lightbulbs lightin up in yer head moments. Aye, that's a fact. An this one is a beauty. A bright one. A real fuckin two hundred an fifty watt job. Bright as fuck so it is. Hey watch out bro, ye'll get blinded. Stick yer shades on. The light goes on an this crackin wee thought pops out my mindpiece.

I know where I'll go. I'll go up to Micky Mulrooney's. Micky's shop is right above Mucky's. I'll nick up there an use his lavvy. Aye, that's the game. Me an Peezi.
Wait here, I tell Peezi. Wait here an watch the cargo.
Peezi waits. Waits an waits. Watches the cargo.
That's a dodgy decision by the way. Really dodgy. Ye should never trust Peezi with a cargo. Ye should never trust Peezi with anythin for that matter. No choice but. Ye know what it's like don't ye? If ye've got to go, ye've got to go. An yer man here has really really got to go.
Ye've heard that auld sayin, shit or bust?

There's fourteen stairs up to Micky's office. Aw fuck man I'm never gonni make it.
Talk about touchin cloth? Fuck, I can't even call it that. This aint the sort of stuff that will touch cloth. Naw. This is hot bubblin lava, this'll burn right through cloth in seconds, burn a big hole right through my keks an jeans.
Aw holy fuck man, honest, I'm tellin ye, I aint gonni make it, has any cunt got a potty?
It's started runnin through my fingers now. Aw the pain man. My

sphincter skin is peelin off the bone. Aw man, aw man, there's a forest fire ragin in my arsehole.

I manage to get to the top of the stairs. I've conquered Everest. I shimmy along the lobby. I'm squeezin everythin tight. I'm tryin to walk just usin my ankles an feet. I smell wee randy Mandy's hard-on perfume. It stings my eyes like paint stripper makin them leak like a pishy auld pensioner's.

She looks at me as if a big lump of snottery slime has just slithered along the floor an threw up an shat diarrhoea all over her nice clean office.

She sighs in deep, rolls her eyes round the room an goes, yes, what is it? She doesn't even wait for an answer. Why the fuck did she ask? Dunno man.

She shakes her head, tuts, then lifts the phone an tells me to wait a sec.

She crosses her legs an drums her false nails on the table.

The leg crossin gives me a glimpse of bare fleshy thigh, horny thoughts start sprintin through my mind an for a small split second I want to hump her head off, but I can't, naw, I fuckinwell can't ye see, because I've got this fine spray of boilin mustard oozin through my fingers.

Hurry up, hurry up for fucksake ya wee snooty cunt. Hurry up or I'll give ye somethin to look down yer fuckin nose at. Yer man here's just about to spray paint yer walls if ye don't get that lavvy door open now.

She tells the bold Micky that yer man's here. It's James McConaughy, she tells him.

Aw c'mon, c'mon, what the fuck's goin on here? All I'm needin's a shit. Can I have a shit? I'm just about to ask really nicely.

Just about to put my hand up an go, Please miss, may I have a shite, can I eh, please, please? Pretty please?

Amazin what ye'll stoop to when yer desperate innit.

But I don't get a chance. Naw. All I hear is Mickey's pissed off voice comin through the phone.

Wee Mickey man. Wee bold Mickey. I hear his voice. Hear it loud an clear. Give him fifty pounds, he says, an not a penny more. Tell him he knows the score.

Oh ya fuckin dancer. I've died an came back to life again. I'm so fuckin happy I could shite. Aye right.

Fifty quid? Well well well then, what the fuck can I say? I mean, it would be rude to say no, now wouldn't it? How can I refuse?

It's nice to be nice an all that, d'ye know what I'm sayin?

Fuckin hell, for a wee split second there I almost forgot that my arse is about to explode an blow this shitty little town off the face of God's earth.

Aye, only for a wee second but. An then it's back, it's back to remind me. The heat. The sting. The burnin. The blazin inferno inside my arsehole.

Alright then, I tell wee Mandy. Alright my wee honeepot. That's helluva nice of the man. What a lovely gesture. So thoughtful an kind. How could I possibly turn down such warm generosity. Tell him I'll accept. But only on one condition.

What's that? she asks me.

On the condition that you let me use yer toilet.

My auld burnt arse hits the lavvy faster than the speed of light an as I sit there sandblastin the enamel of his lovely porcelain throne, I wonder to myself how far Peezi will have got with the carry-out.

Chapter Sixteen.
Deadbeat.

I can't believe my eyes man. D'ye see what I mean when I tell ye to call me lucky?

The Peezi boy's sittin on the carry-out, half sleepin an half shoutin at the pavement. Fuck ye, he's tellin it. Ya shower of dirty bastarts yees. Yees're all a shower of dirty rotten cunts. A wee green puke puddle lies splattered at his feet. He's glad to see me. Peezi boy's always glad to see yer man here.

Awright man, he goes. I kept an eye on yer cargo bro. Safe as houses with the Peezi boy.

We decide to head down to Peezi's house cargo'd up to the hilt. Fuckin hell man, we're talkin about a cargo that's even heavier than Up The Arse Agnes. Honest. The mother, father, auntie an uncle of all carry-outs. It would choke a doss house full of chronic alkies. We heave it up onto a shoulder each. We're nearly draggin it so we are. A pure monster.

Taxi.

The poor driver's stuck for a turn. He must be. Surely to fuck he doesn't need this. Well, actually he does, he does need it. Doesn't want it but. Doesn't want two winos that reek of stale pish in his nice new car now does he? Naw, but he needs it. There's a difference. Must's a master. OK?

An I'll tell ye another thing, we aint the biggest fare he's gonni get all night either, we aint no golden nugget. Put it this way, he's not gonni be able to retire for the night once he drops us off. Naw, we're just goin down to Peezi's house. It aint that far man. It's half a mile if it is that.

Don't put the meter on mate, Peezi tells him, just let the handbrake off.

Aw for fucksake, the guy's thinkin, all this for what?

Peezi's patter's pish an gettin pisher.
Haw, arsehole, he says. Yer tryin to take yer fuckin time on
purpose ya cunt. C'mon to fuck, get a move on. Fucksake man
what did ye come this way for? This is the fuckin long way.
I'll fuckin knock ye out ya cunt. Are ye tryin to act wide?
Cool it bro, I tell him. Easy does it. Easy Peezi. The guy's cool. The
guy's only tryin to make a livin. C'mon wee man. Chill.

We pull up outside Peezi's. I give the guy two notes. He's
delighted. He is, honest. The look on his face says he would've
givin us a fuckin freebie just to get us out the car.
But then all of a sudden relief turns to horror. Aye, just when the
poor cunt thinks he's off the hook his luck takes a turn for the
worse.

Hold it, hold it, says Peezi. A wee bit of blaw would go down
nice so it would. I'd squeeze my left bollock into a lump of mush
for a wee bit of dope. What d'ye say Sonny boy eh, what d'ye
think? We can afford an ounce so we can. We'll get some off the
Shoogly. Wee Shoogly's gear's awesome so it is, the fuckin bull
terrier's baws.
Aw go on Sonny boy. Please. I'll square ye up when I get my giro.
I'll buy the fag papers. Aye, no bother to me mate. I'll get the
Rizlas.

Wee tiny sweat bubbles start swellin up on the taxi driver's brow
now. Then they start poppin an slowly trickle down the side of
his neck. Now he really, really, doesn't need it. Doesn't fuckin
want it either. He's goin to lose his licence so he is.
C'mon to fuck now boys, he's whinin. Aw for fucksake, my
licence, my livelihood. I've got a wife an four weans me. Aw my
fuck.

Just take us round to Shoogly's, I tell him. Here ya silly fucker.
Here's a tenner. Buy yer weans some sweeties.

Peezi's in an out of Shoogly's before ye can say fuck me here's the Polis. That's what I do by the way. I go like that an say to the driver, Aw fuck naw man I don't believe it, here's the Polis. *Aaaaarrggh*. Fuck man. See those wee beads of sweat that were tricklin down his neck, well they've now turned into a waterfall an start to flood his cab.

Aw ya bastart, my fuckin licence, aw my God, aw Jesus Christ Almighty my fuckin licence, my livelihood, my wife, my weans, my house.

Aw for fucksake man, check him out. What's he like eh? I slap him on the back an tell him I'm only kiddin. Christ sake, can ye not take a wee joke. Just a wee joke, fuck.

The wee taxi man starts cryin. Fucksake. See me by the way, I can be a right rotten cunt sometimes.

Here comes Peezi skippin along the path like a four-year-auld toddler comin back from the van. Ice cream an sherbet an a bottle of American cream soda. Gonni make ice drinks. Sharin it with no cunt.

Peezi jumps in an slams the door an tells the driver to put the boot through the floor. Don't spare the horses auld yin.

This is the best of blaw, he says.

Aye the bold Peezi boy loves the blaw.

It changes him. Changes him right away so it does. He starts talkin like a cool dude, starts talkin like a right American crackhead.

Yeah man, real good shit bro, cool man, sound, no worries, don't fuckin sweat it cuzz. Hey mothafucka, he says to the driver, what's yer shit man, why ya trippin?

The wee taxi man's still wipin all the snotters an tears off his face, an Peezi starts makin him even worse tellin about the streets. Aw the streets man, the streets're real bad bro. Peezi boy tells the driver he's from the streets.

We arrive at Peezi's pad. Peezi's hovel. Peezi's midden. Peezi's

fuckin shithole. Take yer pick man. Call it what ye like. Fuck
me, no carpets. Just floorboards. Shiny sticky floorboards. Holy
fuck man. How'd I end up here, here in a hole like this, how'd it
happen?
You tell me.
Yer man here had it all at one time so he did, had it nice an
cushy.
What happened?
I'll tell ye what happened, I pissed it all away, pissed it up against
the wall, down the cludgy, down my leg, down any cunt that
happened to be near. Piss piss piss. Pissed it all away. Yer man
here's a pisser. Piss anywhere. The Martini pisser. That's what
they call me. Anytime anyplace anywhere. Piss beds, piss chairs,
piss trousers. Piss in gardens, cupboards, wardrobes, stereos,
tellies.
You name it, yer man here's pissed it. The bold Sonny Jim boy
has pissed everywhere bar the Moon.
How'd I get like this? So fucked up, so low. Lower than a snake's
baws Rhonda would call me.
I can't blame my upbringin. Naw. Yer man here came from
a good home. It's the company ye keep. Yer judged by yer
company. Ye drink with the winos ye die with the winos.
Wino? Who me? Yer man? Yer man here aint no wino bro.
Well, ye know what they say don't ye? If ye walk like a duck an
quack like a duck, yer a duck.

Me an wee Peezi. The human sewer rat. Wee greezy Peezi.
My best buddy. We stagger up the lobby makin clumpin tearin
noises on the sticky floor.
Angie's out cold on the chair. Peezi's not pleased. He doesn't like
it one wee bit. Right out of the blue he does a Bruce Lee. Yeeee
Hyyyyyeeeee yaaaaa hi karate.
Yer man here can do karate, he says.
His boot comes rammin down on Angie's belly. Up cunt, he
screams. Up, get yer skinny arse up. I've got visitors. Show some

respect ya fuckin slut. Anyway that's my chair. Up.
Angie shakes her numbed an dazed head. Poor poor Angie.
What's the wee soul like? A hairdo like an explosion in a
mattress factory, puffy black eyes an a sad swollen face.
That was him that done that, she says, pointin at her face.
That dirty rotten bastart battered me.

Peezi goes mental an starts screamin an foamin at the mouth.
Ye fuckin asked for it ya cow, yer a right cheeky cunt gettin.
This is my fuckin house, Peezi says, drummin his thumb on his
chest. I'm the fuckin boss.

Angie musters up enough strength to pull her skin an bone out
the chair an drag her ravaged body across the floorboards to the
table. Big blue varicose veins slither like snakes down her legs an
her long floppy tits hang like burst water balloons.
Aw darlin, she says to Peezi, did ye bring me some super lagers?
Aw thanks babes, aw see him, I love him, he's a good man so he
is, he's good to me, good to all my weans. I fuckin love him to
bits so I do.

The wee Peezi boy grabs her from behind an thrusts his groin
into her bony arse an starts pullin at her tits like a farmer milkin
a cow.
Awright doll? he says.

We crack open the cans an bottles. Peezi skins up some joints.
Rollem thick bro, none of yer shit for us dudes, I tell him.
Peezi tells me I'm some man an reminds me he'll definately
square me up on giro day. I swear on my life Sonny boy, he says.
Aw fuckin hell man, I'm vibratin. The booze is wearin off bro. I
can't have that now can I? I start starin at reality. I don't like to
go there man. Reality Avenue is one mean street. Sonny boy just
cannot live there.

I need some tonic. Get it down ye. I crack open the bottle an
wrap my lips round the neck. Instant hit. Bang. The angel juice

kills the gut-curdlin stench an closes the valve in my mind that allows any nasty stuff to enter.

No thoughts, no feelins, no reasonin, no guilt, no remorse, no shame.

Naw, I aint havin any of that shit. No fuckin entry ya shower of fuckers. Piss right off. Beat it.

The angel juice does its duty. Its stingin sweetness singes my tonsils an ignites an inferno in my chest.

Aaahhhhhhh wildfire spread yerself ya fuckin *beeeaaauutyy*. A warm glow flushes right through me. It soothes an caresses my inner skin an slides slowly from my head down to my toes.

I start suckin hard on a big fat joint an watch the soft orange smoke do a classy salsa dance across the room then dive like a graceful swallow into the dim hazy light comin from the top of the soft yellow lampshade.

Every muscle in my body enters voluntary paralysis. It's nice here. Yeah man, cool joint.

Nice pad ye've got here Peezi boy. Yeah nice an cool, cool an warm bro, I love it here, peace man, love an peace. Everythin is beautiful. Every note from the hi-fi comes to life an moonwalks like Michael Jackson across the mantlepiece. I can even see the smile on its face. Dance Mister E sharp dance. Dance for the Sonny boy.

But hey, listen, ye know what happens next don't ye? It's munchie time.

Yer man here must eat. Now. Right now. Munchie munchie munchie. It's the dope ye see. The auld Bob Hope gives ye the munchies. Where's the kitchen bro? I need to eat man. Fuckin starvin. Hank Marvin.

There's a big giant sized hole in the wall where there used to be a kitchen door. It's all ripped open an raw like a savaged carcass.

That was me that done that, says Peezi. Done it with my bare hands so I did. Strong as a horse me. The Peezi boy's as strong as a horse. D'ye like it big man? Open plan. I do all my own DIY so I do. Like it?

Aw for fucksake, check the kitchen. Bare naked shelves an a hollow fridge.

We're de-frostin it, Peezi sneers.

There's not a thing to eat man, nothin but two mouldly rolls in the bread bin.

Aw but I'm fuckin starvin. It's the munchies. They're eatin my brains out. I've got to eat bro. Fuck it. All or nothin. If the blue mould don't kill me the hunger will. There's a big steamie pot on the stove, bubblin an hissin away. The lid's vibratin like an alky in a detox unit. Aw it's pure fuckin stinkin man. What's in it, what the fucks cookin?

It's tripe. Tripe an onions. *Uuuuurggghhh uuuurrrgghhh urrgghh.* I start to boak a wee bit, but only on the inside. Nothin comes up. Fuckit man, I need to eat. I'm gonni die if I don't. The auld belly's makin noises like a gorilla fartin in a metal bin.

Ach well, here goes.

I dook a mouldy roll in an swirl it round fast gettin it all nice an soggy. I open the gub an throw it in. Right, start makin yer jaws go. Aye, get it down ye ya cunt.

Hey, I'll tell ye what, it tastes not too bad at all. Honest I've tasted worse. Yumm yumm have another dook. Easy does it man, gulp, it slides down into the belly.

Aw fuck man, look at me, a fucked up low-life. Driftin in an out of blackouts. In an out of focus.

Things aint movin smooth bro. Everythin keeps stoppin an startin. A mad crazy mixture of fast an furious freeze frames. Stop. Start. Stop.

It aint real. I aint here. I wouldn't do this. How'd I get here? It wasn't yer upbringin. Ye came from a good home.

Who says that? Every fucker.

I can hear a mixture of voices. High-pitched an low pitched. Screams an whispers.

A real sky high glass shatterin squeal pierces my ears. It sounds painful, sounds desperate.

There's the wean greetin, Angie says. Ye better go an see to him. Aw the poor wee babby. Wee greasy Peezi junior. He's no well. Wee mini Peezi's sick. He aint well the wee soul. Poisoned bowels. Screamin for his mammy.

Yer man here's still hungry. Fuckin famished. I need more scran. I dook the other roll in deep this time, swirl it round an round scrapin all the onions off the edges. Yumm yum boiled tripe an onions, my favourite. Hey, aint it funny how ye acquire a taste? Mmmmm, down it goes bro. Nice an smooth.

Angie comes in, she's carryin baby Peezi. Poor wee soul, boakin an shittin all nite long the wee thing.

God love him, she says, he's got poisoned bowels. She looks at me an looks at the pot an goes, What're ye doin, what're ye eatin?

Just a wee roll, I say, I hope ye don't mind, I'm just a wee bit peckish, just had a wee dook like, a wee dook in the pot. Tripe an onions is yer man here's favourite.

Aw fuck fuck fuck, she says. Tripe an onions? Tripe an onions? Tripe an onions my arse ya dopey big fucker, that's the fuckin weans dirty auld nappy. Look, she says, liftin it out the pot with the wooden tongs. He's got poisoned bowels, it's the only way I can get the shite stains out.

She lets it plop back into the pot an my lungs fill up with hot sticky steam an a gut-wrenchin bile starts bubblin up in my belly.

Aw Holy Mother of God. See what I mean? I'm lower than a snake's baw hairs.

I'm tellin ye. I aint jokin when I say this. There's nothin beneath me.

I'm a pure fuckin deadbeat.

I need a drink. More drink. I need it. I light up, drink up. Peezi
boy's out cold an makin all sorts of gurgly noises. Fucksake, he's
chokin, he's turnin deep dark purple, the poor cunt's chokin to
death right in front of our sad an bleary eyes.
I tell Angie to go an check him out.
Aw for fucksake go an see to him, what's the matter, do
somethin do somethin for fucksake.
Och fuckin just leave the cunt, she says, he's only chokin on his
vomit. He does it all the time so he does.
Aw man, chill. Cool it. Nice wee smoke, nice bit of draw.
Everythin's cool again. Floatin. Easy street. Easy easy easy. Mister
Feelgood's back an he's brought all his little soldiers along
to entertain my brain. They swing an sway an do a gentle jig
that makes my mindpiece smile. As they boogie inside me the
warmest flush rushes softly through my body. Happeeee. Man I
feel good, I feel lovely, I feel warm an cool an every single part
of me is light an soft an fluffy.
Peeeaaace maaaaaaan peeeeeeaaaace.
Angie walks towards me. The beautiful Angie. An angel in white
satin.
She slowly shakes her mane. Long strands of black shiny silk
fall gently on her shoulders an wriggle across her neck in slow
motion. Her eyes are sky blue diamonds that twinkle in the
moonlight. She teases me into her soft pink tits. Aw holy lumpin
fuck would ye check those pink pert titties bro?
Ripe an ready, loud an proud an standin to attention.
She dances in perfect timin with the sensuous sex music comin
from the hi-fi.
Come to me. Come with me. She makes me beg for it. Beg for
her body, beg for her sex, gyratin her hips, thrustin her raven
black bush deep an hard down on my face. I'm lyin here helpless.

Her soft pink sweet smellin skin brushes gently across me,
soothin me, caressin me, strippin me, straddlin me. Straddlin
the Sonny boy. Check me out man. What am I like? Lyin here all

tanned an oily. My body ripplin with muscles an a hard-on like a dwarf's arm with a big red shiny cricket baw oozin out of its hand.
Yip, that's what I look like bro. I might not look like that to you. I might not look like that to most folk, but I look like that from where I'm lyin.

Angie baby, Angie. She's on me, doin me. Aye, she's fuckin the brains out the Sonny boy. Oh listen by the way, don't blame me. This aint no dirty trick. I aint no two-faced bastart goin behind the Peezi boy's back. No way sir. The Peezi boy's lyin right there, right there on the chair, right in front of us. A ringside seat. Aye, there he is man. Chokin on his vomit.

An here we are. The Sonny boy an Angelic Angie.
A real handsome couple. Two beautiful people.

She wraps her legs round my waist. We float like exotic butterflies dancin in the sun.
I'm in her, she's in me, we're in each other, we're one, one person, one beautiful fuck we're havin. On the floor, on the couch, on the chair, against the wall, in mid-air, aw holy mother of fuck man, a weightless, motionless, effortless fuck session.
Our bodies brush across each other slowly like a classical violinist strokin the strings of a fine Stradivarius.
My beautiful Angie, my beautiful angel. Angel in white satin.
I'm lickin her like a pussy cat lappin up cream. Lickin her every inch of the way, every inch of her soft creamy skin. Her beautiful smooth body, untouched, unblemished.
The sweet virginal Angela.
I say it. I say it slowly. I hear myself say it over an over.
A-n-g-e-l-a A-n-g-e-l-a.
I love you.
I love you too, she says.
Marry me, yeess baby, yes my beautiful sweetheart, my beautiful drunken slut.

It's the juice man. It's the jungle juice. It's the puff, the blaw, the dope that does it. It's not me, not the real me, it's the dopey fuckin wino inside me that emerges an takes control. The mad crazy monster within.

Oh sweet Lord in Heaven please don't go an let all this die. Please keep me here, don't let it go away. Let me keep this vision, let me stay here forever wrapped in the wings of an angel in the fruit-scented Garden of Eden.

Stay, stay here bro, don't go back. Naw, naw ye can't, can't go back man. Yer man wants to stay here forever in this magical dreamworld.

That's what it's all about ye see. Ye take a cheap flight from reality.

Ye buy a one way ticket. Just one way bro. This flight goes one way only.

But the only thing wrong with the flight that just goes one way is that it bring ye right back here like a boomerang so it does. There's no stops. No stops.

Ye end up right back here where we're standin now, where we're lyin now.

Where I'm lyin. Lyin dyin on this pishy pukey shitty sticky settee. Comin out of this dream that's dyin.

Back to where I started. Planet Reality.

Here in the house of death on Planet Hell. Back amongst the livin dead. Back amongst Angie an Peezi Snr an Peezi Jnr.

Foosty Fanny Angie with her vulgar varicose veins an floppy tits an smelly breath. Wee greasy Peezi zonked on the chair with a throat full of vomit, an wee Peezi Jnr's still cryin because his wee poisoned bowels are makin his wee nippy arse sting like an attack from a hive of starvin bees.

My beautiful Angela has died. Died in my dream. Died in reality. Aw my God, I'm dyin, everythin is dyin. Me Angie an the two wee Peezis.

Death is all around us. I can smell it in the air an on the walls.

Aye, it is, honest, even the sad little burds on the wallpaper are dyin as they try like fuck to flap their tiny wings but can't, can't because they're stuck like fuck in the slimy mustard nicotine that's smeared across the walls.
This is it man, my one way fifty quid fun trip. Yip. That's what it's cost me man. A fifty bucks return ticket from here back to here. A brief relief from the misery of what's in front of me.
What ye see is what ye get.

That's all the ticket gives ye bro. Brief relief. It takes ye away an fills yer belly full of angel juice an yer lungs full of blaw then dumps ye back on yer doorstep when the joy wears off an the pain an heartache returns.
Right back here in this deathhole. Peezi's house.
That's what he calls it. My house, Peezi an Angie's house. The house of death.

I start comin round, comin to. I don't wake up man, I don't wake up cause I aint been asleep, I've been unconscious.
My eyelids are stuck tight. I peel them open slowly. I try not to blink. Blinkin is a bastart, blinkin is so fuckin painful. When I blink my eyelids sandpaper my eyeballs.
My tongue is wearin a fur coat.
I vibrate an shiver. I'm cold an wet, frightened an alone.
The flesh on my face tears as I pull it out of the dried up puke blob that's been my pillow for fuck knows how long.
I stagger onto my feet an trudge along the dim an grimy lobby.
I open the door an clean my feet on the way out.

Chapter Seventeen.
Crabs a Dollar a Dozen.

I took one look at Rhonda an knew I was in bother. Big bother.

How's yer new burd doin, she says, how's she gettin on?
The fuckin prostitute, slut, cow, whore. Wait till I get her, the
dirty filthy fuckin crabbed up bitch.

A plate bounces off my forehead splittin it wide open like a
cow's arse droppin a newborn calf. The next one smashes on
the wall then three cups hit me on the shoulder neck an face.
Fucksake man, the auld Rhonda blade's in good form.
Hey yer a real good shot so ye are honeybunch. Ever thought
about takin up darts?

She's screamin an bawlin an tellin yer man here that she's bein
eaten alive. Says she's half the burd she used to be, aye, she says
she's been gobbled up galore so she is.
What d'ye mean, what d'ye mean? I ask her.
Crabs, ya dirty bastart, she squeals. I'm covered in crabs the size
of rats. Ye've been shaggin some dirty clatty slapper an ye've
gave them to me an now I'm covered in them an they're all
havin a fuckin beanfeast on my poor wee pussy.

Fucksake man, lucky wee bastarts, that's all I can say.
Wait a minute but, this has got yer man here thinkin. Think think
think. Slow down son, take yer time. Ye've got some real serious
questions to ask. Big questions that need big answers. Fuckin
serious stuff man.
Sonny Jim asks himself some important questions.
When did he last hump Rhonda? An here's an even more
important question still. When did he last muff dive? Aye, when
did he last yodel up the canyon?
Questions, questions, questions.

An guess what question number three's gonni be?
Can ye get crabs in a moustache?

Anyway. The point is.
The Sonny boy's in bother. Big bother.
Fucksake. Easy does it bro. Concentrate. Talk slow, think quick.
Ye know the score, ye know what ye've got to do.
Admit to fuck-all. Deny everythin.
It wasn't me, it wasn't me. Deny, deny, deny.
When in doubt deny. Lie. I know nothin about nothin.

Listen hen, it's got nothin to do with me so it aint. The Sonny
Jim's in the clear.
Look.
I point down inside my bawbag.
Look, there's nothin to see down there doll, nothin, honest,
check it out, have a wee squint an see, stick yer dome down
there. Nothin, nothin at all.
One pair of crab-free bollocks.
I tell her she must've got them somewhere else. I tell her exactly
where. I tell her she got them off her big fat arsed sumo wrestler
pal.
Big Sally, big Bawsacks Sally.
That's what she's got man. Honest. Ye see them hangin between
her legs when she walks, two big bawsacks. Two big hippo's
baws.
That's where ye got the crabs hen.

Rhonda works with big Sally. They share a lavvy seat.
But she's havin none of it at first man. The bold Rhonda's havin
none of it. Ye can't get them off a lavvy seat, she says.
Aye ye can, honest to God honeybunch, honest, I swear on my
life ye can.
Ye see the wee warnin signs in toilets all the time.
I saw a right cracker the other week so I did. How'd it go again,
how'd it go?

Before ye sit
Wipe yer seat
The crabs in here
Can jump six feet.

Aye, that was it. Where did I see that now, fuckin cracker innit?
Dead funny.

Yer man here's laughin alone but. Laughin on his jack. Rhonda
aint laughin. Rhonda doesn't see the funny side. No chance. She
calls yer man a liar. Fuckin dirty lyin bastart.
Ye can't, she says. She says she asked the doctor. Asked Doctor
Rajeev. She says she asked him if crabs can jump, asked him if ye
can get them off the lavvy seat.
No chance, says the bold Doctor Raj, no no no. No way José,
can't be done. The one an only way ye can get them is shaggin.
No other way bro.

Who have ye been shaggin ya slut?
Fucksake, who says that? Where did that come from? Did any
cunt hear it? Did I say it, or did I just think it?
Sonny Jim hears these wee voices in the back of his head all the
time. Sometimes it's only him that hears them, sometimes every
other cunt that's there hears them too. Where do they come
from, those voices? They get yer man into so much soapy bubble
so they do. They just come out.
I might just be standin there, thinkin. Aye, just thinkin an sayin
nothin. Then, bang, I end up gettin a hard crack right on the jaw
off some cunt.
Who're ye callin a wanker?
An here's me standin there thinkin I never opened my mouth.
I swear it. I thought I never said a word. I thought I was just
thinkin it.

Fuck me man, see these voices. Bad voices, bad suggestions. I try
to keep them to myself so I do. I try my best. Stay in ya cunt, I tell

them, I don't want no cunt to hear them.

So, anyway. I'm standin lookin at Rhonda an I hear this wee voice in my head sayin, Go on ya cunt, ask her, ask her who she's been shaggin.

Hold it, I keep tellin myself, hold it, stay in, don't come out, please please please don't come out.

The voice stays in. Thank fuck. No cunt heard it. Just me. Good job, it wouldn't have went down well. Not at this point.

Rhonda babe's fired up like a furnace. Fucksake man, look at her boat race. She's foamin through a pair of purple lips an she's curlin up her nails like a malnourished lion waitin to pounce on its prey. Rhonda babe's upset. Upset big time.

But I'll tell ye this. She's bluffin, bluffin like a poker player. She went to the doctor? Did she fuck. No chance. No no no. Went to the doctor my arse bone. How do I know, I hear ye ask, How does the Sonny boy know?

Wait an I'll tell ye.

Rhonda phoned the boozer one time. Well, she phoned the boozer a hundred million times if the truth be told. She's the undisputed boozer phonin champion of the world is Rhonda. Anyway, this time she phones givin it all the usual, booo hoo hoo I need ye honeee I need ye shit.

Fucksake, yer man's here's seen it, heard it, read the book, wore the T-shirt, saw the film, saw the fuckin sequel. Heard it so many times man. The auld honeee I need ye trick. Fucksake, change the record. Hit the fast forward button.

Don't get me wrong though, don't get yer man here wrong. If I'm needed I'll be there. If there's a damsel in distress yer man's right in there. I mean yer hole's yer hole, know what I'm sayin? Anyway after all the boo hoo hooin an the sobbin n snotterrin, I tell her I'll be down when I'm ready. I tell her to sit an wait.

Well it's yer duty innit? I mean ye don't jump for no cunt bro. Naw, never jump in, don't go runnin the minute they shout, naw,

always let the fuckers wait. Fuck aye man. Take yer time.
So eventually I staggers down the frog n toad an she's still sittin
there boo hoo hooin away big time. Rhonda is an Olympic
marathon runner at bawlin. Honest. She could bawl for a world
select.
Anyway yer man wipes away her tears an snotters. Dry yer eyes
baby, dry yer eyes. There, there, there, Daddy's home. A nice
wee cuddle for honeybunch eh? Nice an easy babe, yer man here
knows the ropes.
Well like I say, yer hole's yer hole.

So then she goes an shows me her belly. Aye, goes like that an
pats her belly with her two hands like ye do when ye've just
polished off a big chicken curry an fried rice. Ye know the way ye
do it when yer full to the gunnels?
That's the way she done it.
Look at that, she says. Look, look at it, look.

Well, it's a good job yer man here's in a sensitive mood eh?
I calm her down an whisper sweet solutions in her ear.
Listen honeybunch, it's just like this, ye aint gettin any younger,
but listen, don't worry, most burds yer age have wee pot bellies,
relax, Sonny boy still loves ye.

Naw naw naw, she says, it's not that, it's not what ye think, it's
nothin like that, it's a baby, I'm gonni have a baby. We're gonni
have a baby.
Boo hoo hoo hoo hoo.

Fuckin hell man, the Sonny boy's gobsmacked. Could've knocked
me over with a soggy dog-end. But like I say, the drink numbs
the edges of yer brain an makes these kinda things seem
unimportant. Yer Nat King Cole is all yer man can think about.

So I ask her if she's sure an if she's been to the doctor to get it
checked out. Ye better go to the doctor, honeybunch. Find out
for certain.

Then she tells me she can't, can't go to the doctor's.

Why's that?

Well, she says, she can't go to the doctor because of her ex-man. Wee Dan. Wee Dan the builder man. That was his name by the way. Honest. Dan Dan the builder man. A wee fat cunt. Wee baldy fat cunt with wee tufts of fuzzy ginger hair round the sides. Aye, wee Dan had a head like a See-You-Jimmy hat. Remember them?

The wee cunt was no good to Rhonda. No good at shaggin. A real lousy fuck was our Dan.

He was hopeless in bed honee, she told me. Hopeless. Just threw the leg over, bucked his arse a bit, let out a few grunts, shot his duff, wiped his knob on the sheets then rolled over an went to sleep. That's what he used to do the wee cunt. Rhonda told me that.

He's not in your league, she'd say, not an absolute fuck machine like you honee.

Well, anyway it seems the wee Dan man used to do some work for the doctor. Fix his central heatin when it went on the blink, that sort of thing.

A real good mate. Used to bevvy together an everythin. So she couldn't go to Doctor Rajeev an say she might be preggy. No way. Couldn't trust the auld Raj man. He might get pished one night an let it slip to wee Dan that she was in gettin a preggy test. Then wee Dan might start callin her a slapper, an unfit mother an all that sort of stuff, might even cut her maintenance money. Ye know what burds are like in these sorta situations, it's the auld pride thing. Know what I'm sayin?

Anyway it turned out a false alarm. Rhonda babe was just turnin into a wee pot-bellied pig due to auld age, eatin too many vindaloos an drinkin too many super lagers.

But what it made yer man realise was this. If she couldn't tell the doctor about being preggy, well, she sure as fuck aint gonni be able to tell him about bein eaten alive with crabs now is she?

Naw. No chance.

Can ye imagine it?

Eh doctor, I, em, have these little creepy crawly things runnin riot in my pubes an they are bitin the livin daylights out of my fanny. Is there anythin ye could recommend for them?

Oh an by the way, promise me ye won't tell my ex hubby eh? Promise?

Naw, no way man. No trust. Rhonda didn't trust him. She was never gonni tell him that. There's just no way she's gonni chance goin to the doctor with crabs.

The Rhonda blade's blowin bluff flames out her arse.

Just stand yer ground kid. Aye, hold yer sphincter muscles tight, she's chancin her arm.

Call my bluff ya cunt, go on.

Yer man here stands his ground. Dig yer heels in son, that's the game, dig those heels right into the concrete. She's fucked. Rhonda's fucked. She can't prove a thing. Fuck her.

Just stick to yer toilet seat story. It's a belter by the way. Wait till ye tell the troops that one, honest to fuck.

I just keep tellin her it was big Bawsacks Sally.

That's where ye got yer crabs honeybunch.

Just think about it. Just picture that big floppy arse of hers hangin over the sides of the pan. I mean it aint yer normal sized ass is it? Naw, no way. Imagine it spreadin itself like an octopus havin a wee stretch when it wakes up in the mornin. That's what it would look like.

Now imagine if ye were a crab an ye had to live in a fanny like that. Not yer ideal livin conditions now is it? Naw, is it fuck. So the first chance ye'd get ye'd be offski, offski pop.

Hey chaps, there's a nice shiny toilet seat, let's go for it, let's take the leap, let's go for it when we have the chance, c'mon now let's do it.

Run run run ya bastart, one two three jump.

FRRRReeeeeedddommm.

Then the next thing ye know this nice neat little fanny of yours with its pubes all trimmed an smellin of roses plonks itself down on that seat.

Rhonda liked that bit. Aye. I could see she liked it. Yer man here detected a slight blush. Yer winnin bro, I tell myself, yer fuckin winnin, just keep doin what yer doin.

So then I say to her, Well, what would you do eh? What would you do if ye were a crab, where would you want to stay? A big fuckin sweaty set of flaps like hers, or a nice wee des res like yours? I fuckinwell know which one I would choose.
Right troops, sweet-smellin garden here we come.
Yahooooooo.

Rhonda babe looks convinced. Aye, she snivels a wee bit an blushes, then starts huggin yer man here, tellin him how sorry she is, an that she's so ashamed an feels so dirty an that's she's so so sorry for accusin me of such a horrible thing, an she'll never ever share a lavvy seat with that horrible big Bawsacks ever ever again. The Sonny Jim relaxes. Lets out a huge big sigh of relief.

But the thing is that's only one part of the problem solved. There's still another huge big chunk to be sorted. An ye know what that is don't ye? Aye.
The crabs. Sonny boy's crabs. The other half of the litter. All the wee brothers an sisters of the crabs that Rhonda's got are eatin me into half the man I used to be.
Honest to fuck. I'll tell ye how bad it's got.
I went down to the market the other day. I walks right up to the guy at the seafood stall an says, how much do ye charge for crabs?
Sixty quid a dozen, he says.
Fuck me man, I look at him an a big crazy smile slices right across my face.

Shake hands with a millionaire, I say.
Aye, shake hands bro. Shake hands.

Aw listen, I'll tell ye somethin. See that scratchin? Horrendous.
Drive ye fuckin doolally so it would. Ye just can't stop it.
Ye try like fuck man, ye just try an try an try like fuck. Ye try
everythin. Everythin an anythin.
Ye try drummin yer fingers against yer baws as if yer just sittin
there playin a wee tune.
Ye try pullin yer trousers up every two minutes an give yer hips a
wee shoogle round so that yer baws brush against yer zip.
Ye keep stickin yer hands in an out yer pockets an scratch like
fuck an try to kid on yer just checkin yer change.
Ye lie up on the couch with yer hands down yer baws as if yer
just givin them a wee rub. Ye lie on the floor an wriggle like a
snake, but ye can't get comfy so ye lie on yer belly an rub yer
baws along the deck an then yer in an out the lavvy every ten
minutes to give them a right good clawin.
Aw ya bastart ye, scratch, scratch, scratch.
An hey, listen, ye've got to do all this without ever gettin
noticed.
I'm tellin ye bro, it aint easy.
If she finds out I've got the crabs I'm a dead man.
Sonny Jim no more. Fact.
Every now an then ye get wee spells of relief so ye do. They're
short-lived but. Short-lived.
Ye maybe get ten, fifteen, twenty seconds of bliss, then,
piiiiiiiing, fuck ye they're off an runnin again. All night long bro,
all night long. I wonder if the wee fuckers work shifts. They must
do, they must. Ye can feel them scurryin about. What the fuck're
they doin eh? Is that them shaggin? It must be man, because
everyday there's more. I'm tellin ye, they breed like Coatbridge
teenagers.
The bitches are the killers, the crab bitches, they lie shaggin all
night an lay eggs all day. Ye feel the eggs hatchin. Ye hear them

crackin open. Then the rough edges of the shells cause more scratchin an the more ye scratch the more eggs ye crack an ye release tens of thousands of baby crabs a day man, aw my God it's fuckin torture, pure torture. Millions of little crabs swingin like Tarzan from yer pubes, munchin yer baws, burrowin under yer foreskin. Aw my fuck, aw fuck fuck fuck fuck fuck, it itches till ye can stand no more an ye make a mad crazy lunge for the lavvy an rip an tear at yer bawbag like a demented Eddie Scissorhands. A real flesh tearin frenzy.

Yer clawin an scratchin an rippin an tearin, rip the fuckin lot off ya bastart, that's what ye feel like doin man, honest, ye do, ye just feel like tearin yer baws, pecker, belly button an arse right off yer body. Aye, that's how bad it gets. Just tear the lot off an throw them down the lavvy. Drown ya little bastarts, drown. Yer man here can't stand it any longer. Gonni have to do somethin about it. Cream. I need to get some cream for them. Some cunt told me get this special stuff. Prioderm. It's right good gear man. It doesn't turn yer skin purple an ye don't even have to shave yer baws. The fuckin crabs hate it so they do. It poisons them to death in two ticks.

Aye, good. Good good good. Exactly the stuff yer man's lookin for.
But it turns out it's not that simple. Naw, well, nothin ever is, is it? Ye see the problem is, how the fuck d'ye ask for it? It's all young gorgeous lookin burds that work behind the counters in chemists.

What happens if I bump into them in the street? Fucksake man, I'm blackballed forever. They'll tell all their mates. See him over there, aye him, that right mingin lookin fucker? Well he's got crabs so he has.
Aw for fucksake. Gossip. The burds in this town throw shit about like one of those big spreaders in the field.
Shit sticks to ye like fuck in this town so it does. They aint

invented Teflon up here yet bro.

Anyway listen, a man can only suffer so much. It just gets to
the stage where ye can't stand the pain any longer, the wee
bastarts are eatin away yer bawbag. Aw for fucksake, my poor
fuckin scrotum, look at it, hardly any skin left. It's all red raw an
weepin. It just hangs there like a turkey with its throat cut.

Ye finally pluck up the courage to go in. Ye walk in, ye walk up
to the counter, yer just about to ask for it then ye freeze. Ye
freeze like a British tennis player. Aye, ye do man. Ye fuckin do.
Ye just numb up. Fuck-all works. Fuck-all. Ye try to ask for it but
ye can't, ye can't man, the words just won't come out.
Eh eh eh, can I have eh, can I have a, a, eh?
Ye try an try an try but the words just won't come out.
So d'ye know what ye go an do? Ye end up askin for somethin
else. Fuck ye. Ya bastart. Aye, ye do. Honest. Yer man here's
ended up buyin all sorts of stuff.
Combs, brushes, toothbrushes, toothpaste, hair spray, hair gel,
razors, aftershave, air fresheners for motors, Nicorette chewin
gum, even condoms. Aye, fuckin condoms. That's how bad it got
man. No problem askin for condoms.
I'm thinkin, well, if I can ask for them I can ask for any fuckin
thing. Right?
Wrong.
Can I fuck man. Can't. Just can't.

Then this day I spot it. This chemist. There's a guy in his thirties
behind the counter. Bingo. A guy. Not a burd. A guy. A real
streetwise lookin cunt he is too.
Check him out man. A proper Jack the Lad lookin dude. Ye can
tell he's a man of the world. Easy peasy man. No problemo, in ye
go bro, in ye go.
I stoats up to the counter an right away the guy spots my
unease. He sees me lookin at the cream, sees me havin a wee
glance down at my nuts.

Good good good. He's sussed the situation. Telepathic. He's tuned right into my body lingo. He knows the score, he knows what I'm after.

He's even gonni save me askin, he's just gonni go like that an hand me the cream.

It's OK bro, he goes.

Aye, he calls me bro. Good street talk, right?

No need to blush bro, he goes. I've been there, done it, know the score. Me an you are the same kinda dudes. He taps his hooter with his finger. Take yer pick my man, take yer pick.

But then he turns round an points to the condoms. Aw fuck fuck fuck. Naw naw naw. That aint it for fucksake. That aint what yer man here's after. I could sell johnny bags to him so I could. I could put a whole chain of chemists out the game for fucksake. Condoms?

Listen, you name them I've got them. Mint flavoured, strawberry flavoured, liquorice flavoured, thin ones, thick ones, ribbed ones, extra lub, extra sensitive I've even got ones that glow in the fuckin dark. You name it, yer man here's got it. Could start up my own johnny bag business.

Sonny Jim's Johnnies. Good name that eh? Condoms condoms, roll em on, roll em off.

That's not what I'm after man, naw, naw, naw.

Aw for fucksake, go on ya cunt, just tell the guy, tell him, say, look, I've got these crabs. I shagged a dirty tart an they're havin a beanfeast on my scrotum. Ye know the score man, ye know the score. Aye, he'll get my drift. He already said it earlier. Me and you are the same kinda dudes, he said.

Ye try to say it but the words just stick, they just stick in yer throat, like tellin a burd ye love her when yer sober. Ye just can't get the words out. Ye can't man, ye just fuckinwell can't.

Aw go for it, go on, go on son, just say it, Prioderm, Pri-o-derm, say it, say it ya doss fucker.

120

I say it. Fuck ye man, out it comes like a Sunday mornin vomit after a piss up on a Saturday night. I puke it out, Pri-o-derm.

But then I go an fuck it right up. I should've just stopped there, but naw, did I fuck. I then went an said, Eh I'll tell ye what it's for, it's for my wee boy he came in from school with his head full of lice the other day.
Aye, honest, it's for my wee boy, honest.
The streetwise dude goes, OK bro, cool, chill out. He taps his nose again an says, Here ye are, just shampoo this onto the wee man's head an let it sit for ten minutes then rinse an repeat.
No bother. That was OK, I'm thinkin. Easy. Thank fuck.
But then as I turn an make for the door this wee lassie stackin the shelf shouts, haw big boy, they'll do for gettin rid of yer crabs too. Aye, just give them a good rub on yer plumbs an they'll blow the wee fuckers brains out tee heee heee heeee.

Pissin herself so she was. Aye, her an her four wee pals through the back all start pissin their tiny wee G-strings.
Aw for fucksake, wait till she tells all her pals. Aw my fuck man, the shame. Shame, shame, shame.

I run up the road dyin to get started. Right into the lavvy I go, whip off the keks an study the instructions. Dual purpose, it says. Also effective for pubic lice. Then it says (crabs) next to it. Oh ya beauty. Peace. Relief at last, free from bein eaten to death for the first time in yonks. I smack it on heavy. Big lumpy dollops. Sizzle ya little shites yees, big blobs of napalm. Gonni be a slow painful death. Say goodnight little fuckers, bye bye.
I massage it right into my pores an sit back an wait.
I see it all happenin in my crazy mind's eye. I imagine it hittin them like bubblin hot acid, wormin its way under their shells tearin open their skin an burnin into their raw flesh like boilin hot swords.
It melts their eyeballs into slimy smelly goo that gives off chokin toxic fumes.

A smooth warmth rushes right round my bawbag. Their blood starts to bubble like a sizzlin hot chip pan, I picture them curlin up an screamin for mercy as it melts their intestines.

Mercy? What the fuck does that mean? Die little bastarts. Die. It tells ye on the tube to repeat every day for a week.

I hide it under the sink. Push it right to the back an drop it down behind the pipes. Out of sight out of mind. Out of fuckin Rhonda's sight more like. Ye aint out the woods yet bro. Go cagey.

I walk into the lavvy the next day to cream up an there standin right in front of me holdin a tube of cream is Rhonda. Aw for fucksake man. Caught. Fuckin caught.

She's found it, Rhonda's went an found it. Fuck fuck fuck.

I'm standin there with a look on my face like a ten-year-old laddie that's just been caught wankin with a porn mag. Beetroot. Fuckin scarlet. Check the boat race. What's it like man? I look in the mirror. Mirror mirror on the wall who's the reddest of them all? You are, ya dirty rotten lyin little fuckbag.

Rhonda just stands there starin.

We don't speak. We can't speak. What is there to say? Fuck-all. I'm caught. Yer man here's been caught bang to rights.

Aw fuck it, just come clean. Ye'll have to won't ye, ye've got no choice now bro. Yer man here's clothes are headin for the bin bags.

I'm just about to explain, go into detail, tell her the horrible truth. Tell her I love her more than any man could ever love a woman an that I can only hope an pray that one day she'll find the strength to forgive me. Aye, I'm just about to go off on one, when Rhonda does a quick birly on her heels an marches down the stairs.

I slam the door shut an check under the sink an there's yer man's cream sittin just where I left it. Aye, sittin hidin behind the shampoo exactly where it always was.

Holy fuck man. I'm standin there gobsmacked, haven't a fuckin clue man, I'm thinkin like fuck, tryin to suss the whole thing out when *whooooosh*, the fuckin door flies open an in barges the bold Rhonda with the cream in one hand an the other hand on her hip.

Listen, she says, just in case yer thinkin anythin dirty, I got that fuckin cream out the chemist yesterday. It's for the wean, she came home from school the other day with head lice. I got that out the chemist for her.

Aw for fucksake. Aw ya fuckin beauty bro. Listen, even by the bold Sonny Jim's standards this is the jammyest Get-Out-Of-Jail card that's ever been dealt.
I'm so fuckin happy my heart jumps right out my chest an sucks one of Rhonda's tits an then jumps back in again. That's how happy yer man is.

Chapter Eighteen.
Radar Rhonda.

Things started goin wonky in Rhonda's head.
Rhonda had built-in radar. I swear to fuck man, she had wee
wires in her head that connected to the Polis station.
She didn't need to call them, naw, she didn't need to go near a
phone or even need to mention the words, I'm-gonni-get-the-
Polis. She didn't need to do anythin man, they would just arrive.
Rhonda was goin mad. Polis mad. I'm tellin ye, she didn't half
love the auld Polis. She loved nothin better than gettin the Polis
for yer man. In fact she loved it that much she used to have
about sixteen fuckin orgasms while she done it. Honest.

Ooooh aaaaahh aaah ooooohhh, get the Polis, get the Polis,
aaaawwww yessss aw fuck I'm cummmin aw *yessss*, aw get the
fuckin Polis *awwww* fuckin hell *awww yesss* baby more Polis,
get me more fuckin Polis aw for fucksake *aahhhhh oooohhh
yesssssssssssss*.

She started gettin them for absolutely fuck-all. She'd get them
for no other reason than it made her pussy explode.
We're sittin this night havin a wee nightcap. We crack open
some cans, pour a wee voddy for the bodies, roll a wee spliff, get
all primed up for a nice long deep an easy shaggin session. Usual
ritual.
C'mon get the drink down ye darlin, have a wee puff at that,
that's the game babes, relax, chill, let yer body float, let yer man
here take ye on a helter skelter ride of a lifetime.
We stick on a wee porn vid an dim the lights down low.
I'm lyin back blowin out brown orangey smoke jets an feelin
the inner tingle of the soft slow flow of blood startin to surge
through my body. There's a firmness in my loins as my big hungry
champer starts flexin his biceps. Me an Rhonda are as horny as a

Viking's helmet. Okey dokey babes? Lets get ready to rumble.
Rhonda starts massagin her titties an tweakin her nipples. They
stand to attention, two proud little soldiers in their shiny hard
helmets.

She's rigged out in her favourite black nylon negligée an wee
skimpy panties. Lacy an tasty. I peel them off with my tongue, I
pull her onto me an drive the ramrod in deep.

Yessss, that's it babes, that's me in, make yer arse go.

Rhonda starts rockin. Rockin Rhonda.

C'mon sweet baby mount my ripplin round headed flagpole.
Impale yerself on this big beastie.

Aw Rhonda, sweet horny Rhonda. Lots of cuddles an kisses. A
comfy warmth. Soft lips firm hips.

My baby Rhonda. Straddlin me. I'm in her. In her deep. Her hard
pussy bone grindin round an bouncin up an down. Up an down
an round an round.

Perfect timin bro. Nice an slow, we don't miss a beat in our head
blowin ride to the rhythm of a reggae band.

I bang her silly for an hour or two, nice an hard, nice an deep,
yer man here's in deep bro, bangin his bell-end off her third rib.
We grunt, we groan, our eyeballs roll, our faces are redder than
monkey's arses. My bawbag expands like some cunt's blowin it
up. Up it goes bro, it gets bigger bigger an bigger. Watch yerself
for fucksake babes, we're about to fly around the world in
eighty days.

The big big beautiful balloon deflates an empties its bowels into
Rhonda's ribcage.

Aw that was nice honee, that was so very very fuckin nice.

I roll over an cuddle into her bare arse an go to sleep.

Nite nite, sleep tight, don't let the buggies bite.

That was it bro, that was Rhonda happy, that's all she wanted, all
she needed. I'd give her that an she was as happy as slapper at a
stag night.

I'm in Heaven man, yer man here's snuffed it an gone off to boogie in that big never-endin party in the sky. Awesome, brilliant, mindblowin stuff so it is.

Listen, this is the real Heaven. Fuck yer angels an harps an all that shite, gimmee some of this stuff. Aw man, so smooth, so effortless, just lie there an shut yer eyes Sonny boy, shut yer eyes an dream.

I shut my eyes. The background goes blue. All I see is blue. Blue blue blue.

I hear voices. I hear Rhonda talkin. What's up baby, why ye talkin so rough an gruff? Aw an yer hands baby, what happened to yer lovely lily white hands, why have they gone so hard?

I open my eyes. I open them too quick but, far too quick. Jesus Christ, what a fuckin fright I get. I expected to see Rhonda. Fucksake, Rhonda's had a makeover.

What the fuck have ye done to yerself honee?

Rhonda's grown a moustache an a big fat red nose.

Fucksake, see what I mean, ye'll shag anythin when yer pished.

I rub my eyes an try to put it all together. Yer man here just aint focusin. Take yer time bro, think it through. Break it down into bits. What the fuck's goin on?

Blue hat. Hard hands. Moustache. Big red face. Gruff voice. An the gruff voice is shakin me an sayin, Right, up ye get, c'mon now. MOVE.

Well, I mean, ye don't need to be fuckin Einstein now do ye? The Polis. It's the Polis, aw fuck what the fuck've I done now, how'd they get here? They just arrive out of nowhere. They were beamed in live by Rhonda. Rhonda sent radar.

Rhonda's goin doolally, goin bonkers, screamin the fuckin place down. She's screamin, Bastart bastart get him out of here, he's nothin but a fuckin pussy-teaser.

Pussy-teaser? Fucksake that's a new one. The two Polis look at each other. Rhonda starts to tell them what happened.

That bastart there, she says, he was lyin there batterin his big ramrod off the arm of the chair, squeezin the head off it an wavin it about like a fireman's hose. The cunt enticed me onto it so he did, got my fuckin hopes built up, got me screamin for mercy, then he goes an falls asleep, next thing I know I'm jumpin up an down on a raw link sausage, fuckin terrible so it was, never been so humiliated. I want him charged, want him prosecuted. Cruelty, fuckin mental cruelty. I want the bastart done so I do, want him fuckin put away.

The Polis look at each other. I look at the Polis. We've heard it all now bro.
She wants me charged. Charged with possession of a floppy dick. A dick like a fuckin raw link.
They tell me it's time to go. Ye've got to go Sonny boy, ye know the rules, tenants' rights an all that shit.
They walk me out. The walk of shame. Fucksake man, shame.

Fuckin hell, what time is it?
I'll tell ye what time it is. It's Mucky time. Time to get Mucky. Hit Mucky's bar. Mucky's timewarp. Honest, Mucky's place is stuck in a timewarp, time doesn't exist in Mucky's place. Open all hours so it is, mornin noon an night.

Mucky's muckhole. Dark an depressin. Just like yer man's mood. I'm in a mood bro, the Sonny Jim boy's a real fuckin Mister Angry.
The walls of Mucky's are fallin down on top off me, closin in, squeezin me, crushin me, depressin me, stranglin me to death. Dark an dingy, dirty an grey. Grey grey grey. Look across there, there's a big slobbery greyhound lickin its arse, its eight floppy teats are like a pensioner's paps.

Drunken cunts blootered out their boxes lie here there an everywhere. Everywhere ye look man. They're lyin snorin under duffle coats, spread out on burst foamy benches, sittin blootered at the bar with their faces stuck in ashtrays. Faces, sad yellow faces dyin with the jaundice, pancreatitis an liver failure. Failure, every single one a failure, a loser, a bum, a no-user.

Dyin, they all lie dyin under the dull hauntin drones comin from the auld crackly juke box.

Yer man here's crackin up inside, the mist is comin down bro, get yerself to fuck, I just can't be arsed, got a real bad mind, I'm cold an tired an badly need numbed up. I'm a mixed up fuck-up, I dunno if it's New York or New Year.

The place is jumpin, my head is thumpin, aw fuck man, my head, my poor poor head. Fuck yees, fuck the whole lot of yees. I hate this whole wide world so I do. Stop spinnin ya cunt an let me off.

I start to drink. I drink an drink but can't get happy, some cunt's stole my happy head, I've lost the key that opens up the happy gates an lets me laugh again. I'm a fuckin headbanger, my head is bangin, my head is thumpin, all these noises rumble round my head, my head, my fuckin humdrum head.

I keep drinkin, keep tryin to chase away the grey, the grey slimy demons, my dark an twisted tormentors, but it just aint happenin bro, the mist is comin down, the steam is boilin up an the fierce savage tiger is tearin at my insides tryin to get out. Aw my God in Heaven man, all this rage. Hatred. The world, yer man here hates the whole wide world an every fucker in it.

I hate myself the most but. I hate me, hate my fuckin guts, it's the hatred that does ye in so it does, the Sonny Jim boy's full right up to the gunnels with self-loathin.

Look at me, I'm standin starin, starin straight ahead, starin at an ugly sad lookin baldy bastart, a real bad lookin cunt, a baddie in a Bond movie. Me, that's me, that's what Rhonda calls me, a baddie in a Bond movie. I'm starin at the man, the man in the mirror, the man in the mirror starin back at me. Me, me? You lookin at me?

Bad expressions. Faces turnin ugly. Distorted. Two faces starin each other out, playin intimidation games. Don't dare blink ya bastart.

The fastest draw wins.

Fuck it man, go for it.

My arm whips back an a quick flick of the wrist sends a half inch thick pint measure spinnin through the air. It skins the edge of Mucky's ear an smashes the cunt in the mirror right on the middle of the forehead.

The mirror explodes sprayin slithers of silver though the air like a big gigantic sparkler.

Mucky slams the till shut. Turns. Points. Stares.

You do that again an yer barred, he says.

Aw ya beauty, see what I'm sayin? Wee Mucky man. Mucky's bar. The greatest place in town. Aye, go'n yersell wee man, ya fuckin bold wee cunt ye.

Do that again an yer barred, he says.

Listen, ye always get another chance at Mucky's. Mucky's bar. This is where ye come to when yer barred from the last chance saloon.

It's time to go bro. Yer man here's birlin like a Morris dancer. There's vomit stewin in my belly, my eyeballs have got varicose veins an there's green foamy goo comin out my nostrils. The monster in my head is bangin on the door to get out, I'm dizzy, I'm faintin, I'm zoomin to the Moon.

Dyin. I'm dyin man, I'm dyin. Wake me up when I'm dead.

I've got to go bro.

Got to go where? Just where do I go?

Nowhere to turn to, nowhere to go.

All the doors are closin.

All the doors are closed.

Closed. Bang. Shut. Locked. Double locked.

Folk just don't want to know so they don't.

They don't want to know yer man here. Dont want fuck-all to do with the Sonny boy.

I'm a mad crazy fucked-up bastart. A wino, an alky, a drunk.
Aye, that's me bro. That's what I am. That's what people call me.
That's what I'm really good at. That's what I do best.
Bein crazy. Bein a cunt. Bein a fuck-up.
Yer man here's pure shit hot at bein all those things so he is. No
doubt about it man, especially the last one. A fuck-up.
The Sonny boy has the biggest fucked up head in the universe.

Who says that?
Every cunt an their auntie says that.
Sonny boy, they say. Yer a fuck-up, yer a waster, yer a pure crazy
cunt.

Fuck them, I say. I'm a waster, a fuck-up, a pure crazy cunt.
So what man, so fuckin what? Who cares, who gives a fuck?

Chapter Nineteen.
The Horizontal Door.

I come to. I'm in my auld man's, I'm lyin on his floor. I know it's
my auld man's cause he's here, right here, right now, towerin
right over me.
He's starin like a madman. He's bawlin shoutin swearin.

Hey Da, I say, whaasssap? What's the problem auld dude?
Why so mad?
Why so angry?
Why're ye so upset?
My auld man is really beelin big time.

Ya bastart, he's screamin. He's callin me a bastart. A nutter, a
ravin fuckin lunatic.
Well well well now, where the fuck've I heard all that before?

Yer a looney, a total fuckin looney tune, he's screamin. I dunno
how ye got here, dunno how the fuck ye landed on this planet.
What the fuck did me an yer maw do to deserve ye. Can't blame
me, he's shoutin. No way was it my fuckin fault. Ye haven't got
any of my genes, ye didn't come out of my fuckin loins. No way,
ya crazy fuckin cunt.

I dunno what the score is bro. Dunno what's the problem.
My auld man's upset. Big time. Gigantic time. He's standin
over the top of me with a hammer. A hammer. He's swingin it.
He starts swingin it round his head. He's gonni hit me with a
hammer. Naw he's not. Well, not yet anyway.
He starts bangin on the door, bangin all the facins, hammerin in
the nails.
All the frames of the door are loose an hangin off an broken an
bent an splintered. There's nails stickin out an shreds of glass an
wood shavins lyin all over the door.

The door. Aye the door. The door is on the floor.
Not in the space in the wall where it should be. No way man,
naw, it aint there, it's on the floor. Who the fuck put the door on
the floor?

Ye forgot to knock ya crazy bastart, he says. Yer supposed to
knock. Every other cunt in the world knocks. Look. Wait an I'll
show ye how it works, he says.
Knock knock.
Who's there?
Hold on, here I'm comin to open it an let ye in.

That's the way it should work. That's what normal people do.
But naw, not you. Not you.
Knock knock, no answer, kick the fuckin door in. That's what you
do. That's what ravin fuckin lunatics do, kick the fuckin door in.
It wasn't me, says me.
Well it fuckinwell wasn't me, says the auld man. An if it wasn't
you then it was some cunt that looked like you. Aw aye, a dead
fuckin ringer so he was. An the cunt must've took a loan of yer
clothes an gave ye them back again without ye knowin eh?
Aye, he must've whipped the gear right off yer back, came up
here an kicked the fuckin door in then went back an slipped
all yer clothes back on yer back again without ye fuckin noticin
they were fuckin gone. Well, as ye do eh? Oh fuck aye man,
these kinda things happen all the time don't they? An everyday
occurrence so it is.
He's squeezin the hammer tighter an tighter an gettin madder
an madder. His eyes are bulgin like balloons that are about to
burst.
He's gonni swing the hammer. Hit somethin hard. Dunno what.
The door? The nails? The facins? He starts hammerin the facins
back on to the wall.

Then he stops. Turns. Walks towards me with the hammer. He's
squeezin it tight an then tighter still. The skin on his face is

stretchin to the limit. His veins are burstin an gonni explode an blow blood all over the place.

His big swollen eyes are at the poppin stage an in his face is screamin out pure venom, rage, murder.

Oh fuck man. My dear auld dad. A venomous ragin murderer. What the fuck've I done to him man, what the fuckinhell have I done?

He raises an arm an his teeth are gritted an grindin an he's snarlin an foamin at the mouth.

An then all of a sudden the light inside his head goes out. Some fucker's pulled out his self-control plug. All's lost now bro. He's zoomed right past the point of no return. He's lost the plot completely an he's made up his mind that he's gonni kill me. Aye, his mind's made up so it is. He's just about to hammer me to death an he thinks yer man here's gonni shit his keks.

But I'll tell ye what. He better fuckinwell think again bro cause the auld cunt has another think comin. Yip. A brand spankin new one's on its way. It's in the post with a first class stamp an should arrive in his brainbox any time. Aye, think again ya auld cunt. An I'll tell ye why.

Because the bold Sonny Jim boy just does not give a fuck. I don't give a fuck so I don't. I don't. Honest. Don't care. Don't care if I live or fuckin die. This is the end of road an it really doesn't matter. Yer man here's prepared to die. Die an go to Hell. Listen, auld Nick the Devil doesn't bother me none. Fuck him.

I start screamin an foamin at the mouth, forcin my eyeballs to look like a frog's throat.

I start screamin, Do it do it do it. Hit me, hit me. Fuckinwell hit me ya auld cunt. Go'n, do it. Swing it, bang it, burst my fuckin face open. Bury the fuckin thing right in there, I tell him. Cave my fuckin head in, hit me right on the temple, hard. Go on. Do it.

Now it's my turn. Now the roles are reversed. Two sets of crazy

scary eyes. Not a pretty sight by the way. Fucksake man. Father
an Son playin a deadly game. Call My Bluff it's called. Have ye
heard of it? Great game. Fun game. Oh fuck aye man, funny
fuckin haha. A game for all the family.
Stop right there man.

FREEZE.

Enter big bad Frankie boy. It's big Uncle Francis. He's standin at
the door. Well, he's standin at the space where the door used to
be.
Hey there Franky boy, how's it hangin?

Sorry to interrupt, he says. I don't like to disturb a domestic.
Aw for fucksake, check him out. Big Frank's just back from
Turkey. The cunt's as black as Birmingham. Black as broad
daylight to a blind man. Oh an look what he's brought us back,
well look what he's brought my auld man back.
A bottle of the finest Turkish rotgut. Twelve pence a bottle an it
goes straight to yer fuckin liver. Pickles it in seconds so it does.
Great stuff man. Lovely jubbly.

Get the glasses, he says, an make sure they're manky. What the
fuck's been happenin here? he says. Where the fuck's that big
lump of wood that used to be in that gap? Fuck me lads, do yees
not think yees're takin the auld open plan a bit too far? I mean
it'll be helluva draughty in the winter. C'mon now boys. Chill
out. It's family.

The big man does a right good Marlon Brando impression so he
does. Remember the film *The Godfather*? Heeyyy it's faahhmillly.
We pull out three glasses an three chairs. Peace man. Peace on
Earth. The big black man from the east brings peace. Honest
to fuck, see once we get a few glasses of the auld liver disease
down us we all start to love each other.
Fuckit, black Frank says, it's only a lump of wood.
An then the auld man agrees with Franky.

Ach aye, it doesn't matter, hey, does any cunt know any good joiners? What the fuck does it matter? It's only a door. No cunt cares.

We all start sippin away nice as ye like.

The rotgut starts fryin up my brain cells like sausages an ignitin tiny fuses in my mind sendin electrifyin eruptions through my body. Shootin stars an tiny spaceships zip across my hazy vision. Explosions go off in my head, my ears pop, my tongue goes dead an I can't feel my feet, hands, belly or arms. Everythin is numb man. I'm numbed up an don't give a fuck. That's me man. That's the Sonny boy. I don't give a fuck for no cunt an I hope tomorrow never comes.

All my brain cells sizzle up an die. I don't care, I've got no need for them anyway, I don't have to think or work anythin out anymore. I just sit back an relax. Take it easy man, life's a cool breeze. Fucksake, aint life just the berries? All those dark an scary demons that haunt yer man to death have gone an done a runner. Aye, they have, they're fuckin offski pop so they are. I've now got crystal clear vision. Me an my auld da are lovin each other.

Aw yer the best wee da in the world so ye are.

Aw fuck aye son, yer the best boy any father could ask for.

I fuckin love ye Da.

Love ye too son. Yer a good boy so ye are. The best laddie in the whole wide world.

We have another glass. Then we have another, an another, an another.

Aw for fucksake, is that the time? That rotgut's strange stuff so it is.

It gives ye the feelgood factor. Well naw, it doesn't. What it does is it just gives ye a wee loan of it. Aye, it only gives it to ye short term an then it takes it back an gives ye somethin in its place. What? What, ye might ask?

Wait an I'll tell ye what. The big bad black scary monster that's what. The big black dude comes along an kicks Mister Feelgood's ass.

Fuck off, it tells him, get yerself to fuck out of here, I'm the new kid in his box. I call all the shots from now on.

My name's Mister Nasty.

I start growlin at my auld man. My auld man starts growlin back. Ya crazy cunt, he snarls. Ya fuckin crazy bastart.

Fuck ye, ya auld bastart, I never liked ye anyway, stick yer house right up yer arse, can't stand the fuckin sight of ye so I can't. I'm gonni change my fuckin name.

Ye owe me big time ya crazy fucker, he goes. Five hundred bucks for a new door.

Take it out of there ya auld cunt, I tell him. Take it out my fuckin chin. I hate ye ya auld cunt, ye never came to see me playin football when I was wee. Where were ye when I needed ye.

Fuck off, he says. Who reared ye? Who put food in yer belly? Who put clothes on yer back?

I never asked to be born. That was your responsiblity anyway ya auld waster. You brought me into the world.

Aye, I brought ye into it, he says. An now I'm gonni fuckin take ye right back out it. Where the fuck's my hammer?

Bastart. Auld bastart. Brought me into the world to hit me with a hammer. What fuckin chance have ye got?

That's where he's off to now.

Auld Pop. Auld super Pop. He's off to get his hammer an he's gonni smash my head in. My auld man. My dear auld dad, gonni bludgeon me to death so he is. Gonni kill me, kill me with his hammer.

Franky boy's the peacemaker.

He aint havin it. He says he's seen enough. Aint nothin worse than a family feud. A fuckin real ferocious thing to see so it is. A father an son fightin.

Let's hit the road, he says. Let's go for a wee wander. Let's take a wee stoat down the town. Aye, c'mon. C'mon we'll go for a beer or ten.

We walk out the door an the auld man's still rantin an ravin an fuckin an cuntin an callin me all the crazy cunts under the sun an tellin me never to darken his door again.
Ya bastart, he shouts. See when I get a new door, ye better never darken it again ya crazy cunt.
We trample across the door an out onto the landin. Big Franky boy stops an smiles.
He lifts the door up an checks under it.
What the fuck're ye doin ya cunt? I ask him. What the fuck're ye doin?
I'm just checkin to see if there's any mail, he says.

Chapter Twenty.
The Valhalla.

Take a walk, says Franky boy. Aye, take a walk. Walk walk walk. Clear yer head. C'mon son.

Big black Franky takes me a walk. We go walkin. Walkin through the streets. Me an Frank strollin.
Strollin's no good though. Naw, I need more pace, more gutty, more steam. Man, I've got to get this sizzlin hot steam out my system.
Big Franky's huffin an puffin an can't keep up.
For fucksake big man where's yer iron lung, I say to him. Did ye leave it in the house? It's a good job it's a guitar ye play an not a trumpet.
It's these fuckin things he says, pullin a soggy dog end out his lips.
Fuck, soggy aint the word. Squelchy. Splungin.
Fuckin hell man, it looks like he's just pulled the thing right out his nose.

On ye go, I tell him. I need time. Yer man here needs time. Time to think, let the head clear, let the red mist fade an die. Die ya bastart.
The mist. It comes down like a damp blanket on the Sonny boy. It presses down on his dome like a too tight crash helmet. Squeezin. Squeezin out all the pus an shit.
There's never any warnin signs. I can never feel it comin on me. Never. All it takes is the tiniest wee thing an BANG, yer man's a loaded gun. The slightest little thing pulls the trigger an pushes me over the edge.
Fucksake man. Don't push me. My head. My melon. My melon's swellin. Painful pressure. Blackness. Depression.
I see all my horrors, my nightmares, my realities. All my

yesterdays. All sorts of fuck-up scenes go racin through my head. The past, the present, the future. Hammers. Blades. Screams.

Pain pain pain. Misery. I keep seein all sorts of faces. Faces of friends an family. They're friends no more but. No more friends, no more family. They've all shown me the door. They've all had enough.
They're all frownin, tuttin, pointin. Pointin at me. Go. Go away an don't come back. Go go go. Nutcase. Crazy cunt. Madman. Drunkard. Wino. Jakey. Go go go. Don't come back. Don't ever ever come back. The doors, all the doors are shut man. Shut. Slam. Bam.

I say adios to Franky. Big black Franky. I walk on alone. On my own. No choice. Nowhere to turn to. Nowhere to hide. All the doors are closin.
All the doors are closed.

The Valhalla. Even the fuckin Valhalla's doors are closed bro. I can't get into the Valhalla. Honest. That's how fuckin bad it's got.
There's two big bruisers squeezed into the doorway. Suited an booted. Dicky-bowed up. Look at them. What the fuck're they like? Two fat heads with no noses or necks or charisma or wit. None. No sense of humour either. They've both had their sense of humour genes booted out their arseholes.

They hold their arms out an show me their palms. This big fat sweaty palm starts gettin nearer an nearer. It comes right up to my face an presses hard against my nose.
I aint gettin in. No entry. Another closed door.
Well I'll tell ye somethin Mister, the bold Sonny Jim aint havin that. I'm havin fuckin none of it.
Why aint I gettin in? I ask.

Too drunk, they say. Too dirty lookin, too mad lookin.
There's no way they're lettin me in.

I look at them an flash a real crazy smile.

Can I ask one question? I say.

Sure, go ahead, they say.

Why do they call those things round yer necks dicky-bows?

Do ye know, do ye?

They look at me. They smirk, they shrug, they push their fat heads into their shoulders. They're fucked. Clueless. They aint got a scoobie.

I'll tell ye why, ya pair of fat cunts. They're called dicky bows because they're wrapped round dicks.

Well, I'm definately barred now eh?

So, if I'm barred for doin nothin, I'm as well gettin barred for doin somethin.

Their faces do even more sleekit smirks. All ye can see now is their wee tiny foreheads keekin out their collars.

All the cunts inside the boozer have stopped what they're doin an start starin out to see what's happenin. Hundreds of disgusted faces all lookin down their noses at yer man here. They shake their heads an draw me dirty looks.

The Sonny boy looks in through the big tinted window. It's huge. I see right inside. I see all the faces. They turn round an they all start laughin, smilin, singin. Havin such a good time. Happy faces havin fun.

What does that mean? Fun? Happy? Laugh? How the fuck do ye do that?

They're all laughin, laughin at me, laughin at my dirty face, my clatty clothes, the dirty dried in pish stains down the front of my trousers, laughin at the madness goin on inside my head.

They are man, they're all fuckin laughin, sneerin, smirkin, lookin down their snooty fuckin noses.

Who the fuck're ye lookin at? What the fuck's so funny?

Me?

Ye lookin at me?

D'yees think yees're fuckin funny?
Wait an I'll show yees somethin funny ya cunts.
Did ye ever see the film *One Flew Over the Cuckoo's Nest*?
Remember the big guy, the big Indian? What's his name now?
Can't remember. Doesn't matter. What does matter is what he
done.
Do ye remember what he done?
See if this reminds ye.
There's a big ugly fucker of a concrete bin sittin yards from the
pub door. It sits there stinkin, it's full of auld fish suppers an fag
ends an empty wine bottles. Right big heavy lookin cunt it is too.
Looks like the bouncer's sister.

Haw ya big cunt, is that yer sister?

Hahaha. So yees think it's fuckin funny do yees? Well, wait an I'll
shove those smiles right out yer arses.
I walk across to the bin. I roll up my sleeves, bend, take a deep
breath an wrap my arms right round its big fat waist.
I breath in deep. C'mon now, inhale, exhale. In through the
nose out through the mouth. I squeeze hard. I tilt my head back.
Right, dig those heels in bro. Now pull.

Up she comes, *eeeeeaaaassy*. I'm a fuckin powerliftin champ me.
Used to squat three hundred an eighty pounds easy.
Her big arse comes up off the ground. My head spins like a merry
go round an wee electric sparklers burn the insides out of my
eyes. I'm standin up straight. Head back, arms locked.
My face burns like an over-fried tomato.

Hey check them all out now. Smilin faces no more. Now it's my
turn to laugh.

Where's the two pricks gone, where's the two big dicky bow
boys?
They aint here. I can't see them. All I see are freaked-out faces.
Panic stricken. They're all tryin to move but can't. There's no

space, they're all crammed in like illegal immigrants. An they were all havin a party too, havin a ball, havin such a real fun time.

An now they dunno what's about to hit them. But they soon will. I'm tellin ye. Any second now the party's over. Fun time no more. The party pooper's here to haunt ye.

I start to trundle forward like a steam train pickin up pace. Here I come ready or not. Look out fuckers, there's a crazy bull chargin at the window.

I'm goin for the jugular so I am, this crazy bull sees red. Red red mist is droppin down.

Here I come, chargin, gruntin, snortin. Me an my big ugly bin. There's two hundred pounds of shit doin an almighty charge an there aint no stoppin us now bro.

I hear high-pitched wails screams an shrieks as any second now slithers of broken glass will explode an spray through the sky causin hysterical chaos, bedlam, carnage.

But then it all goes dark. Blackout. I feel a baw-burstin crunch as I hit the ground face first.

Sixty stone of blackness obliterates me an turns out my lights. Haw, where the fuck did my fat arsed bin go?

Fucksake, there it is over there, upside down with all sorts of smelly shit spewin out its arse.

The Polis, it's the fuckin Polis practisin their rugby tackles. The Polis. Who the fuck phoned the Polis?

Fucksake man, check the faces on the people inside the pub now. Relief. Total relief on freaked out faces at the thought of what might have been. Me an my big fat bin have been taken out the game so we have.

We never made it, never crossed the touch line, never scored a try. A match winnin tackle by the boys with the blue tits on their heads. We never fuckin made it man. So near but yet so far.

Fucksake, I'm breathless, I can't breathe, I'm passin out.

There's these big black arms round my neck an legs squeezin my windpipe, squeezin my baws, rippin my scrotum, twistin my two arms up round my neck an across my face.

I'm screamin kickin bitin scratchin.

I see faces. I hear shouts. I hear radios cracklin.

I feel round-shaped thuds bouncin off my head, ears, neck, belly an baws.

Chapter Twenty-one.
Banged Up.

Ye come to. Ye don't wake up. I never waken up. I don't man, honest. The bold Sonny Jim just never ever wakes up.
Hey, listen. I don't fuckin want to.

I say the Lord's Prayer. My own little prayer to the Lord.
Don't let me wake up Lord. I say it every night so I do. I don't want to wake up. Wake up to what, reality?
Fuck right off man, I can't stand the sight of it. Can't. Never ever liked the place. Never ever took to it.
So I mean it when I tell ye that I really really don't want to ever wake up.

Like I say, ye come to, man. Ye do. Ye just arrive here. Where ye are now. Right here, right now. In this mental no-man's land, this empty nothinness.

Aw fuck man. I'm awake. Bastart.
I open my eyes. I close them. Open. Close. Open. Close.
A thin sheet of sandpaper rubs hard across the surface of my eyes.
Oh ya bastart. Fuckin dead sore.
I'm gonni keep the auld peepers shut for a while.
Aye, just you two chaps stay closed for a bit an keep the big bad world away. Keep it out of sight man. Out of sight out of mind.

A new day dawns. Say hello to Horrorville. Good mornin ya horrible lookin bastart.
What's yer name? What day are ye called?
Monday? Tuesday? Wednesday?
Dunno man, dunno what day it is. Don't really care. What difference does it make anyway. The name of the day don't matter bro. Don't matter one single jot.

What does matter is, where?
Where the fuck am I?

Ye don't realise right away. Naw, ye don't.
Yer first thought is, aw fuck don't tell me she's been re-decoratin, she's moved the bed again, moved all the furniture. She never fuckin stops so she doesn't. Can't leave things alone.

Then ye see tiles. Oh fuck, tiles. The lavvy. I must've been well pished last night man, I slept in the fuckin lavvy. Ye know yer in the lavvy cause there's a piss pot in the corner. Stained with deep yellow pish an browny-black shite. Dead giveaway innit? Fuck me man, ten out of ten for observation.
OK, yer in the lavvy. Ye've gathered that much. So far so good.

Then ye see the big metal door. Jesus Christ Almighty. Drug dealer.
Ye think, drug dealer. Ye've went an flaked out in a drug dealer's lobby.
Aye, that's where ye are man. Drug dealer. Why? Why am I here in a drug dealer's den?
Me, I don't do drugs. Naw, I'm no junky bro. The Sonny Jim boy's an alky, a jakey, a pisshead, a drunk. Everybody says so, they tell me all the time man, every cunt an their dog. Well, let's face it, they might have a point so they might.
Fair do's. I cannot argue. Alky. Alcoholic.
Alcoholic yes. Drug addict no.
Yer man here aint no junky. Drugs just aint my thing man. I take a wee bit of blaw now an again, but nothin heavy.

Drink's my thing, drink's my darlin, drink's my fuckin God.
The juice. The juice. The good old jungle juice. Juice me up baby.

But then ye see the bars. The bars on the window an the wee thick-paned glass squares on the ceilin that lets in the light.
There's thirty-six in all. I count them. I always count them. I don't need to. I don't. But I do. Thirty fuckin six. Six across, six down.

Lavvy in the corner.
Thick metal door.
Bars on the window.
Tiles on the floor.

No prizes for guessin where I am.
An I aint alone. Naw.
There's another cunt in here beside me, lyin over there, over in
the corner on the floor. He's beneath me. Aye, beneath me. Hey,
I'll tell ye somethin by the way, there aint many cunts beneath
me bro. I'm up above. I'm on a concrete ledge. I'm lyin on a thin
strip of rubber. I'm sweaty an sticky. Soggy an stale.
Jail man jail. Yer man here's in jail.

My hands are holdin my baws. My cold wet shrivelled up baws.
Wet, they're wet. Soakin wet baws.
Who done that man?
Well it wasn't fuckin me.
Don't blame me, I'm forty-three.
Ye take the blame for nothin man. That's the golden rule. If ye
piss the bed ye blame the blankets.

What're ye in for mate?
Nothin.
What about you, an you, an you? Nothin nothin nothin.
Honest yer honour, I never done a thing.
The jails are full of innocent souls. Dossers an deadbeats.
Decrepit lookin degenerates all sprawled across the floor.
I've been picked up off the streets. The filthy smelly streets.
I never done a thing officer. Was just lyin on the streets. It aint
the fuckin drink.
I aint got no problem. I drink, I get drunk, I fall down. No
problem.
They lift ye off the streets an bring ye here so they do.
In ye get ya cunt. A free guest at the Oddball Hotel.
Except it aint free mate. Naw, nothin's ever free. No such thing

as a free drink. Ye do the crime ye pay the fine.

Ye pay at a later date. Drink now pay later.
Roll up roll up, great new deals goin down.
I'm gonni plead not guilty.
Not guilty yer honour. To whatever it is ye say I've done, I'm not fuckin guilty.
What the fuck have I done?
I dunno, but I'm just about to find out.

The bin. The window. The bouncers. The Polis. The struggle.
The verbal abuse. The physical abuse. Vandalisin public property.
Resistin arrest. Assaultin four officers of the law. Foul an aggressive language an behaviour. Drunk an disorderly.

Ah well, just wee things eh?
Not guilty yer honour. Honest to God, it aint what ye think. I'm not guilty.
The whole fuckin thing man, it's not as plain an simple as was read.

I was just being a good citizen so I was. Aye honest, yer man here just saw this big heavy concrete bin lyin across the road.
It was rollin back an forth so it was. Aye, it was rollin about an I started thinkin, fuck me man that big bin's gonni cause an accident, gonni cause damage, some poor innocent soul's gonni get hurt, hurt real bad so they are. It's just about to roll across the road, hit a car or a bus, a bus full of children perhaps.

So I thought to myself I better lift it, lift it an put it out of harm's way, put it in a nice safe place.
An that's what I was doin m'Lord. I was just liftin it when I was subjected to all sorts of verbal abuse from the two scary guys at the pub door.
They were very abusive to say the least m'Lord, callin me all sorts of disrespectful names. An here's me only tryin to be honest an decent an make the world a safer place.

So I then started strugglin, strugglin under the severe weight of the bin an goin a bit light in the head, very dizzy, started to sway back an forth so I did, becomin more an more disorientated. I was very very unsteady on my feet sir. Honest. Then I felt as if I was gonni faint.

Faint, I'm gonni faint, gonni pass out. An then it happened. I thought I had fainted at first, but then I felt a crushin sensation. All these bodies landin on me. Heavy black bodies. I thought it was the two big scary guys at first, but then I heard the noises, the radios, the sirens.

Then I felt the restraints on my wrists, the pressure on my throat. I couldn't breathe m'Lord. Couldn't. Couldn't get a breath. I felt my windpipe bein crushed an twisted. I'm gonni die, I thought. Aw my God I'm gonni die.

So I started scramblin desperately for my inhaler. I am a chronic asthmatic m'Lord, have been since childhood.

So I'm lyin there screamin for my inhaler but no one's listenin. I'm kickin, screamin, bitin, beggin for mercy an I can't find my inhaler, my lifeline, my only hope of survival. I'm gonni die I'm thinkin. I just know I'm gonni die.

I saw the big picture flash across my mindscreen in seconds so I did. Saw the whole lot. All my yesterdays. My whole life from the tit to the grave went zoomin right past me faster than the speed of sound.

Aw my God Almighty, my inhaler. Where is it, where is it, where has it gone?

I can't find it. Dunno where it went to. I know for a fact I put it in my pocket when I left home, I carry it with me everywhere, never leave home without it.

I guess it must've been lost while I was bein attacked. Yes, attacked m'Lord.

I thought I was being viciously attacked by some gang of thugs. It wasn't until I felt the excruciatin pain of the handcuffs grindin through the bones of my wrist that I then realised it was officers of the law. I am so sorry m'Lord, but I really do panic when suffocatin. It was such a vice-like pressure on my windpipe. What a horrible nightmare. Never experienced anythin like it in my life. I pray to God I never do again.

I honestly thought I was a gonner, thought I was gonni die. Die. Yes sir, die. I really thought I was gonni die.

Chapter Twenty-two.
Pay the Fine or Do the Time.

Ye know the auld sayin, If ye do the crime, ye pay the fine?
Well there's a problem. Aye.
The problem is, yer man here never pays the fine. I won't pay no
cunt so I won't. I won't even pay attention.
I've been warned. The auld judge man, the judge told me, ye've
done the crime now pay the fine or ye'll do the time.
Yep, that's what's he told me bro.
He laid it on the line. No nonsense. A two hundred pound fine.
Ye better pay on time. Wednesday. Just make sure ye pay every
Wednesday. It's important that ye pay on that day. It's all to do
with discipline, all to do with obeyin the letter of the law, d'ye
understand? Obedience.
How much can ye pay? he asks.
A fiver a week, I say.

He hmms an haws, shrugs his shoulders, screws up his nose an
shakes his head.
No, he says. A big NO. A firm NO.
It's very very clear to see he fuckinwell means NO.
Ye'll have to do better than that, he says, I'll set it at twenty.
Twenty pounds a week. Every week. Every week until it's paid.
Make sure ye don't forget, he tells me. Pity fuckin help me if I
forget.

No problem, I say, no problem.
I mean, I actually say it as if I mean it, like it aint a fuckin
problem, d'ye know what I'm sayin? No problem. Yer man here
says no problem to every fuckin thing.
But the problem is, that when the time comes, it is a problem,
every tiny little thing is one big gigantic problem.
Ye see, the problem with me is that I can't remember. Yer man

here suffers blackouts.

Black. Out. That's what I do man, I black out. Everythin just goes black.

One minute yer there, the next thing, nothin. The whole wide world goes black an yer out. Out cold.

I have all these fines to pay but I forget, I can't remember, sometimes I dunno what day it is, I lose all track of time. The fine goes right out my mind.

My whole life's so hazy m'Lord, I go about in a daze, I dunno where I'm goin or where I've been, I can't remember a thing. It's the drink so it is, it's the dirty demon drink.

He agrees. The judge agrees. He sees my record, he looks at my files.

Drink-related, drink-related, drink-related.

He's gonni give me a second chance, he says, but part of the deal is that I attend alcohol counselling. I must report to a counsellor. He says he's gonni set it up with a probation officer that I will report there twice a week.

I am giving you one last chance, he says. Now, for your sake, don't blow it. Let me down and I'll send you down.

As he says that last bit, his eyeballs turn ten degrees colder.

Chapter Twenty-three.
The Therapist.

My name is Liz, she says. I'm yer addiction worker.
Big Liz. Big Lizzie. Big Dizzy Lizzie.
She's a beanpole, she's got big floppy tits an she's ten feet tall.
Oh man, check that hairdo. Pure erotica. It's like an explosion in
a fireworks factory. Sharp shocks of violet pink an yellow spray
out of her head like a sexy cockatiel's tail.
Educated eyes, thin lips, sharp features with smooth rounded
cheekbones.
A plain Jane but beautiful. Ordinary but gorgeous.

I love her. I'm in love. Yer man here's in love.
Naw, not love. It aint love. I dunno what it is really. The comfort
zone maybe.
Aye, that's it. Comfort. Safety. I'm gonni get sorted. She's gonni
sort me.
D'ye know what I'm sayin? It's the same way ye fancy a wee ugly
fat-arsed nurse. She tends to yer wounds, she soothes yer pain.
She's a comforter. A safety valve.

Lizzie's gonni sooth my sorry mind. My mad demented brainbox.
Lizzie's gonni fix it.
Lizzie. Thin Lizzie.
She's strong an she's firm.
She scares me to death.
She's overpowerin an intimidatin. Like a bank manager.
Aye, a bank manager. D'ye know the type I'm talkin about?
He might be a wee frail specky cunt, but ye owe him money, an
he wants his money back. Now, he doesn't have to throw ye in
a chair an threaten to batter the fuck out ye, does he? Naw, but
he puts it over in a certain way that ye just know yer gonni give
him his money back. D'ye know what I'm sayin?

He carries those vibes. He's the boss. He's gonni get his cash.

Lizzie is the boss. She strikes the first blow.
I know ye don't want to be here, she says, but it's part of yer
court order. Failure to comply with a court order will mean
referral back to yer probation officer, who will in turn refer it
back to the judge, who will in turn throw ye right into jail. It's
either this or jail, she says. Take yer pick, it's your choice. We all
have choices, she says.

Well put like that it's dead easy, I say. Simple fuckin Simon could
suss this one out in seconds.

She eases up now. She sits back an becomes more friendly.
She smiles. Her eyes light up. She looks so sexy. Sexy but scary. So
near but yet so far.

I start feelin horny now, I want her, I want to reach out an grab
her, stroke her, squeeze her, but aw fuck I can't man, I'm fucked,
I'm shattered, I'm weak an scared an she's strong, so strong an
fearless an she'd grab me an break my fuckin arm.

She says she's on my side, says she's here to help me not hinder
me. It's her job to try an investigate some underpinnin isues, get
inside my head, get to the root of my problem.
That's where it all lies, she says, in here. She taps the temples of
her freaky lookin head. In here, it all starts in here, it's between
the ears, she says. Everythin starts in here.
All my offences are drink-related. Some violent.
We have to get them out, she says, we have to talk about them,
find out why I done them. What makes me go so crazy, what
makes the dreaded red mist descend on me like death?
Ye must tell me everythin, she says. It's the only way. Ye have to
open up, open up the gates, let it all flood out.
She tells me it's completely confidential. Only me an her'll ever
know. She tells me there are some things she might have to refer
back to the probation officer, but it'll remain private between

us three. Trust me, she says, not another soul or their auntie will ever know. Trust me, ye have to show trust.

Fucksake man, trust, what does that mean?
Some cunt get me a dictionary.
Trust? Yer man here's a complete fuckin stranger to trust. The bold Sonny Jim boy doesn't trust no cunt.

But then she goes an says somethin that blows me right off my feet, aye, honest, fuckin sends me spinnin like a waltzer in my chair.
She says it AINT necessarily all to do with drink.

Well fuck me hard man, play a heavy drumroll on my head with a pair of stiletto heels.
Now she has my full attention.

It AINT about drink?
Fuck, maybe I have it all wrong. Maybe I'm sane. Maybe it aint the drink. Maybe she has some magic solution, some hocus pocus potion to splash on my face, rub into my skin, soothe my worried soul, ease my troubled mind, take away my problems, take away my pain an let me drink like a good guy.
I want to be a good guy, honest to fuck I do. Drink makes me a bad guy. All my problems are about drink. All the shit that's ever happened to me has always happened when I'm drunk. It all goes tits up the minute I touch the stuff.
I'm a good guy sober. I am, honest, every cunt says so.
Yer a good cunt, people say. See you Sonny, yer a good cunt. A right good cunt when yer sober.

It aint about drink, she says. Lots of people drink, but not everybody goes on benders, drink till they drop, have blackouts, wet beds, vomit daily, explode into fits of uncontrollable rage an piss an shit blood. Not everybody does that every time they drink, she says. So, ye see, it aint the drink. It's the person.
The mind of the person, the history of the person is what makes

that person do these things when drunk. We have to examine the mind, she says, the underpinnin issues. But don't look so worried, she says, there's no rush, we'll take it nice an slow, but we have to be thorough, leave no stone unturned, it's all to do with soul searchin. We'll go right back to the beginin, back to my childhood, clear out the wreckage of the past.

She says it won't be easy, in fact it might be pretty painful, but if approached in an honest an sincere manner it will be so very very rewardin.

She says all that with a soft an gentle smile that has the same effect as the wee nurse sayin yer poor broken arm will soon be all better. There, there, little plump nurse is here to help ye. Gonni make ye well again.

Lizzie asks me questions. Questions about drink.
She asks me how much I drink.
I tell her I drink as much as I can get.
She asks me how often.
As often as I can, I tell her.
She asks me what I drink an I tell her I drink anythin that's wet an blows my fuckin brains out.
She then asks me why, why do I drink?
I tell her I drink to cheer myself up an to stop me feelin like shit an stop me hatin, hatin the world, I hate the whole wide world an every fucker in it. I hate you. I hate me I hate every cunt that's dead or alive.

We talk about how drink makes me feel.
How it makes me feel good, at peace, happy, makes me want to laugh an tell jokes. Aye, I want to laugh, I want to make you laugh, I want you, me, an the the whole fuckin world to laugh together. But ye see, if the truth be told, that just aint the case no more. Naw. The laughin, the fun, the happy heads. That's all gone now so it is, gone an done a runner.
Some dirty rotten bastart went an stole my little laughter valve.

Yer man here don't laugh no more. I cry. I cry an I make other people cry.
Just look at Rhonda. I tear her apart, tear her to bits an make her cry. We break each other up so we do. We make each other cry. Rhonda makes me fuckin cry. The whole wide world makes me cry.

Yer man here don't like no cunt. I don't like people, I don't like life.
I drink so that I don't have to live here, in reality, in this shithole. The whole wide world's a piss-pot an I hate every inch of it. Hate it so I do. Hate every fucker in it. I'm tellin ye, Planet Earth's a fuck hole.
So I drink an drink an drink till I hit oblivion, till my head don't belong to my body, till my arse is sittin firmly planted on the Moon.

So there. That's why I drink. I drink because it zooms me to the Moon.
Yes, the Moon, the Moon is where I live. I'm not from Planet Earth, me.
I'm the man on the Moon.

She asks me to name five things I like about myself.
I sit. An sit. An sit.
I keep sittin an thinkin but come up with absolutely nothin.
I feel scared. Panicky. I don't like this road we're goin down. I feel like a drink. The glow comes over me.
I tell her this. I feel like a drink an I feel good. I like myself when I'm drunk. But only when I'm drunk. I can't think of anythin else. Nothin. Oh fuck. Oh my fuck. Nothin. Zilcho. There's not one single thing I like about me. Not one.
She asked me to name five an I can't even think of one, not one. None. I'm a no-user, a nobody, a complete and utter nonentity.
Jesus Christ Almighty man, what a piece of shit.
Why is she doing this?

I'm sweatin, I'm cryin, but ye can't see it so ye can't. Naw ye can't, cause I'm cryin on the inside only. Don't let the tears fall. Never drop yer guard.

I dunno any nice things. I fuckinwell don't.

I'm in a mess, I'm strugglin. She sees this. There's a panic attack on its way. She waits. She watches. She's a professional. It's her job to do this, take me to the edge. She takes me to the edge but she won't let me fall, won't let me break up an crumble into pieces. Break down. She won't let me break down. She won't. I trust her. Please sweet Lizzie, don't let me fall.

Ye see, she says, there's nothin. Not one single thing ye like about you. So if ye can't think of one thing ye like about you, how are ye gonni like anybody else?

She says I have to start lovin me, have to start lovin me first. I have to love me before I can love anyone else. More love, less hate. Love an hate can't live together, she says.

Hate. I'm full of hate. Hey listen, I can tell ye five things I hate. No problem. Easy. In fact I can tell ye five fuckin hundred things I hate.

She asks me to name number one. What's my number one hate? What do I hate more than anythin in this world? That's easy. Easy peasy. Ask me a hard question.

Rhonda. The answer's Rhonda. I hate Rhonda. Hate her with a passion. A desire. I love to hate her. I get a kick from it I do, honest. I get a right stiff hard-on hatin Rhonda. It makes me feel good. It justifies my shitty fuckin existence. It's her fault I'm like this. It's because of her I'm such a giant-sized fuck-up. It's all her fault. Rhonda. Rhonda made me like this.

I hate her, hate Rhonda. Rhonda rubs me up the wrong way, she's an alky, a tyrant, an absolute control freak.

Rhonda, my one-time sweetheart, my one-time gorgeous angel. She's my problem. She's my number one hate. She's my number

one, two, three, four an five hate. She's a schizo, a nut job, a
pure fuckin rantin ravin lunatic.
It's her her her. It's all her. All her fuckin fault so it is.
Why don't ye leave her? That's what people always say. Why do
ye keep goin back?

Most frequently asked question. Why, why, why?
Even the Polis ask me that when they throw me out. Why d'ye
keep goin back Sonny?
Do yerself a favour son, don't go back. That's what they told me,
the Polis.
Do us a fuckin favour an stay away, they said. We're fuckin sick
an tired of this.

Why do I keep going back? Why, why, why?
Dunno. You tell me.
I just can't leave. I can't live with her an I can't live without
her. I crave her like fuck so I do. She's my habit. My drug. My
obsession. She fixes me, she soothes me. We need each other, we
feed each other.
Rhonda is my cheap bottle of rotgut.
D'ye know what I mean?
She's bad for me, but I want her, I always keep goin back for
more an more an more. That's how it is bro. We are imprisoned,
the two of us, we are each other's prisoners. Handcuffed
together at the heart.
No explanation. Just complete an utter insanity.
I keep on tellin myself that this time it will be different, this time
we'll take it easy, talk things over, agree to disagree. This time
we'll take time out, count to ten, give each other some breathin
space, give each other lots of hugs.
Let's start again honeybunch. This love affair will last forever.
This time we won't attack each other, waste each other, kill each
other. This time it will be so very different. This time. This time.

Aw Lizzie. Lovely Lizzie. What the fuck's wrong with me?

Tell me. Well that's yer job innit? That's what yer fuckin paid for.
Give me all the answers. Sort me out, fix my fucked up mind.

She tells me straight. Tells me I won't like what I'm about to
hear. She tells me the truth is gonni hurt but I need to hear it. It's
for my own good after all.
I need to hear it an act on it or I'll never be able to move on.
She looks at me coldy with scary green eyes. She takes a deep
breath an starts to rant. Words start flyin out her mouth, words
that I relate to, identify with. They are her words but they're my
thoughts. She's sayin exactly what I'm thinkin but I'm not able to
put them into words, but they are all my words flyin out Lizzie's
mouth, my words, my voice.

Lizzie's lips are movin but it's my voice I'm hearin.

Ye need Rhonda cause she feeds yer ego ya cunt.
She loves ye, she tells ye she loves ye. It's ego inflation. Yer a
man, ye need to be made to feel like a man, a real man, ye need
confirmation, constant reminders. Love love love. Security.
Ye have sex. Durin sex ye tell her that ye love her.
Durin sex, it's always durin sex.
Sex is love.
Do ye love me?
Yes I love ye.
Are ye sure, are ye, are ye sure yer sure?
What if ye don't really mean it, what if ye go off me?
What if ye stop lovin me, Rhonda? Then what?
What does that make me?
I'm not a real man.
She won't give me sex. She doesn't love me.
What does sex mean? What is sex all about? Sex means love. Sex
is love.
If she doesn't give me sex then she doesn't love me.
If I don't give her good enough sex she won't love me.
Good sex, I can't give her good sex anymore, aw Holy Christ I

can't last long enough, not as long as I used to, I don't hear her moanin the way she used to. Oh my fuck I can't do it, can't give her satisfyin sex no more. I can't concentrate. My cock, my cock is soft an floppy an it won't go hard, I'm never ever gonni be able to have sex again, I'm useless, totally fuckin useless. What does she see in me?

Nothin. I'm nothin.

She wants another man, a real man, a man who can make her happy, give her sex, treat her like a lady. She doesn't love me, nobody loves me. I need love. If I don't have love I'm nothin. I must learn to love myself. I can't love myself when I hate myself. I'm so so full of fuckin hate, I hate me, I hate you, I hate Rhonda, I hate every fucker.

Aw my God I really fuckin hate her. Why do I hate her?

I don't hate her. Lizzie says I don't hate anyone. Apart from me, that is.

I don't hate Rhonda, I hate me. I make comparisons.

When I feel bad I look at Rhonda an she looks good an that makes me feel worse, makes me feel inferior, inadequate. So I set out to make her feel bad.

I tell her she's a fuckin crap shag, an ugly lookin bastart, a fuckin pathetic excuse for a mother. I call her all the fancy names to bring her down to meet me. I try to talk her down to my level, below my level. Fucksake, is there anythin below my level?

Control. It's all about control. I'm a control freak. Lizzie says I'm a control freak.

I can't do that. No one can do that. No one can have total control over another person's mind.

We are all powerless over people places an things. Live an let live.

I can't control her, I can't make her feel things she doesn't feel, or say things she doesn't want to say.

I want her to tell me that she loves me an that she'll never ever leave me.

But I can't, I can't get inside her head an control her thinkin, make her feel the way I want her to feel, the way I want her to speak. I want to make her love me, make her make me feel good.

I can't do it bro, I can't control her, it can't be done.

Powerless. I'm powerless.

So Lizzie says. Lizzie lays it on the line. She gives it to me straight between the peepers. She doesn't miss me an hit the fuckin door. Lizzie gave my baws a good hard kickin for the girls. One for the girls it was.

Fuck you arsehole.

Girl power.

Yer man here can't change no cunt.

No point in even tryin. Got to ditch the hatred.

Hatred's no good bro. It just festers an festers an eats ye all up.

Ye've got to let it go, move on, let Rhonda be Rhonda. Sort yersel out.

Mark yer own card. Stay away from her. Sort out Sonny boy first. Let Rhonda sort out Rhonda.

Aye. Yer man here. Sonny Jim. Powerless. Powerless an hateless an problemless. Just for now anyway. Just for now an feelin good.

Chapter Twenty-four.
The Bad News? Or the Really Bad News?

I'm bein a good guy. I'm watchin my units.
Lizzie told me all about units.
Count yer units, she says. Here's yer little diary. Fill it in every day.
Every drink ye have mark it in.
It's roughly two units per drink an yer allowed twenty-one units
a week. Ye have to tell the truth but, be honest.
Count yer units, she says.
I'm countin my units. I'm countin the cost of my life, my sanity.
It's all in here bro, all jotted down in my little red diary.

But the thing is, ye still need money don't ye. Yer man here
needs money.
I mean, I don't need a fortune, naw, I don't need loads an loads
cos I aint drinkin loads an loads.
But ye still need money. Security. Money in the pocket.
Walkin about money. It's all mine anyway, all mine.
It's an open an shut case after all, a forgone conclusion, the
money's as good as mine.
Mickey Mulrooney says so.

I go for a swift stroll round to Mickey's place. Somethin's wrong
bro, somethin just aint right. I can suss it. Mind what I told ye
earlier about yer man here bein able to suss things?
A really strange look is spread right across the bold Mickey's boat
race.
Aw fuck aye man, a real strange one so it is, I can't quite explain
it, I aint really got the words to give ye a proper description.
Can't describe it.
Well, I suppose I could if I tried.

Let me try.
His face is a mixture of smug an serious. It has a frown with the hint of a smirk.

Sit down, he says.
The look on his face changes now. It's serious. It's just plain serious. All the other stuff's gone.

Ye've been a right naughty boy Sonny Jim, he says.
He's shakin his head. The look on his face changes again. It's now serious but also a wee bit pleased.

Ye should've been honest with me Sonny, ye should've came clean. I don't like dishonesty.
Look, he says, look at yer fuckin track record. There it is there, have a gander.
He lays it out on the table. He covers the whole fuckin table with my brief.
For fucksake, look at it Sonny, he says, it's longer than a pornstar's plonker.

So what? I tell him. So fuckinwell what?
Why're ye fuckin moanin? I say to him, I mean I'm keepin ye in a fuckin job.
Listen, see if it wasn't for cunts like me, there would be no need for cunts like you. Cunts like me keep cunts like you in big fancy villas in Spain. Ye should fuckinwell love me Mickey boy, ye should want to blow my fuckin bell-end every time I walk into yer wee office so ye should, I'm yer bread an butter bro, I'm yer fuckin toast an jam.
But naw, that aint what he's on about. He keeps goin on about me not comin clean. Says I should've told him all the nitty gritty. The whole shebang, all the gory details.
He's shakin his head. The game's a bogey, he says, yer number's up Sonny boy.

Then his big fat face goes frosty cold.

He asks me what I want first. Do I want the really bad news, or the really really bad news.
I tell him I want the really bad news first.

He slides a slip under my nose.

One thousand, seven hundred pounds.
No fuckin way José. There's no way on God's fuckin Earth I'm acceptin that.
Fuck right off man, Listen ya wee cunt, I was stabbed, jumped on, kicked unconscious an left for dead.
I was in a fuckin coma for fourteen days an nights, I still get double vision, dizzy turns, blackouts an hairy scary nightmares.
It's a fuckin miracle yer man here's still alive, I was a midge's baw hair away from losin my life so I was.
Is that all my life is worth for fucksake, is it eh? A fuckin lousy seventeen hundred bucks?
No way bro, I aint havin it, aint acceptin it. I am fuckin deeply offended so I am, cut to the bone in fact. Haw, listen, yer man here's lookin for ten times that at least. An even then I'll knock back the first offer. Tell them to go fuck themselves with a boilin hot dildo dipped in mustard.

The look on his face blows the smugometer right through the rafters.
No, he says, that's not what they're offerin you.
That's what you owe me, not what I owe you. I owe you fuck-all. Jack shit.
Zilcho. Zero. Blank.

What d'ye mean man, what the fuck d'ye mean?
Yer man here's confused, gettin dizzy, my mind's goin all fuzzy an grey. This is one grey day bro. What the fuck's goin on?

Let me put ye in the picture, he says.
The Criminal Injuries Board have informed me that ye've got a criminal record that would embarrass the fuckin Kray twins.

They do not pay money to anyone who has a criminal record, especially if it's for violence. An a big huge chunk of yours is for violence. Resistin arrest, Police assault, domestic abuse. All violence-related.

Mickey's smile broadens with each sentence.

Ye see, they reckon with all the damage ye've done down the years, that given the law of averages, some of the heads you have cracked might have came to them lookin for money. So what they're sayin is, they have paid out a right few bob all because of you bein a naughty boy.

You have cost them a right few grand Sonny boy. So why the fuck should they go an give you anythin? Why should they?

Get yerself to fuck, they're sayin, they owe ye nothin, zilcho. You an them are quits, even steven, eeksy peeksy.

Basically what they're sayin is, because you are a bad boy an caused a lot of havoc in yer time then the law considers you a liability.

So, in a nutshell Sonny, in our lingo, the language of the streets, you are onto the middle of a fuckin doughnut.

Mickey sits back, smiles, stretches out an claws his big sweaty baws.

All this makes a big lump of boak in my belly decide it's time to start enterin the Earth's atmosphere. I feel sick an dizzy an empty an depressed.

Then he starts again.

So, Sonny boy, he says, slidin the slip right under my chin.

This is the really, really, bad news.

That's what you owe me.

Seventeen hundred pounds. Seventeen hundred big ones. *You* owe *me*.

My boak baw is now bouncin about doin backflips, frontflips an cartwheels but can't quite make up its mind yet.

Fuck off man. I aint goin down without a fight, the Sonny boy's

no quitter. I never ever give in so I don't. No chance.
I tell him I never ran up that amount. No way man.
He pulls out another sheet.
There it is right there Sonny boy, he says.
Look, it's all signed, sealed, delivered. All the dates of all the fifty
pound loans, all the wee fifties up front that I gave ye over the
last two years are all marked right down there in front of ye. All
signed for.
Take a look. Look, see for yerself. Thirty-four of the wee fuckers.
They're all your signatures Sonny. Signature signature signature.
All down in black an white. They're all there with all the times
an dates.

Aw man, aw man. Aw Holy Christ. What the fuck? Oh my God in
Heaven. I dunno, I just don't fuckin know. Yer man here dunno
nothin.
I don't remember. I don't remember yesterday never mind last
year. Honest to fuck, I dunno if this is today or tomorrow. I don't
man, I swear it.
Days mean fuck-all to me. Mondays are no different from
Tuesdays or any other day.

There was one day I came in here lookin for my fifty quid so
I did. I'm sittin spinnin on the big fancy leather chair. I starts
spinnin one way, my head spins the other.
Spinnin, spinnin, spinnin, man. Spinnin out of control.
I started demandin fifty. Where the fuck's my fifty? I'm shoutin.
Mickey boy came out, started shoutin no way ya cunt ye've
already been in earlier, ye've already had yer fifty Sonny boy.
Fifty a day I told ye an not a penny more. That's what we agreed
on, c'mon to fuck.

But I'm spinnin on the chair adamant, swearin, swearin to God
that I wasn't in earlier, I wasn't in. No way. That was yesterday,
that wasn't today man, not today, naw, yesterday, I was last in
here yesterday.

I sat an swore to God that it was yesterday.

Ye see what I'm sayin? Yer man here dunno the difference between today an yesterday. Can't remember. Can't remember signin anythin.

But I must've done. Look, there it is like Mickey boy says, all down there in black an white. One thousand seven hundred pounds. All wee fifties. Aye, all thirty-four of them. Fuck me it sounds worse when ye say it like that.
Aw man, all those fifties. All signed for. Yer man here's signature. Fucksake, he must be right. The Mickey boy is always right.

The big foosty lump of boak that's bouncin about in my stomach can wait no more man. All this dancin an birlin around inside me is causin it to get restless, it's had enough. Ye know what it's like, shite an vomit wait for no man.
Here I come ready or not, it growls.
Up it comes.
There's an almighty splash as all these lumps an gooey bits splatter all over Mickey an all over his desk an chair an all over his nice paperwork an pictures of his wee fat kiddies with their wee spoilt faces. He grabs the documents, wipes the puke off them an rubs them on his shirt.

I stand up defiant. Proud an pukey. Fuck ye ya cunt. Fuck ye right up yer big fat spotty arse.
My pockets are empty. Aint got no dough bro.
I tell him he'll have to take it out of somewhere else.
Take it out of there ya prick, I say. Take it out my nose, take it out my chin if ye like. I'll tell ye what ye can do. Ye can even rip my heart out an take it out of there.
Aye, go on ya cunt, do it. Do it. Rip my fuckin heart out.

But the fucker then goes an stands up an starts slappin his big meaty arse an tells me that he's gonni take it out of there. Aye that's where he's gonni take it out of. My arse.

He's pointin at my arse now.

I'm gonni take it out yer arse Sonny boy. I'm gonni put ye in jail for this. Ye can't pay. No way. Ye've no way to pay. Ye'll go to jail son. Jail, where some big twenty-stone hairy-arsed lifer is gonni make ye his little sweetheart.

Yer gonni pay, he says.

Mickey boy says it's payback time, says I'm gonni pay one way or another.

This is payback day. Payback for all the shit I've caused him.

He says he's sick, sick of the sight of me an my crazy fucked up face comin in here every day sweatin, stinkin, steamin drunk. Stinkin of piss an shit, shittin all over his lovely clean lavvy, demandin money, forcin him into a corner an makin him look a proper cunt. Extortin money from him as well.

Extortion, he shouts. The wee cunt's shoutin at me now, callin me a wee bastart. Ya wee bastart, he goes, ye've been screwin me to fuck for long enough. Day in day out all I've listened to is, fifty, fifty, fifty, gimmee gimmee, gimmee.

Aw Mickey this, Mickey that, aw please Mickey, gimmee another fifty, c'mon Mickey, aw Mickey Mickey Mickey.

He's had it, he says, had it up to here. He's sick to the back fuckin teeth lookin at my greasy sad pathetic beggin face. For months now he's had to listen to all my drunken sob stories, all my verbal abuse, all my demands, had to look at me day in, day out. My face, my sick pleadin face. No more, he says. No more payin up. He's payin up no more. Now it's my turn to pay.

He's gonni make me pay so he is. Micky's gonni make me pay for it the hard way. Fucksake, one way or another man, I'm fucked, fucked in the arse. Mickey boy's just fucked me in the arse.

Chapter Twenty-five.
Rhonda's For a Slash.

I take the drink. Then the drink takes me. It takes me on a trip. A one-way trip to Hell. Aye man, it takes me to Hell. Then it takes me further. Further down that big black shit-filled hole. I'm tellin ye the truth, ye've no idea how fuckin low it takes me.
Lower than Hell. Hell's a halfway house.
The drink takes over. The drink is in charge. The drink is runnin the show now. The demon drink. The demon an all his cronies are hauntin me to death. I'm spaced out. I take blackouts.
Did I ever tell ye that before? I can't remember.

Well I do. The Sonny boy takes blackouts.

        Black   Out.

Just like that. That's how it happens bro. Pure blackout. Total nothiness.
One minute there's somethin. The next minute, nothin.
Nothin that I can remember anyway. Can't remember a thing.
Nothin.

There's bedlam. There's mayhem. There's pure fuckin hell to pay.
The Devil's craziest disciples are on the fuckin rampage.
What the fuck's goin on man? What the fuck's the matter. Where am I? What the fuck's the score?
There's murder. Blue murder. The big bad boys in the wee blue bunnets have come to take me away.
I can't move. Can't. Why can't I move? I'll tell ye why. Sonny Jim's in the auld smelly brown stuff right up to his baws.
The copper tells me to change my name. Change yer name to Bob Fosbury, he says.
D'ye know why ya wee cunt?
Because yer for the fuckin high jump.

I'm in trouble. Big soapy bubble. This is a domestic. I'm gettin huckled. There's a big set of chunky silver bracelets bein snapped tightly round my wrists an I'm bein huckled down the road. The Polis don't do that for nothin so they don't. They don't shackle ye up mate. Naw, not for a domestic. Not unless there's been violence.

There's been violence.
There's blue lights flashin an sirens wailin. Blue men an green men. Polis an paramedics.
There's people all shoutin. There's walkie talkies cracklin. There's a stretcher. There's blood. There's loads an loads of blood.
There's Rhonda. She's on the stretcher. There's blood on Rhonda. Rhonda's on a stretcher an she's covered in blood.
Where am I?
Dunno. Dunno whether I'm here or if this is just some big mad crazy story bein told down the boozer. A story that happened to somebody else an I'm just standin listenin.

I pinch myself.
The pinch is painful. My wrists. My wrists are sore an I look down an they're swellin up like yer baws do when some cunt's booted them. Fuck me they're sore.
I'll tell ye how sore they are. I'm drunk an they're still sore. Nothin's ever sore when yer drunk. That's why yer man stays drunk. It takes away the pain, drink. It takes away the hurt. I'm bein huckled away. I'm goin all the way down the road. This time there's no gettin dropped off at the boozers, this time I'm completin the journey.
Aint no stoppin bro, I'm headin right on into the terminus. I'm takin my final trip. This time there's no way back.

The Station. They take me to the Station. I'm stayin the night. Might be stayin a few nights. This time it's serious. No wee slap on the wrists. The wrists hurt really bad so they do. I feel cold steel on bone. Icy chill.

I still aint sure if all this is real.
Is it? Is this the real deal?
I dunno man, I really dunno.
It's all so vague. There's heavy duty fog. There's flashin lights an squeals an walkie talkies an voices all runnin through each other. Words. There's loads of words. Words all twisted an knotted.

Screams. I hear screams. Ya bastart, ya dirty evil bastart.
Blood. Loads an loads of blood runnin through my mind an stainin my brain. Turnin it red. Red. A deep deep red. The finest red mist wafts across my hazy vision like misty red rain sprayin against a window. There's blood runnin down my glassy eyes man.
My eyes. My poor auld eyes, so heavy an tired.

Tired eyes, tired bleary eyes. The red. The big red. I can't stop seein red. Red red red. Blood, so much blood. A bloodbath, a slaughterhouse.
What the fuck's goin on man? Everythin's so stained, so stained an damaged. My brainbox it just aint workin. All the little cogs aint runnin in rhythm, aint clickin in time.

Everythin is broken. Broken. My heart. My Rhonda. My sweet Rhonda. I've broke my sweet Rhonda's heart.

I'm here but I'm not here. D'ye know what I'm sayin?
I dunno where the fuck I am. Is this real, all this right now, all this I'm tellin ye?
Real or imaginary?
It's real. It's got to be real because I've no imagination. Naw, I don't fuckin have one.
My tortured mind's too fucked up to imagine, too fragile to fantasise, too lifeless to create any activity. Too many dead brain cells. Brain dead. Yer man here's brain dead.

Flashin lights an walkie talkies. Men an women in green an blue uniforms.

People starin. Talkin. Shoutin. Pointin. Pointin at me. Shock.
Horror. Disgust.

I'm cuffed. Cuffed an shackled an taken away. That's a sure sign
it's serious. A sure sign I aint just goin down the road for a lie in.
Yer man's goin down for a long stay this time.
The cell door clangs shut. I fall face first onto the floor. Let me
sleep man. I need sleep. Please please let me sleep.
Sonny Jim needs his sleep. I've got to sleep. Go to sleep an dream
it all away.
I'm gonni wake up an it'll all be gone. It'll all be away. None of
this will have happened. It'll all be better in the mornin. Aint
that right?
Nite nite, sleep tite, don't let the buggies bite. Don't have nasty
nightmares.

Fucksake man. Oh my God. I'm dyin. I'm lyin here cold an wet as
the hauntin howls of madness echo through the night.
I'm all alone again. Just me an my madness. My neurosis my
paranoia my delirium tremens. Aye, they're all here. All bringin
me my daily helpins of Hell on Earth. They're all served up on a
platter so they are, all burnt an black an drippin in hot smoky
grease.
All my worst nightmares delivered to me daily by the ghosts of
Hell's kitchen.
All the melted-faced monsters with purple an yellow eyes an
spiky metal teeth. Monsters. Ghosts.
All my yesterdays. All my sins. Ghosts of people who hate me.
People I have hurt. All comin to get me. Comin to haunt me.
Comin to take me away.

Mickey Mulrooney in leather straps an buckles, pierced nipples
an a red hot poker stickin out his peehole. He pulls it out, points
it, waves it, pokes it in the fire. Waves it around like a magician's
wand. He whooshes it round his head an bright golden sparkles
come sprayin out the black heavy smoke. Sparklin stars start

poppin an burstin in mid air an form the shape of gold coins. They fall through the sky like heavy golden snowflakes. Coins, pound coins, millions of them bein fired at me by the nasty man with leather straps an the big fat sweaty belly. Hot metal coins hittin me hard, stingin me, burnin me, burnin big holes through my body, sizzlin an stingin an stickin to my flesh, meltin my skin, bubblin up an soakin right through to my bones. Gold coins, stickin to me, burnin me.

Get them to fuck off me. I'm screamin like fuck man but no cunt can hear, no cunt's listenin. I'm clawin an scratchin, diggin my nails in deep, prisin them out my body pullin out handfuls of flesh an hot burnin gold runnin through my fingers. Wee fat Micky boy's laughin, snarlin, sneerin.
Money money money. *Haaarghh haaarghh haaarghh.* He's grabbin his big pointy poker at the end of his peehole, he's pointin it at me, he's smilin an dribblin at the mouth, he's gonni ram it up my arse, aw my God my poor poor arse, a big fuckin red hot boilin poker.
Pay up, pay up ya pathetic little prick, pay yer dues to Mickey boy.
Mad bad Mickey boy's gonni make me pay.

An Dizzy Lizzie's here too. Squealin. High-pitched squeals. Her an her big butch battalion of hairy-arsed lesbians. They're out on the war path, out on a manhunt, gonni sodomise every man on the planet. She's wavin a foot-long black rubber dildo above her head. It's covered in rusty razor blades an smeared with burnin hot mustard. She's wavin it, wavin it about like a Samurai warrior. She batters me with it, batters my head in, sticks it up my arse, rams it down my throat. I'm screamin but I can't scream.

The screams man, desperate terrifyin screams, I'm forcin them out but they're muffled, choked, they can't come out. I'm gaggin, can't breathe, chokin. I'm chokin to death on a razor-studded dildo. No one can hear me. No one would care even if they did. Dizzy Lizzie an her big butch bears. They're tearin me apart, rippin my insides out, smearin my intestines all over each other. Lizzie an her lezzies, squealin like hyenas, rubbin their pussies, squeezin their tits. Screamin an chantin. Death to all men. Girl power.

Aw an they've captured Rhonda. Oh my God man.

Rhonda, my sweet Rhonda, take a look at her now, aw holy fuckin hell, aw hen, aw what the fuck have they done to ye? Big bad black-eyed Rhonda. The Devil's daughter. She's snarlin hissin spittin. They're eggin her on, the big butch bunch of man eatin lesbos.

Get him, eat him, kill him, tear him to fuckin pieces.

Rhonda's got black eyes an lips. There's burgundy blood oozin through pointed metal fangs. There's big pointy steel talons shootin out of her fingers. She gonni slice me to pieces, she's lashin out at me vicious as fuck, aw Holy Christ almighty man she's gonni slash me to shreds.

She drags them down her face first to try them out. Oh ya cunt ye. Fuckin hell, four perfect parallel lines run down each cheek. Four lines, four lines of pipin hot blood run like watery snot down her face an into her mouth.

She licks her lips an her tongue darts out an splits into four. She hisses an spits in my eye.

Ya bastart. Ya bastart ye, she squeals, ye ruined my life, ye screwed up my head, ye tore out my heart, ye filled my poor wee pussy full of flesh eatin crabs. She hacks hard at her fanny with her steel nails an blood pishes through the air like a slashed jugular vein.

It's your time to die, she howls. Die ya bastart, yer gonni die. She draws a foot-long dagger out her arse, she whirls it round her head, she's gonni chop my head off, gonni slice me up. She licks the blade. The hot blood hittin metal hisses like piss hittin a coal fire. She runs it down her tits an right across her belly then draws it up quick choppin off her nipple. She squeals with delight. A sexy orgasmic squeal. She's lovin it, she's wallowin in her masochistic delight. She lifts the dagger above her head an turns the blade in. She drives it down hard into her arm an starts hackin an slicin. She slices off her arm, aw fuckin hell man Rhonda's sliced off her arm, her arm, her lovely sexy arm. She grabs it by the fingers an swings it round her head. Aw holy lumpin fuck, all the gungy entrails are oozin out the end. She swings it hard an fierce, smashes it down on my head, starts clubbin me, beatin me, batterin me into submission. Submit ya bastart, submit. Do ye fuckinwell submit?

Aaaargghh aaarghhh, aw Jesus, aw Holy Jesus Christ, OK, OK, I give in I submit, I'm sorry, I'm sorry, I'm so so fuckin sorry.

It's mornin. Dunno what part of mornin, dunno what time, but it's the mornin. It's light so it must be the mornin. It's the mornin an it aint gone. The pain aint gone. No way José. The shit is all still here. Very much still here.

I'm in a wee room. A wee naked room except for a table an three chairs.
I'm sittin here.
Two Polis sit across there. Starin. Starin at me. A man an a woman. A tidy young woman. Lovely. Sexy. Nice teeth. Nice tits. Nice woman.

Nice Polis woman. I'd love to shag her.
Bad Polis man. Fierce, he looks fierce. He looks feart of no cunt. Really.

Sonny Jim says that all the time, feart of no cunt. But Sonny Jim don't mean it. That's the difference. This cunt means it. He's feart of no cunt. He doesn't say it. He doesn't need to.
WPC Carol somethin an Detective Inspector Jim somethin.
I bet he's shaggin her.
An who's the other dude, the big skinny cunt that just walked

in? Six feet eight, thick specs, greasy hair an a face full of ready to squeeze plooks.

He's a lawyer. Oh fuck, he's a lawyer, my lawyer. Check him out man. What's he like? The big cunt's just walked out of high school ten minutes ago. Ah well. Fuck it. Call me lucky.

At least it can't get any worse can it?

Of course it can ya silly cunt.
In fact it's just about to.

Jim somethin asks me what happened.
Fucksake. Funny cunt eh? Maybe he aint as fierce as I thought, maybe he even has a sense of humour.
What happened? What happened where? I ask him.
What? When? Who?
Dunno. Sonny Jim dunno. I'm waitin to be told. Aint that the script? You tell me. That's why ye brought me in here. Aint that right? He lays it on the line, he tells me Rhonda's in a mess, a bad mess.
It's her arm, her arm's shredded. Shredded fuckin wheat. Wait till ye see the state of it, he says. Slashed, stabbed, call it what you like. Her arm's raw mince. It's gutted an filleted. The muscle tissue's been ripped right off the bone, cut to the core so it is. Fuckin serious. Emergency surgery, loads an loads of stitches.
He paints a vivid picture.
The place was an absolute fuckin bloodbath, he says.
Fucksake, he ain't half layin it on thick. He must've been talkin to Mickey Mulrooney.

How did it happen? he says. Who dunnit? Tell me, tell me the truth. Tell me. There was only you an her in the house. The neighbours say they all heard screams, shoutin an bawlin.
Your voice, her voice.
There was glass everywhere, broken furniture, broken coffee table.

There was a bloody knife. We've found the knife, he says. It was lyin on the kitchen table. A knife covered in blood, her blood. Only you an her in there.

An open an shut case, he says. What more do we need?

Man, I can't remember. Like I say, blackout. Sonny Jim takes blackouts. Aw fuck man, I'm tryin to think. Think think think.

They point the finger.
Him an her point. Jim an Carol pointin at yer man.
Pointin at me. It must be me. Only me here. Nobody else.
The fingers all point at me.

There was nobody else in the room at the time, just me an her. Me an Rhonda.
You done it, he says. Jim somethin keeps on sayin it was me, it had to be me, there was nobody else there. Everythin's pointin back to me.
Point point point. All fingers comin at me bro.

No way man. No way. Not me, not the Sonny boy. There's no fuckin way I used a knife, never. Yees can say what yees like but I'm tellin yees this, knives aint yer man's game. Never used a knife in my life. Not a fuckin chance in hell of it man.
I wouldn't. I couldn't.
Could I?

I'm so tired. So drowsy.
I aint here.
Am I?
I'm scared. So fuckin scared. Dunno what I'm doin. Dunno what I'm sayin. He puts it to me that I done it. You done it, he says, didn't you?
It was you. It was you. You done it. You you you. You done it. You slashed her. You were drunk, you lost the head, you took the knife an slashed her. Didn't you?
He keeps on drillin, keeps on bangin on my brain.

Bang bang bang. You done it you done it you done it.

Aw fuck it, fuck it. I've had it up to here, can't take it no more, my brain, my poor auld bruised an battered brain. Beaten black an blue by Jim somethin.

OK, for fucksake man. Look, I say. I might have, I dunno, I might have been provoked, I can't remember man, I dunno. OK if you say so, fuck it, I'll say anythin ye want. I'm so tired, so tired, so scared, so sorry. Oh my Lord. My sweet Rhonda. So sorry.

I remember wee bits. Flashbacks. A struggle. A table smashin. Her callin me names. A struggle. Screamin. Lots of screamin. Blood. Lots of it. Lots of blood.
I dunno man, aw fuck, I just dunno. Dunno what I'm sayin. I can't remember, can't remember nothin man. I didn't do it, I never used no knife. No way. Sonny Jim aint no chib man.

Well, he says, we believe, my colleague and I, that there was a struggle, a vicious struggle. Both of you were drunk. Maybe she hassled you a wee bit, provoked you, it's possible you were provoked. But you have hit your girlfriend so many times now, twelve previous arrests for domestic violence. I reckon that this time you went too far, this time you snapped, and through a drunken haze you lost it, lost control completely.

You went into the kitchen lifted a knife an lashed out at her. Isn't that the truth Sonny boy?
You slashed your girlfriend's arm. Is that not the case? Do you remember? How much can you remember?
I put it to you that you remember the whole sorry episode fine well, but you sit there an you play this blackout card all the time don't you? As far as you're concerned, if you tell yourself you can't remember it then it can't have happened. You can't remember so you can't have done it. Out of sight out of mind. Put it out your mind. That's your game son isn't it? But I know you done it, he says. An I know you remember. I know you

slashed your girlfriend. Didn't you? Didn't you?

For the last time, he says, did you, in a drunken rage, lift the knife an slash Miss Turnbull's arm?

But it wasn't his last time. Was it fuck.
He asks me again an again an again.
Didn't you, didn't you, didn't you?

No, I tell him. No no no.

But he won't let up, keeps askin an askin, Who then? Who done it? Only you an her an the canary were in the room. Who done it son? Who done it?

I dunno man, I just dunno. I might have. I must have. If you say so sir. I must have, it was maybe me.
Fuck. Did I say that, did I just say that?
He nodded. Nodded at me then nodded at the tape recorder.

No, I tell him. Take that back. Retract that part man. I dunno. It wasn't me. Honest to fuck. I dunno. I had a dream so I did. I had the DTs.
I had a dream she slashed herself, cut her fuckin arm off.
It was her man, not me, she done it to herself so she did, she cut off her arm an hit me on the head with soggy end, I swear to God man.

Aw holy fuckin hell, my eyes have bricks hangin from their lids. Big bricks, big heavy grunters. I just want to sleep, please man let me sleep. Sonny Jim feels dead, feels lifeless, my eyes are heavy, so fuckin heavy, so much weight on tired shoulders, all this pressure on my weary soul.
The walls are closin in bro, the room is gettin smaller an smaller, I'm bein crushed, suffocated, the walls are squeezin me to death, the walls, the ceilin the floor all comin together, crush crush squeeze, squeezin me to death breakin my bones burstin my baws.

This is the end of the line, he says.
You done it.
You say you done it, then you think you done it in a dream, then you say Miss Turnbull done it to herself. Of course she did. She chopped her arm off an hit you on the head Sonny boy, didn't she? Oh aye, of course she did.
OK, enough's enough. We have heard enough, he says.

He reads me my rights an my wrongs. Charges me with this an that.
I just take in wee bits an pieces. My rights? I have rights?
Me, Sonny Jim has rights? I don't deserve them bro, I fuckinwell don't.
I have the right to remain silent. I wish to do so sir. Too fuckin right I do. Silence, I want silence. I want sleep I want unconsciousness, I want comatose, I want death. Yes sir, death. Death is the answer. See when death comes knockin, I'll tell ye this right now bro, I'm grabbin its baws an squeezin them tight an never lettin go till it takes me away an never brings me back again.

Yes man, death. Dr Death, death is the answer to all my shit.
Sleep, let me sleep, let me vanish off the face of this shithole, let me fade away forever, let me disappear an die.
I will die an be reborn an all this horror will be gone, none of this will have happened.

There'll just be me an Rhonda. My sweet Rhonda standin in front of me draped in silky white softness, doin a dance, an erotic slow dance. Sexy an seductive. Poutin her petals, flashin her pearly whites. Pullin me in. Holdin me tight. Lyin on a bed. Me an Rhonda. A waterbed of soft warm waves. Holdin hands, lookin at the sky, the lovely warm sky, a soft orangey purple scattered with fuzzy tangerine dots with starbusts of deep red punchin through the blackness. I hear her voice, her sweet heavenly voice, an angel pluckin a harp.

Shut yer eyes honee, shut yer eyes, she says.

I shut my eyes tight. Shut. Please stay shut. Stay shut forever an ever.

My head shoots forward an my neck cracks like a branch breakin. I'm still here, I haven't moved, I'm still sittin on this wee chair in this wee room.

Me, Jim somethin, Carol somethin an the plooky fuckface lawyer are all still here an there's all these words comin out that I can see but not hear.

Words words words with no real meanin man, all breakin up into letters. They whirl round the room like confetti then fall to the floor an blow away in an icy chill wind.

I'm up. I'm on my feet. I'm walkin. Dead man walkin. Here I come, I'm walkin, walkin down a dimly lit tunnel, there's hollow clunkin an clankin an screamin an bangin. Scary mad voices howl along the cold yellow walls.

I walk through a thick metal door covered in big rusty bolts. It bangs shut, a heavy boom bounces like a billiard ball round the walls of the cell, boom boom boom boom round an round it goes man, the tinny echo bangin through my eardrums ringin out forever, round an round an on an on it goes, it bounces off the floor an hits the roof an booms back off the four walls again, a never-endin hum slowly gettin thinner, thinner, quieter, quieter, quiet, stoppin, stop.

An inch-thick slice of foam lies on top of a bed of stone. I collapse on it. I pull my legs up into my chest an curl up an try my very hardest to die.

Chapter Twenty-six.
The Last Supper.

They kicked my arse out onto the street. They gave me my date.
My court date.
My date with the Devil. Be in court ya cunt. That's yer date, don't
be late.
Fuck ye man. Go fuck yerself. My date. Too late, too late man.
That was yesterday. Yesterday's a mystery. It's been an fuckin
gone so it has.
I'm on my last legs. I'm on the way out. Yer man here's finished
this time. Finito. The walls are closin in. There's a warrant out for
my arrest. The Polis are after me. They're waitin to pounce. Fuck
this bro, yer man's too tired.
He can run no more.
Gonni hand myself in. Put on the crocodile tears. Play the poor-
me card. Leniency.
Gonni go for leniency.
Tomorrow. I'll hand myself in tomorrow.

But listen, ye need to feed the face first don't ye?
A man can't go to jail on a hollow belly.
Naw, no way bro. A man goes to jail on his stomach. Have to
scran up first. Aye, that's right. C'mon to fuck. Have ye ever
tasted jail grub?
It aint no fine cuisine.

I round up all the troops like the Lord an his Apostles. It's my
grand finale. The last supper. My great big fond farewell.
They all look stunned so they do. Shocked an stunned.
A slap up meal? What the fuck d'ye mean Sonny boy, what the
fuck's that?
A restaurant, what the fuck's a restaurant? Never been in one of
those before. This is a first for the troops.

Deek, Peezy, Shoogly, Stan, Ernie, Moggsy, Paddy Pie, Boaby Breech an Heed. All the likely lads. The dead end kids. Check us out bro. What're we like? Sonny Jim an his disciples struttin through the streets.

Time for some serious nosh. It's on the house. Yer man here's payin. I'm goin away forever, never to return.

We head for the Kooh I Noor. The trendiest joint in town. Aye, nothin but the finest. Fuck me, talk about glitzy. Aw fuck man, check those prices.
Ach well, never mind. I mean it aint everyday yer goin away to prison for years an years now is it?
C'mon, in we go troops.
We go for the full monty. A table for ten please sir.

The guy in the turban looks well chuffed. Really pleased to see us so he is.
Oh yes, table for ten sir, no problem, he says. He snaps his fingers an all these wee turbans appear from behind a curtain an start pullin tables together an decoratin them with knives, forks, spoons, glasses, cups, saucers, the works.
They hand us all menus an tell us there's also a buffet for ten quid. Ten quid. Fuck me. Eat all ye like for ten quid?
I tell the troops to fill their boots. Eat all yees want boys, the treat's on me.

The big turban then goes an asks a right fuckin silly question. Would we like some drinks?
Fuck me. He's never met us dudes before. Never. It's obvious.
Drinks all round. Six pints of lager, four pints of heavy, five vodkas, three whiskies an two gins.
Fuck it. Have one yerself dude.
Oh, an get the two lovely girls at the table over there a drink as well.

Two dolly burds. Two real stoaters. Yer man here's on fire, he

winks across but they aint too friendly.
Ah well, who gives a fuck? Get the drinks up.
Oh what a night, aint this just the fuckin business?

He asks us if we'd like starters.
We tell him of course we do, we want every fuckin thing, we
want starters, middlers, finishers the lot. Lay it on big boy.
Nan bread, pitta bread, jappatis, spiced onions, pakora.
I snap my fingers, Another round of drinks please kind sir, my
guests here are real thirsty chaps.
Oh an those two girls over there, give them a drink too. Fuck
those two who aint smilin, give those two lovely ladies a drink
instead.
Care to join us ladies? Feel free. This aint no private party.
They look at us an look away quick. No takers. No problem. Who
gives a fuck?
But wait a wee minute though. There's a big problem bro.
All these knives an forks an spoons. What the fuck're they all for
again? D'ye work from the inside out, or the outside in?
Fucksake, none of us know where to start.
There's two of every fuckin thing.
Why's there two? Is that in case you drop one?
Aye right.

Now the big picture starts.
Main course.
We're all hungry mongrels. Aint eaten like this in yonks man.
In fact, maybe never. Here comes the grub. We slabber all over
the table at the smell of it. Aw the smell, ye can actually taste it,
taste the fuckin smell, feel it ticklin the edges of yer tonsils.
We're gonni eat like fuck so we are. Me an my bold brothers
here are gonni eat an eat an eat forever, eat till we drop man,
eat till we die. Get it fuckin down ye troops.

The big turban man is slabberin too. Slabberin at the thought of
all that cash rollin in. This is well beyond his wildest dreams man.

Fucksake, a table for ten. Ten hungry horaces. Check those big brown eyes bro. Rollin like dollar signs on a Las Vegas puggy. Serve them up, he snaps. The three wee turbans start to cover the table. Curries, dopiazas, biryanis an bhoonas. Fried rice an boiled rice.

An there's the buffet deal too troops, don't forget the buffet deal. Eat all ye can for a tenner.

Imagine tellin that to Moggsy. The wee Moggsy man had a brain op an they damaged the wee bit in his brain that gives ye a shout an lets ye know yer belly's full. Aye, poor wee Moggsy, he doesn't know when he's full.

The wee cunt doesn't eat till he's full up, he eats till he's fed up. The wee man could eat for a world select so he could. Team captain.

How d'ye like yer steak sir, rare, medium, or well done? Moggsy doesn't know, doesn't care, he just tells the dude to wipe its arse an pull its fuckin horns off. Tells him he doesn't even have to kill the fucker first if he doesn't want to. Moggsy boy will eat it while it's still moooin away like fuck. This big cow's arse arrives on a plate. It's all for Moggsy. He dives on it like a cowboy bringin down a bull at a rodeo.

He starts rippin it to pieces man, munchin away, his head's stuck right up its arse. Aye, honest, ye just see two big ears stickin out the side of this steak.

More curries arrive. Vindaloos an madrases. We shout on the big turban an tell him we need more drinks. Loads of thirsty soldiers here dude. We need more drinks. Keep it flowin.

Big bowls of rice an bubblin juicy sauces come next. Moggsy aint carin, he's still muchin an munchin an there's no way he's stoppin for no cunt.

Oh ya beauty, he goes, lovely bubbly gravy, *mmmm Bisto*, that'll do nicely.

He grabs it an pours it all over his steak.

Big Deek jumps up an goes, Haw ya wee bastart that's my curry sauce.

Moggsy just keeps on munchin, aint listenin, Ooohh ya beauty ye, this is lovely gravy.

Poor big Deek, check him out, the poor cunt's sittin there starin at a plate of boiled rice.

Hey Deek dude, don't sweat it, yer man'll sort it, the Sonny boy'll sort it.

A swift snap of the fingers, snap, snap, Another bowl of curry sauce for my sad lookin hungry-faced friend here please.

Comin up. It's on its way.

Yer man here's gonni make sure he enjoys it. The next load of grub the Sonny boy'll eat will be served on a plastic tray with plastic knives an forks.

Aw fuck man, it's hot stuff. Hot hot hot.

More drinks please mister, keep it comin, we're burnin up, keep coolin us off.

Bottles of wine, big cold pints of lager, wee vodka an whisky chasers. A big silver bucket of ice appears on the table for the boys.

We sit back burstin, sweatin an blowin steam out of arses an ears. It's time for dessert. We all want dessert. Yes man, yes.

Aw yes just what we need, the icin on the cake. Bring us everythin ye got dude. Ice cream, banana splits, knickerbocker glories, trifles, black forest gateau, cheesecake, sticky toffee puddin. Aw fuck man, you name it, we're eatin it.

Listen, some cunt open the windows an doors an let some fresh air in. Ten hungry soldiers boilin over an just about to explode.

I'm gettin heavy in the head now, could do with a wee nap.
I sit back an relax. I feel like a small aperitif.

What would the gentleman like sir?

Give me some of yer finest brandy.

Aye, brandy makes ye randy, well so they say. Sonny Jim aint
randy, naw, Sonny Jim is bleary-eyed an ready to piss shit an
puke, but not randy, naw, randy don't live here no more.
The brandy kicks in quick, delivers the killer blow.
Brandy for the boys. Two bottles. Sittin on the table. Four star,
five star, as many stars as ye like bro, yer man can see them, lots
an lots of tiny shootin stars pingin out my eyeballs.
The night slows down, the clock stops tickin. Time stands still. We
just sit an sit an sit. Sit an stare at the walls, the faces, the tiny
little stars. Communication's over bro, words won't come out no
more. The wee box in my throat that makes the words appear
has shut its eyes an gone to sleep.

The man in the big turban aint smilin so wide now. He asks
me again if I enjoyed my meal. He says he enjoyed havin us an
hopes we come back again to his very fine restaurant very soon,
but would we mind payin the bill now an movin on as other
customers are waitin on this table.
He brings us a wee silver plate with wee After Eights.
Fuck me I'm full, couldn't eat another bite.
I sit back an belch an fart an scratch my big fat belly.
He looks at me.
I look at him.
I shrug.

He frowns.
He looks at me as if I look like somethin's wrong.
A battle of wits begins. A game of mental arm wrestlin.
He's dyin to ask a question, but scared to because he already
knows the answer.
Stalemate.
Then he goes for broke. Pops the question.
Is there something wrong kind sir?
Is there anything I can get you?

Yes, I say. The words come out slowly.

There is somethin wrong. In fact there are two things wrong.

The first thing is, I am numb from the head down.

The second thing is, I'm skint, broke, penniless, rooked.

An there is somethin ye can get me. A pair of Marigolds.

In fact make that ten, ten pairs, any colour, any size. Me an my buddies here will scrub yer kitchen squeaky clean. There ye are, can't say fairer than that now, can we?

He looks at me, smiles, an for a split second the expression on his face says this might be a prank, just a wee joke, an that I'm gonni laugh an say I'm only windin him up an I'm gonni go into my wallet an pull out a big wad an tell him to keep the change. But it only lasts a teensie weensie second. Then his hint of hope dies an goes to Hell. Reality hits home. Ten winos. Ten skint winos. Ten skint winos who don't really give a fuck.

He erupts an starts bawlin an shoutin, wavin his arms at the kitchen. What seems like a hundred men in turbans come screamin out the kitchen howlin an bawlin an tooled up with meat cleavers.

Time stops. We just sit there an stare. We've all got too much drink in us to feel scared. Numb. No fear. We fear fuck-all, we just sit an wait for the cleavers to come an take away our misery. Chop chop chop. What a way to go man, what a rock 'n' roll endin. It aint gonni happen but. Naw, no chance. There's too many people about.

They don't attack us, they keep on runnin, runnin right past us. They bolt the door an stand across it, stand on guard. They start signallin for people to go out two at at time. Fucksake, they're gonni empty the place then they're gonni do us in. Fuck me, aint it funny how the drink wears off fast?

I look at all the troops, they look like they've just emptied all their curries into their keks.

They start snarlin, snarlin at yer man here, Sonny Jim. Sonny.

Good auld Sonny boy. Took them all for a lovely big nosh up.
Or so they fuckin thought.
They thought I was treatin them, aye, a nice wee treat from yer
man here. Too good to be true but. Aye, cause there's nothin
nice about this fucker. No such thing as a free meal mate. Aw
what a dirty rotten bastart.

I told them it was on the house too, they thought it was a treat,
they thought it wasn't gonni cost them.
Cost them?
Fucksake, it's gonni cost them big time so it is, gonni cost them
dear.
They're all gonni pay, pay with their lives, an it's all because of
me, dirty lousy scumbag me.
It's safe to say yer man here aint too popular a dude. Listen, I'm
not too sure who wants to kill me the most.

I sit back, light a fag an get ready to die. Die an go to Hell. This
is where it's all gonni end. Here. Here at the jaws of the growlin
dogs.
Still. Not to worry, I daresay I wouldn't have liked that jail grub.
Or my big hairy arsed cell mate.
An look on the bright side. I won't have to pay all those fines.
Or Mickey Mulrooney either.

As the draught from the door blows cold air on my neck it
catches the end of the tablecloth. It starts flappin an flutterin.
I dunno, I really dunno man, I really can't explain this but for
some reason my mad crazy mind goes into overdrive.
I crack a match on the wall an let it flicker slowly under the edge
of the cloth. It smoulders slowly an starts turnin brown givin off
thin waves of smoke, then thick flicks of yellow flame dance up
onto the table.
The flames man, they're wigglin an weavin, they start runnin
faster an faster across the table up the wall across the ceilin,
spreadin quicker than gossip at a hen night.

In seconds the place is a burnin furnace. Orange red an yellow flashes of fire come screamin through big brown an black smoke balls.

There's tables crashin, glasses breakin, fire sirens wail in harmony with screams of blue murder. Then this big gigantic black face appears from nowhere. It aint one of the troops or the customers an it aint wearin a turban.

It's a big black face with big firey horns an he's growlin snarlin hissin.

Welcome to Hell, he howls.

Welcome to Hell on Earth.

The doors fly open an the stampede squeezes through the space. Bodies crush each other, a mad scramble of men women an children makin that last-gasp bid for freedom. I'm caught up in the crowd. It lifts me up an carries me out the door.

Fuck me man I'm free, I'm walkin up the main street cryin big black tears of joy. I'm chokin on the stale-smellin stench of burnin wallpaper an paint.

I'm dyin, I want to die, I don't want to be here man, this aint livin.

I go walkin. I dunno where I am, dunno where I'm goin, anywhere'll do. There's sirens, there's Polis, there's ambulances, there's fire engines wailin.

They scream right past yer man here. The stranger on the street standin watchin in amazement.

Me? I could be any cunt.

But this cunt's gettin to fuck out of here.

Hey legs, are ye ready? Start walkin.

I'm walkin walkin walkin. Gonni walk forever.

That long long road to nowhere. The road to ruin. Been walkin that road forever so I have. I've worn it down to nothin bro. Me an that road go back donkeys so we do. I know every crack in its sorry auld face.

I'm walkin. Sonny Jim's walkin. Aint ever goin back. My head starts poundin. It's all gone wrong in my melon. A mechanical malfunction, a red alert in the headpiece. The auld headpiece is birlin an swirlin. I'm stoatin under orange burstin streetlamps that don't do it for me no more. Naw, they aint got that romantic vibe now. Now all they do is burn me, glare down on my sorry head like an angry August sun.

Speedin cars with angry blarin horns swerve to hit me, aye, they try their best to run me over cause they hate me, hate me, every fuckin thing hates me, the whizzin cars, the swayin buildins, the burnin streetlamps, they all fuckin hate me, hate me to death so they do cause I'm one dirty rotten sorry lookin bastart.

I'm gonni die, I want to die. Death is the answer. Death will solve my problems. Death will chase them all away.

Problems? Go an take a fuck to yerselves, yees can't catch me cause I aint here, I've died an gone to Hell.

Judge, jury, Mickey, Lizzie. Take yer pick man. I don't really care. I'm dead. Well, I soon will be. Yees can't catch me, yees can't get yer money back, can't get a piece of my arse, yees can't lock me down Sir, yees can't take me away.

I'm dead man, dead. Death is the answer.

Look at those dark grey buildins. Tall an dangerous.

They're swayin. I'm swayin. We're swayin, me an those buildins swayin in perfect harmony.

I've got it now bro, got it now. I'm goin up there. I'm goin up there to jump.

Jump. Aye, there ye are, easy peazy. Climb to the top an jump. I'm gonni jump off an flap my wings an fly away.

That would be nice, that would sort me right out. Me, up there on that big tall buildin.

Hey but listen, once yer up there ye've got to do it bro. Once yer up there there's no way back. Once that big crowd gathers ye have to do it.

Jump jump jump jump jump.

Listen to them. They're all eggin ye on, they all want to see ye do it, see ye bounce off the slabs, see yer head burst open like a big baboon's arse.

Ye have to fuckin jump ya cunt, c'mon to fuck, we've been standin here for ages, jump ya cunt, jump ya fuckin shitebag, they shout, jump, c'mon, there's only one way down. Can't let the team down. Can't lose yer bottle, don't be a shitebag.

Yer man's a broken man. Broken into pieces. Broken heart an dreams.
My sweet Rhonda. Broke her heart in two. Ripped it out so I did. Stripped off all the flesh, squeezed it hard an drained out all her love.
Oh my God. My sweet Rhonda. Kill me Lord, take me out of here.
Give me the strength to go up there, give me the courage to jump.

I'm rooted to the spot.
I can't move. I can't walk, can't climb, can't jump, can't die.
Oh ya useless fucker, ye can't even die right. Can't. Can't even kill myself. Can't do myself in. I can't go up there, I can't jump off.

Shitebag. Coward. Yellow-bellied bastart.

God aint in. He aint listenin. He hates me like every other cunt. He's not helpin me, he won't let me jump, jumpin's too easy, the easy way out, no chance, yer man's not gettin off light, he's gonni let me suffer, gonni make me pay, I'm gonni pay, pay for all my sins. Here. Now. In this life.
Gonni pay man, gonni pay big time. If ye do the crime, ye do the time.
Yer man here's gonni do the time. Big time.

The Sonny boy's sick. Really fuckin sick. I'm one sick cookie. Been told so many times. Ye need help ya cunt, yer sick.
I am sick. I'm spewin sick.
All that shit that went down feels like it's time to come back up.

I can feel it stirrin in my baws, workin its way through my belly.
It starts with pins an needles an then jabs with knives an then
big sharp stabs with poisoned swords that slice right into my
guts.

I'm burnin, I'm on fire, I feel faint, I'm gonni die.
I'm gonni choke on my own vile poison. Poison, that's what it is,
it's poison an it's bubblin molten lava ravagin my insides burnin
into my gullet an it hisses an spits as it swirls round inside me.
Round an round an round it goes, rippin raw flesh from my
tonsils an *whoooosh* man, up it comes like concrete spewin out a
mixer.
It splatters on the ground like a multi-coloured splash of skittery
cow dung.
Its burnin embers hiss like a serpent as it hits the pish puddle
runnin through my legs. I'm finished so I am, there's fuck-all left
of me. This is it man, this is all that's left. I drop to my knees an
fall face first onto the deck.
I'm lookin down smilin like fuck at the Devil.
Me. Aye, this is me, my whole life, here, look at it, a pailful of
piss an puke dribblin across the cold black tar.
I'm a shell, hollow, empty. This is me. Lyin here dyin. No dignity
man. It's gone an done a runner a long long time ago. We
parted company for good so we did.

The end of the road is nigh. The end of the road is now. The end.
The end of my life. My life. This is my life.
Mr James McConaughy, this is your life.

Hey listen by the way, there's not a great deal to tell. There's very
few pages in the big red book of Sonny Jim.
You were born 1961. You went to school. You left school. You
went to the boozer. You drank a lot. You shagged a lot. You
were absolutely shite at both. You trampled on the toes of
every fucker you ever met. You were a loser, a user, you took
every cunt for granted. Always a taker, never a giver. You lied an

cheated an stole.
You broke your poor mother's heart.

You died in a puddle of your own piss and puke.
James Aloysius McConaughy. That was your fucked up life.

I lie on the road spreadeagled, I roll over onto my back. I'm
Christ on the cross only I'm on the ground. I'm wide-eyed an
watchin the shootin stars. Peaceful. So very very peaceful. It
reminds me of those evenins, those sweet romantic evenins, me
an my sweetheart, me an my sweet Rhonda watchin the twinkly
starspangled sky.
Aw look at it man. Just look at it.
Shiny dancin dots on soft black velvet.
That deep black sky, illuminatin my mind, so black, so shiny, so
alive an bright.

But those lights go dim. Dimmer an dimmer.

     Fadin.

   Fadin to gray.

Fadin away
         Black.
            Jet black.

      Blackout.

I'm trundlin along lookin out a window.
I'm watchin passin faces. Faces watchin me watchin them.
The crackle of a wireless makes me jump. I'm in the back of a car.
I'm lookin out the front. Fuck, I'm bein chauffeur driven. Two
chauffeurs.
Aye, two, an they're wearin fancy hats with lovely chequered
braidin. Chequered bunnets.
Oh fuck, guess where I am?
I'm in a Panda car headin south. South Street cop shop.

They know me. I know them.

Hey look, one cop says to the other, sleepin beauty has come alive.
Wakey wakey how's it goin Sonny Jim? It's time to go home. Yer arse is out the window now boy.
They take me down the Station, through the doors, along the corridor an up to the desk.

Look who it isn't, says the copper at the desk.
Fucksake Sonny, he says, yer in here more often than me an I'm here every day.
He reads me all my rights an my wrongs.
I can't stand up, can't stay awake, I'm faintin, dyin, ready to drop.
I'm huckled along the hall an dumped in a cell. I tell the cop I want a bedtime story an to give me an early alarm call around tenish. Oh, an I'll have two rolls an bacon with brown sauce for breakfast. An a big mug of tea with milk an two sugars please.

Nite nite, sleep tite, don't let the crab-infested mattress bite.

I dunno what time it is. He's just told me but I've forgot.
It's dark. It aint light. It's still night.

I'm out of my cell. Who brought me here?
I'm back in my favourite room now. The bare room with the table an three chairs.
Two cops. They sit across there. I sit here. Waitin, watchin, shakin, sweatin.
I'm so tired, I want back to sleep, I want to sleep an sleep an never wake up.

There's no good cop, bad cop, routine. Naw, this time they're both goodies.
Take it easy Sonny, we want to help. Let's all help each other eh?

He reads out all my shit, all the usual.

Breakin interdicts, breakin court orders, non-payment of fines, bein prosecuted by solicitor for non-payment of loans, breakin probation, breach of the peace, resistin arrest, non-payment of restaurant bill, domestic abuse.

An last but not least, arson. Aye, arson they call it, settin fire to a restaurant tablecloth.

All that shit an more. I tell them my favourite joke, tell them they should be out there chasin the real criminals. Nobody laughs. Nobody ever laughs.

They've heard it, I've heard it. Change the record. Don't ever play it again Sam.

I've got loads an loads of excuses. I've got them all ready.

I tell them that I dropped my fag on the table an there was no ashtrays.

I should've listened when my mum told me smokin was naughty.

I was gonni pay, I forgot my wallet.

I was scared to go to my counsellor because her pointy fuckin face frightens me.

The cheque for the lawyer's in the post. Honest. Honest.

Look, they say, the bit about the fire can be covered up.

It was just an accident. They are prepared to reduce the charge to causin fire by accident, the are prepared to do a deal an go easy on all the lesser charges as long as I plead guilty to the biggy, the serious assault charge. Plead guilty an the dude with the curly wig an fishnet stockins an suspenders will give me a break.

What d'ye say Sonny boy, what d'ye say?

I'm all for it man. Guilty, yer man's guilty.

Give me the forms. I'll sign my life away, I'll sign any fuckin thing ye want sir. I want sleep, I need sleep.

Guilty will do. I want a guilty, I want away for a wee holiday, that's what I need bro, I need a rest. It aint easy bein me ye know. I need a break, I need away from every fucker an their auntie. No more man, yer man can't take no more. I'm guilty, it's the easy way out eh?

Just think, no more debt. No more cheatin, lyin, thievin. No more judges. No more lawyers. No more Dizzy Lizzie.

No more booze, no more pain, no more dazed up days. Give me the fuckin sheet. Where do I sign? Get me out of here. Take me to Hell.

I'm back in my single cell.

I lie on my back an stare at the pitch black ceilin.

All night long the walls boom an bang. There's squeals an screams an high-pitched howls. All night long the animals dance in the jungle as the drums beat to the sound of the Devil's boogie.

Yer man here's got that jungle fever.

Welcome to the jungle.

Chapter Twenty-seven.
Jekyll an Hyde.

The court is heavin. Burstin at the seams. Surely to fuck they aint all here to see me?
Naw, I'm guilty. We're all guilty, all us dudes sittin here are guilty. All the guilty men.
There's no jury. Don't need one. I've been tried an found guilty by my conscience.
My mind, my guilty mind.
All the little jurors in my mind say guilty. Unanimous decision. All twelve. Twelve zero.
I sit on my hands. Stay steady ya cunts. Stop shakin. Easy does it now.
It'll soon be all over. I'm hot an sticky, I'm burnin under my skin. I'm overheatin.
We shuffle our arses in our seats. There's a soft hush of whispers an mumbles an murmers. The hollow sad empty tones of the convicted.

All stand.
We stand.

My heart starts boomin. My breathin's heavy. My chest, aw fuck, my chest, my lungs, my heart, it's tightenin up like fuck man, aw man I'm bein squeezed to fuckin death. Stop squeezin ya bastarts. I'm bein crushed, crushed in a crowd. Crushed to death by the bad mad crowd. Get to fuck ya cunts, get off me, let me breathe. Aw dear Lord please let me breathe.
The room starts spinnin, goes waltzin. People do birlies. A day at the fairground.
Then my eye catches Rhonda. My heart stops beatin. Rhonda.
The place goes into freeze-frame. Nothin else matters.
She looks at me.

She melts me with her big Maltesers. Her lips move but my eyes can't read what they say. I can't read them, I can't look.

What's her face sayin?

I dunno. Is it love, hate, forgiveness, revenge?

Nothin, her face says nothin. Well I don't think it does, ye see I'm guessin, just guessin cause I can't bear to look.

Maybe her face is sayin, I forgive ye my sweetheart.

Yes, I see her face sayin that.

Is it?

I dunno.

I know that's what I want it to say. Her face, her gorgeous face, sayin so much, sayin so little, her face, her everchangin face, like a crazy anti-drugs video on the telly.

I can't take it man, no way, I can't. I'm fuckin dyin to look but can't, can't look at her gorgeous lips in case they say what I can't bear to see.

What if she says, I hate ye an I hope ye die an rot in Hell ya dirty rotten bastart?

Aw man, what if she says that?

There's no way I can take it.

Can't look, won't look.

A sharp bang bounces round the room. A hammer hittin mahogany. The bang of the hammer tells me the Wig wants my attention, my full attention.

My mind snaps. My head jolts to the side. My name. I hear my name. McConaughy. Pay attention. You. Aye you ya cunt. Listen here to me.

This is yer fate, yer fuckin destiny.

The PF reads out all my charges, all my shit.

Aw fuck man, go easy.

Drunk an disorderly. Resistin arrest. Causin fire damage to property. Serious domestic abuse. Assault with an offensive weapon.

All these an many many more.
Like I say, who cares, who gives a fuck?

There's movement from Rhonda, I can see her out my side view.
Tiny trickles of sweat roll down like tears. I wipe them away.
I keek through the space in my fingers for a millionth of a
second an catch a glimpse.
She has her arms outstretched.
I look away. I wipe more sweat. A steady flow runs down my
cheeks.

What's she doin? Fuck me. Arms wide open. My baby wants a
hug.
That's what I see. Or do I?
Is that what I see, or just what I want to see?

My lawyer pleads my case. Big Plooky. Go for it son. A plea for
leniency. Go for it, go on, make me cry, make the whole fuckin
world cry. Oh fuck aye man, c'mon now, let me see some tears.
Leniency, he goes for leniency.

Please be lenient on the boy m'Lord.
A poor boy, a sick boy, came from a broken home, a
dysfunctional background. The boy has never really had a chance
in life. Been dragged up, was bounced from pillar to post as
a child, ping-ponged from home to home. Admittedly he has
made some bad choices at times with the company he keeps
and also had serious problems forming relationships with the
opposite sex.

He suffers from a range of serious illnesses. Alcoholism.
Asthma. Panic attacks. Also suffers serious blackouts an has no
recollection of what went on during these episodes. He often
comes to in strange places with no recollection of how he got
there. My client clearly cannot account for his behaviour when
intoxicated. But I have to say m'Lord, he has gone to great
lengths to tackle these horrible afflictions.

He has attended alcohol counselling and has also attended anger management classes. He clearly carries a lot of anger, anger at everyone he feels has let him down.

My client really has been badly let down sir. We feel he clearly has a case. Does society do enough for the the James McConaughys of this world, does it give them a fair break, do they get the chances that the rest of us get?

I think not m'Lord. So for this reason I ask you to be lenient. Please take some time to consider the injustice of this poor boy's upringing.

A good boy, a boy who needs a break. Could this be the break he has been waiting for? Are you willing to make this the turning point in this poor unfortunate chap's life?

I ask you to be lenient sir.

We offer a plea of leniency your honour.

Oh for fucksake man, get the Kleenex out, the big plook is playin a stormer. Not a fuckin dry eye in the house. Tell me this, is that a little trickle of the auld salty stuff runnin down the wiggy boy's cheek?

Fuck me man. Yes, the big plook filla's pullin it off so he is. In fact, I think it's time for yer man to start cryin now too, aye, that's an idea, give it the auld tears, crocodile tears, hundreds of them, show some emotion, show loads of remorse, cry like a cunt, let them all see how sorry ye are, cry ya bastart cry.

I try like fuck to cry but can't, naw, can I fuck man, can't even fuckin cry to save myself, save my sorry arse from goin to jail. Fucksake man, the auld macho pride. Pride, aye, pride comes before the fall. Yer man here's in freefall but fuck that cryin shit.

Ye see, the thing is, the Sonny Jim boy doesn't know how to cry. Was never allowed to. It's all to do with yer past, yer childhood, yer rough tough council estate upbringin. Cryin's for poofs, cryin's a sign of weakness, start that cryin an every cunt'll pick on ye.

Don't you cry ya wee bastart, yer auld man used to shout at ye.
Start that fuckin cryin an I'll give ye somethin to cry about.

Naw, the Sonny Jim boy aint too hot at cryin. Still, nice try young
man.
The young plooky dude's doin real good but.

There's more activity comin from the gallery. I get another
sharp glimpse of Rhonda. I see her again out my side range, my
peripheral.
Movement, serious movement. Arms swingin. Slowly at first, like
a windmill goin round an round.

My head is pure fuckin spinnin now, spinnin out of control, can't
stop it, I'm gonni faint, gonni pass out, aw fuck c'mon ya cunt,
stand up strong bro, be a man, take it on the chin, hold on tight
to yer two baws, aye, baws, ye need big baws at times like this
so ye do.
That's one thing ye can say about the Sonny boy, he's never been
known to have wee baws.
I need blinkers but. I don't want to see her. I can't see her, I can't
bear to look but I'm dyin to look, aw my God I want to hold her,
grab her, cuddle her in my arms an squeeze her.

Fucksake man, concentrate. Forget her, get her out yer head
ya crazy bastart she's jail bait. Look at the state yer in. Pay
attention. Focus. It's verdict time. My destiny dawns.
The judge starts talkin, starts tellin me the score.
Says he's taken into account my plea of guilty. Good boy. Yes,
look at all the court's time you haven't wasted.
But.

An accordin to wee wiggy this is a big BUT.
I have disobeyed him.
I was told to stay dry, stay sober, be a good boy. But I haven't
done that, haven't been a good boy at all, in fact, I've been a
very very bad boy, very naughty boy, have broken interdicts,

have missed counsellin appointments, have shown bouts of aggression, an most of all, a total disrespect of people's property an safety by playin silly games with fire. Now we all know what happens to naughty little boys who play with fire don't we? He uses fancy jargon but I get the gist. What he means is I'm back on the swally with a vengeance, I'm a no-use rotten cunt, a disobedient rotten cunt at that. Aye, that's what he can't stand, disobedience, doesn't like little fuckin insignificant cunts like me not doin what he tells them. It's disrespectful, it lowers his credibility, his street cred, he doesn't like any cunt not takin his threats serious, so he aint fuckin havin it.

That's what he means, aye, that's what ye mean ya auld cunt don't ye?
Just say it, spit it out. Never mind the snooty shit, speak my language ya dirty auld sussy wearin fuckpig.
I dunno if I'm sayin all this out loud. I am sayin it. I am. I can hear it bouncin round my brain like a boulder in a tin bin. Why can nobody else hear it?
I am speakin out loud, I am sayin these words but no cunt listens, no cunt hears me, every cunt in the court has turned to stone.

I stand.
He stands.
We all stand together.
Waitin. Waitin for the hammer to fall.

It aint lookin good bro. Mister Negativity has moved into my mindpiece an the dirty rotten cunt's livin rent free.
My poor demented mind reels off its own private horror show.
Fucksake man. Talk about a vivid imagination. It's all up here bro, all in my little private cinema, the scenes are so real, so vivid.
Pull up a chair, sit back an relax.
Lights, camera, action, let the big picture roll.
He slips off his wee curly wig an slides an ugly black cap onto his big baldy napper. He sits there like an emperor in the Colosseum,

his arm raised, fist clenched, ready to drive the thumb down on the dyin gladiator.

The dirty Grim Reaper comes wailin out the walls swingin his blood drenched blade. Aw man. Aw my God. Blades. I've seen enough of fuckin blades to last an eternity.

I shut my eyes. I pray. I pray for mercy.

Dear Heavenly Father... For what I am about to receive.

What's it gonni be?

Five years, ten years, fifteen, twenty?

My eyelids seize shut, my jaw locks an my stomach plummets like a spacecraft re-enterin the earth's atmosphere. There's silence, there's nothin, not a sound. Time stands still for hours an hours. Waitin an waitin. What the fuck's goin on bro, is this a wind-up? Maybe I'll open my eyes an they'll all have fucked off home.

Go on ya cunt, go for it, open yer eyes.

Fuck off man, no chance I aint doin it, fuck it, c'mon, c'mon, here it comes, the verdict, what's it gonni be?

Auld wiggy boy rolls it off his tongue quite the thing.

Mister James Aloysius McConaughy

I hearby sentence you to

nothin
    nothin
        nothin nothin's happenin man,

I stand, he sits, I wait, he waits, every fucker in the place just sits an waits, waits an waits, there's no noise, no rufflin no shufflin, just silence, not even a breath, nothin, nothin, just one long everlastin pause like we're all tryin to see who can hold their breath the longest, nothin nothin nothin no cunt breathes, no cunt.

Then it happens, a sound, a slight hiss, a *sssss*, a long *sssss*, a *sssss* that sounds like the beginin of the word SIX.

Fuck, oh fuck oh fuck oh fuck it's six, aye six, it's a sixer, it's six fuckin years. He's just about to give me six years

when a noise comes from over there, over where Rhonda is.

It's a shrieeek, a squeeal, a high-pitched squeeal.
Then a loud sharp NO, then a pathetic panic-ridden NO.
A desperate NO of a loyal lover screamin a too-late plea for
mercy.

It's Rhonda. The good auld stark ravin looney-tuned bonker
brained Rhonda. She's cryin, sobbin, begin for mercy. No no no.
Sad an desperate words.
Nice try doll, but there aint no words in the whole wide world
that's gonni save this dude.
But Rhonda has more than just words, fuck the words, actions
speak louder than words. Actions. Rhonda resorts to actions.
She lifts her arm up, her bad arm.
She screams, Guilty.
Guilty guilty guilty.
Every cunt's lookin about, shruggin, as if to say, fucksake hen
don't state the fuckin obvious.
But it's not me she's pointin at. Naw, it's her, she's pointin at
herself.
She starts whippin herself across the arm in this frenzied mock
slashin gesture.
Then she starts screamin that SHE is guilty. Not HIM, she says,
ME.
I am guilty. It was ME. I done it, I done it, I cut myself, she shouts,
I done it, I hate him, I love him, I hate me.
I'm sorry, oh God in Heaven I'm sorry oh somebody please please
help me.

The cries an sobs crackle across the courtroom.

There's rumblin an mumblin an gasps of disbelief. There's
shocked an stunned expressions. There's all these mouths hangin
open an every cunt's lookin at each other an then lookin at me

an then lookin at Rhonda.
A woman at the back shouts God love ye hen.

Auld wiggy swings his hammer like a navvy breakin up rocks.
Order, order, order, he shouts, in perfect sync with every beat.
Someone see to this poor lady.
Aw the sin, the poor lassie, there there.
Cunts with hankies in their hands surround poor Rhonda.
She's ushered out the courtroom like a badly beaten boxer.

But wait a wee minute man, hold that result. This changes
everythin.
Looks like Rhonda's played a master stroke.
The wig, the plook an the PF all do a huddle round the dock.
Three heads an six shoulders all noddin an shruggin.
C'mon to fuck, they're sayin, we want to get this done an
dusted. Remember we're goin for a round of golf.

There's more hush-hushes an more shouts of order, order, an
more thumps on the mahogany.
Wiggy says this changes things.
He signals to the sexy brunette on the typewriter to strike the
assault charge from the sheet.
Clickety click like fuck she goes. She wipes it off the slate.

Different ball game now bro. The plook sticks his shoulders back.
Stands there lookin big an proud, a job well done, a majestic
piece of law work.
What's the big cunt like man? He looks as if he's just whipped a
plate of cream from under a pussy cat's nose an lapped it all up
himself.

All I'm left with now is the lesser charges, aint that right?
Aye. They said it, the two screws back at the nick said it in front
of the lawyer, aye, admit to the BIGGY an they'd go easy on the
LESSER charges.
Well the BIGGY is out the way now, all I'm left with is gettin

pissed an resistin arrest, the broken interdict charge, the non payment of some fines, failin to attend counsellin sessions an failin to pay the big man in the turban for the curries. Oh, an that wee accident with the match.

Well I mean it aint too terrible now is it? Wouldn't exactly call it the crime of the century. It hardly makes me a hardened criminal eh?

I breathe in more smooth air than I have done in the last ten years. Oh my God man, don't that air taste good?
My eyes are wide open, my jaw hangs loose an relaxed.

Wiggy leans on one elbow. Is that the teensiest hint of a wee smile I see?
He asks me if I have anythin to say.

Yes, I tell him, yes m'Lord, yer honour, whatever they call ye. Two things. Two words. Jekyll an Hyde.
I'm a Jekyll an Hyde m'Lord. It's the drink, it's the auld demon drink, it changes me so it does, it totally changes my personality, turns me into a madman, a loony tune, makes me do things I don't want to do.
I am a nice guy at heart but drink splits me in two, brings out this other guy, this guy I hate, this Mister Hyde character, this person that really isn't me.
I hate this other person, hate him, want rid of him, this other guy, this nasty guy, this guy I don't want to be no more.
It's the drink, the drink changes me so it does, I'm two different people, honest yer honour, there can be no doubt about it, I am a Jekyll an Hyde.

He curls his bottom lip down an wrinkles his brow. He looks as if he's interested, like he might even believe me.
Oh fuck yes man, yes yes yes he does believe me, he tells me so, he says it loud an clear.

Yes, I believe you are, he says. That clearly seems to be the case.

He takes a final deep breath, leans back, chest out, fills his lungs an exhales through his nose.

OK, Dr Jekyll, he says with a smile.
You are admonished.

My heart races, my head goes white, my blood swooshes through my veins like a speedboat.
I howl, ya *beeeeaaaauty*, I punch the air an start jumpin up an down like a maddy huggin an kissin the plook.
Aw fuckin thanks man, thanks thanks thanks.
I look across at the auld judge. I'm just about to run across the floor an pull his wig off an plant a smacker on his auld baldy dome, when he shouts,

WAIT.

He clears his throat an stares at me.
His glassy green eyes turn two hundred degrees colder.

Mr Hyde, he says.
You will go to prison for six months.

The Tar Factory
Alan Kelly
ISBN 1 84282 050 8

We needed bigger rakes an bigger wheelbarrows. Ah'm tellin ye, our own little private tar factory was rakin it in. Hey listen, we were gettin beggin letters from Donald Trump. Swear it...

Meet the Crazy Gang. There's Crazy D, Big Chuck Mcfuck, Mad Dog an me.

Crazy D had planted the idea in Mad Dog's head. Slice yer leg off, accident like, an it's worth forty gran. But Crazy D bottled it and Mad Dog he lost his happy-head – had to go elsewhere for his forty Gs didn't he? Least he still had his leg but. Of course when Denzo Doom minced ma hand with the gulley motor he called me 'buddy', thought I had bigger balls than a West African elephant. It was only a fuck-up.

So how does a tarman make a few extra bob for the boozer? Ah'm warning you it's not pretty. Gang bangs, bribery and scams, this is some story. Noir as tar. Wait till I tell ye...

Unpretentious, human, moving and funny. Alan Kelly gives us a man with true grit and a real practical morality. Mad Dog protects the underdog but beware those who misuse their power. This deserves to sell more copies than Trainspotting. The Tar Factory *is f**kin magic. A surprise hunner quid Giro on a wet Tuesday in February.*
DES DILLON

The Tar Factory *has a brash energy and undeniable linguistic authenticity.*
SUNDAY HERALD

Luath Press Limited

committed to publishing well written books worth reading

LUATH PRESS takes its name from Robert Burns, whose little collie Luath (*Gael.*, swift or nimble) tripped up Jean Armour at a wedding and gave him the chance to speak to the woman who was to be his wife and the abiding love of his life. Burns called one of the 'Twa Dogs' Luath after Cuchullin's hunting dog in Ossian's *Fingal*.
Luath Press was established in 1981 in the heart of Burns country, and is now based a few steps up the road from Burns' first lodgings on Edinburgh's Royal Mile. Luath offers you distinctive writing with a hint of unexpected pleasures.
Most bookshops in the UK, the US, Canada, Australia, New Zealand and parts of Europe, either carry our books in stock or can order them for you. To order direct from us, please send a £sterling cheque, postal order, international money order or your credit card details (number, address of cardholder and expiry date) to us at the address below. Please add post and packing as follows: UK – £1.00 per delivery address; overseas surface mail – £2.50 per delivery address; overseas airmail – £3.50 for the first book to each delivery address, plus £1.00 for each additional book by airmail to the same address. If your order is a gift, we will happily enclose your card or message at no extra charge.

Luath Press Limited
543/2 Castlehill
The Royal Mile
Edinburgh EH1 2ND
Scotland
Telephone: 0131 225 4326 (24 hours)
Fax: 0131 225 4324
email: sales@luath. co.uk
Website: www. luath.co.uk